The Duke of Her Desire

The reel followed, then a country dance and the minuet, which had to be repeated three times since Lady Amelia continued to falter. But rather than show any sign of defeat, her posture grew increasingly rigid, until making further mistakes became almost inevitable.

"You must try to relax," he told her gently while he guided her forward.

She was silent for a moment as they made a few complicated steps, before quietly saying, "It is difficult to do so when I have to concentrate on my every move." As if to accentuate the point, she made a mistake, prompting her to mutter something Thomas chose to pretend he hadn't heard.

"What you need is—"

"Shh!"

He blinked. "Did you just shush me?"

By Sophie Barnes

Novels

THE DUKE OF HER DESIRE
A MOST UNLIKELY DUKE
HIS SCANDALOUS KISS
THE EARL'S COMPLETE SURRENDER
LADY SARAH'S SINFUL DESIRES
THE DANGER IN TEMPTING AN EARL
THE SCANDAL IN KISSING AN HEIR
THE TROUBLE WITH BEING A DUKE
THE SECRET LIFE OF LADY LUCINDA
THERE'S SOMETHING ABOUT LADY MARY
LADY ALEXANDRA'S EXCELLENT ADVENTURE
HOW MISS RUTHERFORD GOT HER GROOVE BACK

Novellas

MISTLETOE MAGIC (FROM FIVE GOLDEN RINGS:
A CHRISTMAS COLLECTION)

SOPHIE BARNES

The Duke of Her Desire

Diamonds in the Rough

AVONBOOKS

An Imprint of HarperCollinsPublishers

THE DUKE OF HER DESIRE. Copyright © 2018 by Sophie Barnes. All rights reserved. Printed in the United States of America. No part of this book may be used or reproduced in any manner whatsoever without written permission except in the case of brief quotations embodied in critical articles and reviews. For information, address HarperCollins Publishers, 195 Broadway, New York, NY 10007.

First Avon Books mass market printing: January 2018

Print Edition ISBN: 978-0-06-256682-9
Digital Edition ISBN: 978-0-06-256679-9

Cover design and art direction by Guido Caroti
Cover illustration by Chris Cocozza

Avon, Avon & logo, and Avon Books & logo are registered trademarks of HarperCollins Publishers in the United States of America and other countries.
HarperCollins is a registered trademark of HarperCollins Publishers in the United States of America and other countries.

FIRST EDITION

18 19 20 21 22   QGM   10 9 8 7 6 5 4 3 2 1

To a wonderful author and friend,
Codi Gary

Chapter 1

Huntley House, London, 1818

When Thomas Augustus Heathmore, 3rd Duke of Coventry, came to call at Huntley House one Monday morning, the last thing he expected was to find the Duke of Huntley's sister, Lady Amelia, sprawled on her backside in the wet grass.

And yet that was precisely what happened, thanks to a bit of serendipitous timing. Because he'd actually been heading toward Huntley's study. Except the French doors at the end of the hallway stood open, allowing him to hear Huntley's youngest sister, Lady Juliette, shout, "Careful!" at precisely the right moment.

It was the sort of warning that could not, nay, *should* not, be ignored, so it was only natural for him to walk past the study where Huntley's butler, Pierson, stopped to knock, and continue on through the French doors to the garden.

"Oh my goodness!" Juliette exclaimed. Her eyes met his from behind a beam of muted sunlight that sifted through between the branches of a nearby elm. His gaze swept sideways, falling directly on Lady Amelia just as she turned to stare up at him. Her eyes widened a fraction, filling with something he could not define, before looking away as she pushed herself up off the ground.

He felt the edge of his mouth twitch with amusement. "I see you're putting your sister-in-law's advice to good use."

Lady Amelia rewarded his comment with a glare, which was unsurprising, considering the Duchess of Huntley had been trying to teach Lady Amelia proper comportment for the past month.

Having spent most of their lives in the slums of St. Giles, Raphe Matthews, the Duke of Huntley, and his sisters, Amelia and Juliette, had found their lives turned upside down when their brother had inherited his title. Since their arrival in Mayfair, they had all been doing their best to adjust themselves to Society's expectations, which as Thomas understood it, had not been easy.

"Is it not fashionable for young ladies to have grass stains on their skirts?" Lady Amelia inquired in a dry tone. She swiped her hands against her gown, leaving streaks of moisture and dirt upon the white muslin.

"Not as far as I am aware," Thomas replied. Looking her over, he couldn't help but sigh at her messy appearance. "I trust you are unharmed?"

She gave a slight nod, prompting a chestnut curl to drop dramatically over her forehead. It bobbed in front of her hazel eyes until she blew it aside with a puff of air. "Quite," she muttered.

"Well then." He shifted his gaze to Lady Juliette, who appeared to be admiring the roses with great intensity, before addressing Lady Amelia once more. "That is the most important thing." He paused, observing how flushed her cheeks had gotten, before he asked, "Will you tell me what happened?"

A moment passed before she pointed toward some branches in a nearby tree. "I was returning a fallen nest and ended up losing my balance."

He nodded. Of course that was what she'd been doing. She was invariably compelled to help the less fortunate creatures of the world. According to her brother, she'd taken in several stray cats, for which he'd since been forced to find new homes. "You should probably have asked the gardener to assist you," Thomas said. After all, climbing trees would not improve her reputation. Especially since the garden shared a fence with Green Park, and anyone strolling along the nearest path might witness her unorthodox behavior.

"Of course." She crossed her arms, and he wondered if he ought to say something more.

After all, what sort of friend would he be if he didn't offer his honest opinion? He pondered that thought for a moment and finally told her, "I would also suggest you remove those twigs from your hair and put yourself to rights. It will be calling time soon."

Seeing how flushed her cheeks grew, he chose to retreat before embarrassing her any further. So he dipped his head and turned away with the intention of seeking out Huntley, only to find that the man in question was leaning against the doorway behind him.

"Pierson said you were here." Huntley smiled. "Now that you've finished berating my sister, I'm thinking you might like to have some coffee?"

"Yes, please." Thomas followed him back inside. "I am sorry if I overstepped in some way, but I believe it was prudent to tell her that falling from trees and getting dirty is not the sort of endeavor she ought to be focusing on."

Huntley threw him a humorous look as they entered his study. "You needn't apologize, Coventry. I appreciate your critical evaluation. It actually happens to be one of the reasons why I wish to speak with you. Will you please sit?" He gestured toward Thomas's favorite armchair.

"Thank you." Thomas sank down onto the velvet seat, leaned back and crossed his legs while eyeing the other duke. "What is this about? Your note did not specify."

Huntley studied Thomas for a moment, then pinched his lips together and said, "You know I value our friendship. Correct?"

Wondering what might have brought on such a question, Thomas shifted slightly but nodded. "Yes. Of course."

"It's been bloody difficult, you know, what with my past and all, to find people I can trust." Huntley's expression turned thoughtful. "But you . . . you had no obligation toward me or my family, and yet you didn't turn your back on us. Indeed, if it hadn't been for you, Gabriella might very well have married that rotten bastard her parents favored."

Thomas flexed his fingers. "Fielding," he muttered between clenched teeth. "The man did not deserve her."

"No. He did not." Huntley tilted his head. "But there was also my murky upbringing to consider, my boxing match and my connection to Carlton Guthrie. Many suspect him of being one of the greatest criminals in the country, and yet none of this seemed to trouble you."

Thomas shrugged. "I found it intriguing—a puzzle to be solved. And once I got to know you better, I realized you might be one of the most honorable men I have ever had the pleasure of knowing, not to mention your title demands respect, regardless of your past. Mostly, however, I like how different you are from the rest." Tilting his head, he arched his eyebrows. "You are a refreshing peculiarity, Huntley."

The duke chuckled. "Well, thank you, Coventry. Your support has certainly been of great value to me and my sisters." His expression sobered as he held Thomas's gaze. "I hate having to ask you for anything else." A knock sounded at the door and a maid arrived. She set a tray on the desk between the two men and swiftly departed. Huntley poured two cups of coffee, pushing one in Thomas's direction. "But the thing is, I don't really know who else I can turn to."

The seriousness with which he spoke gave Thomas pause. He took a sip of his hot beverage before saying,

"Just name it, Huntley, and I will see if I am able to help."

"How's your mother, by the way?" Huntley asked while he raised his own cup to his lips.

The question threw Thomas completely off guard. "My, er . . . she's very well, thank you." He felt his eyebrows draw together with concern.

Huntley nodded. "Good. Good." He set his cup aside.

Thomas's frown deepened. He waited a second and finally exclaimed, "Oh for heaven's sake, Huntley! Will you please tell me what this is about? I already—"

"Chaperone Amelia and Juliette for three weeks—four tops."

Thomas almost spat his second mouthful of coffee all over the desk. Fortunately, he managed to keep it down with a slight cough and a wince. "I beg your pardon? *What?*" The last word came out strangled.

Folding his arms across his chest, Huntley looked back at him as though he hadn't just made a preposterous request. "Gabriella and I haven't really had much privacy since the wedding. She feels she has a responsibility toward Amelia and Juliette. In spite of the scandal, invitations have begun trickling in again, and preparing to escort them to these various events is taking up a great deal of Gabriella's time." He expelled a deep breath. "I'm 'opin' to invite 'er on a weddin' trip. If we can just get away fer a bit . . ." He scratched his head and offered Thomas a loopy smile.

As was oftentimes the case when his emotions ran high, Huntley had fallen back into the unrefined dialect he'd spoken during his life in St. Giles. Thomas arched an eyebrow. "I understand your reasoning completely, old chap, but ordinarily, one would ask a female relation to help with such matters. Certainly not a bachelor."

Huntley frowned. "Gabriella's mother and father remained in Gloucester after the wedding in order to have more time with Gabriella's sister." Having fallen from grace when she'd married a commoner who'd since abandoned her with child, Lady Victoria had made a new life for herself with Huntley's friend Benjamin Thompson, the recently appointed caretaker of Huntley's estate. "But Gabriella's aunt, Lady Everly, is in residence, so we have naturally spoken to her. In fact, she has agreed to move in during our absence."

"Excellent."

"However . . ."

When Huntley paused, Thomas raised an eyebrow. "Yes?"

"Have you ever met Lady Everly?"

"Of course. She has an excellent sense of humor and is far more relaxed than her brother and sister-in-law. If I am not mistaken, I saw her smoking a cheroot once during a ball—didn't seem the least bit bothered by how shocked people were by it."

"Forgive me, but are ladies not allowed to smoke?"

"Not in public and certainly not in the middle of a ballroom. It is considered terribly gauche by most."

"Which leads me to the point I'm about to make." Huntley looked directly at Thomas without wavering.

"As much as I like Lady Everly, I'm not entirely sure she will offer Amelia and Juliette the proper guidance they require. I worry they will get into trouble if she's the only one supervising them. Which is why I am hoping you will keep an eye on them too—especially since it is my belief that their association with a respectable duke will be of great advantage to them."

Pressing his lips together, Thomas puffed out a breath through his nose. He was beginning to understand why Huntley had asked about his mother. Clearly, he didn't trust Lady Everly to make a success of his sisters and was hoping the Dowager Duchess of Coventry might fill any gaps that remained in their education. Taking a moment, Thomas considered the proposition with greater seriousness than he had earlier, and eventually asked, "Do Lady Amelia and Lady Juliette know about this scheme of yours?"

Huntley broke eye contact. "I thought I'd ensure your willingness to help before mentioning it."

Thomas nodded. "I suppose that makes sense."

Arching his fingers, Huntley gave him a frank look. "I actually think my absence might help them."

"How so?"

"I'm still working on salvaging my reputation, but you are well respected. With your support and my absence, the *ton* might start to view them in a new light. And with Amelia's age taken into consideration, the time to find her a husband is limited. Another year and she might be firmly on the shelf."

Thomas stared back at Huntley with increasing uncertainty. "In other words, you are not only asking me to chaperone your sisters, but to try to get them settled, as well?"

"Just Amelia. Juliette still has plenty of time."

"I don't know, Huntley. What you are asking of me is not only unusual. It is . . ." How could he continue that sentence without causing offence?

"Something of a challenge?" Huntley prompted. "Believe me, I am aware. The fact is that adjusting to our new way of life has been particularly difficult for Amelia."

"More than it was for you?"

Huntley nodded. "Yes, I believe so."

Shocked, Thomas sat back against his seat. It hadn't occurred to him until that moment that being put on display would be more difficult for her than it had been for her brother. "I always imagined she would enjoy shopping for pretty things and dressing up for balls. Most young ladies do."

"Most young ladies have also spent their entire lives preparing themselves for their debuts. I think both my sisters found the experience to be more intimidating than enjoyable, but now that they are out, there is no going back."

Acknowledging the dilemma, Thomas set his jaw and considered Huntley's proposal. "Three weeks, you say?"

"Four at the most," Huntley assured him.

"Very well then," Thomas said. "I will do it. And I will even ask Mama to help."

A smile slipped into place on Huntley's face. "You knew I would ask?"

"I knew you inquired about her earlier for a reason."

Huntley's eyebrows dipped a little. "Do you think she'll object?"

"I cannot say." Thomas tapped his fingers against the armrest. He looked away briefly before meeting Huntley's gaze once more. "She has been very withdrawn these past few years, but if I can manage to convince her, it might be a welcome distraction."

Huntley's expression turned tragic. "How thoughtless of me," he whispered with deep apologetic undertones. "I forgot about your sister. I—"

"Don't." Thomas felt his teeth clash together as he clenched his jaw. "I would rather leave Melanie out of this."

"Coventry . . ."

"I am not the only one who has lost a sibling. Am I?" When Huntley expelled a tortured breath, Thomas said, "Might I suggest we speak of something else?" He waited for Huntley to nod his agreement before saying, "I will speak to Mama and let you know what she thinks by the end of the day."

"Thank you, Coventry." Rising, Huntley walked Thomas out toward the foyer. "I hope you will need a favor in exchange soon so I can repay your generosity."

Thomas smiled. "We are friends, Huntley. It is my duty to help you as best as I can." And perhaps in doing so, he would thwart the demons that chased him and find some measure of peace.

"**I** do hope the two of you have a lovely holiday together," Amelia told Gabriella as she embraced her in the foyer a week later. Dressed in an elegant gown cut from lilac muslin, the duchess looked every bit the Society lady she'd been raised to be. What set her apart from the rest of the *ton* was her lack of aloofness and modesty. Amelia had liked her for both of those qualities since the moment she'd first met her.

"Are you absolutely certain you and Juliette will be all right during our absence?" Gabriella asked for what had to be the tenth time. "We can still cancel our—"

"No. Absolutely not." Amelia stepped back and met Gabriella's pretty blue eyes. "You and my brother deserve to enjoy each other's company somewhere far away from here where we won't be a distraction. No need to worry, I assure you."

Gabriella paused as though on the brink of saying something more. But whatever it was remained unsaid since Raphe entered from the street where he'd been overseeing the preparation of the carriage. "All the trunks have been loaded," he said, picking up the beaver hat his valet had placed on the hallway table. Examining it for a second, he shook his head as if confounded by the item. "Are you ready to depart?" The hat was returned to the table midquestion, its existence seemingly forgotten by Raphe, who'd already turned his back on it.

"Yes." With a reassuring smile directed at Amelia, Gabriella went to say goodbye to Juliette and Lady Everly, who were standing closer to the front door. The house would feel empty without them. Especially since Raphe had given his valet and his secretary leave to visit with their families during his absence.

"We'll be back before you know it," Raphe told Amelia. He bent his head to kiss her on the cheek. Straightening again, he met her gaze with a somber expression. "In the meantime, I hope you will take advantage of Lady Everly's and the Dowager Duchess of Coventry's guidance. Both ladies have a lot to teach you."

Responding with a smile that hopefully hid her concerns, Amelia walked her brother to the door where Gabriella stood waiting. She watched as he guided her sister-in-law down the front steps and helped her into the awaiting carriage before climbing in beside her. The driver whipped the reins a moment later, and Amelia stood beside Juliette and Lady Everly, waving until the conveyance rounded a corner and vanished from sight.

"I do hope I get to go to Paris one day," Juliette said with a wistful sigh as they returned inside. "It's supposed to be terribly romantic."

"So it is," Lady Everly said. "I have no doubt the duke and duchess will enjoy it. Shall we take tea while we await Coventry's arrival?"

"Certainly," Amelia managed to say in spite of the tightening in her throat. Ever since her brother had told her of the agreement he'd made with Coventry a week earlier, her nerves had caused such riotous thoughts that succumbing to sleep in the evenings had proven a chore.

"I must confess I'm a little bit anxious about making the dowager duchess's acquaintance," Juliette said when they entered the parlor. Crossing to the bellpull, she gave it a gentle tug before joining Amelia and Lady Everly, who'd seated themselves on a sofa upholstered in silver damask silk. Juliette claimed a matching armchair, leaving the adjacent sofa vacant for their guests.

"You need not be," Lady Everly said. "The dowager duchess is extremely pleasant and kind. Much like her son, actually, and I know you have no qualms where he is concerned."

"Of course," Amelia murmured while trying to ignore the sudden swing of her stomach.

Just the thought of spending an increased amount of time in his company, of him bearing witness to all of her flaws when he himself was so utterly perfect, was making her feel rather queasy.

She'd hoped to continue her lessons in etiquette and proper comportment while keeping him at a distance, the plan being he would eventually marvel at her progress the next time they happened to meet. Instead, he'd stepped out onto the terrace last Monday and found her looking a fright. The experience had been mortifying—a definite blow to her self-esteem.

"Coventry has been extraordinarily good to us." A tiny smile formed upon Juliette's lips to convey her appreciation. "Frankly, I cannot imagine what we would 'ave done without him."

"*Have* done," Lady Everly corrected.

"Oh yes." Juliette's smile faded. Her brow knit with concentration. "*Have* done."

After little more than a month of intense tutoring, the uncultured dialect Amelia and her siblings had grown accustomed to using during their life in the slums had been mostly replaced by precise pronunciation. Certainly, there were times when they forgot themselves. Amelia knew this was especially true of herself and her brother when they were feeling stressed or irritable. But as long as she set her mind to the task, proper diction could be managed much easier than correct posture.

Catching herself at that thought, she deliberately straightened her spine and pulled back her shoulders just as a maid arrived to take their order.

"I believe Coventry has benefited as much from you as you have from him," Lady Everly said once the maid had gone to fetch the tea they'd requested. "There has been a distinct sense of quiet agitation about him for years—ever since his sister passed. If you ask me, helping your brother succeed was precisely the sort of challenge he needed. He has loosened up since he made Huntley's acquaintance."

"Forgive me, but how did his sister die?" Amelia couldn't help but ask the question. Since the moment he'd invited her to dance at the ball her brother had hosted three weeks earlier, the Duke of Coventry had filled most of her thoughts with fascination. Devastatingly handsome, his sand-colored hair was tousled enough to deny him the look of a pampered lord, his eyes a warm shade of brown that crinkled at the corners whenever something amused him, while his mouth . . .

"As I understand it," Lady Everly said, forcing Amelia out of her reverie, "the poor girl caught influenza while traveling Europe. She died shortly after returning home."

Amelia shuddered. She understood all too well the pain the loss of a sibling could cause. Bethany's death had torn her world apart at the seams. It was something she knew she would never get over, even if time did make it easier to live with. "It must have been terribly difficult for the family."

Expelling a breath, Lady Everly nodded. "Well, Coventry's father had already gone to meet his Maker a year before this happened, so he was at least spared from having to bury his daughter. As for the dowager duchess and the duke, nobody saw them for a long time after. You will see that Her Grace still wears black after all these years."

"How long has it been?" Juliette inquired.

"Oh . . . at least four or five years, I should think," Lady Everly replied.

The maid returned with a tray that she placed on the table in the center of the seating arrangement. She was just leaving when Pierson, the butler, entered. "The Dowager Duchess of Coventry and her son, the Duke of Coventry, have come to call," he said. "May I show them in?"

Hesitating, Amelia glanced at Lady Everly, who stared back at her expectantly before finally whispering, "This is your home, Amelia, so it falls upon you to respond. I am merely a guest here."

Appreciating her advice, Amelia told Pierson to show the guests in and then braced herself for the sight that would likely set her heart racing.

Coventry did not disappoint as he entered behind his mother, his height dwarfing the much smaller woman as he looked over her head with ease and offered a smile. Today he'd chosen to wear a navy blue jacket, the cut of which accentuated the breadth of his shoulders. Beneath it, Amelia glimpsed his waistcoat, which had been tastefully cut in a lighter shade. It drew attention to his chest while complementing the beige-colored breeches that hugged his thighs as though they'd been stitched into place.

Amelia's stomach quivered with awareness. No man should be allowed to look so attractive, to possess a jawline so perfectly sculpted or a mouth so sinfully tempting it made her think of couples kissing with wild abandon. She'd seen plenty of that over the years and a great deal more, as well. The inhabitants of St. Giles had not been shy about their desires, happily sating their needs in any available space they could find. Which was probably not something she should be thinking about while enjoying tea with nobility.

So she stood—a bit faster than she had intended due to the tension that strained every muscle in her body—and went to greet Coventry's mother.

"Welcome," she said, curtseying for good measure even though she hated the gesture because of how awkward it made her feel. "It's a pleasure to make your acquaintance, Your Grace."

"Thank you, my dear." The dowager duchess dipped her head toward Juliette and Lady Everly, acknowledging their presence, as well. "After everything my son has told me about you, I simply had to see you for myself." The edge of her mouth curved to form an inviting smile before she turned to address Coventry. "Shame on you for not telling me how lovely the Duke of Huntley's sisters really are."

"My apologies, Mama," Coventry said with a dry tone that would have been slightly severe if it weren't for the twinkle in his eyes. "As you know, I try to avoid stating the obvious."

"Touché!" Lady Everly applauded while the dowager duchess slapped her son playfully on the arm before moving toward the vacant sofa.

Aware that a disconcerting shade of pink was flushing her cheeks, Amelia quickly asked the duke if he'd have a seat as well before turning away to resume her own—thankfully, with an entire table and tea set wedged between them. Because although she knew that complimenting ladies was second nature to him, and he'd spoken not only of her but of her sister as well, her heart had responded with a wild beat that could be tamed only if she managed to keep her distance from him.

All she had to do now was pour the tea without spilling it.

Perfect!

Reaching for the pot, she curled her fingers firmly around the handle in an effort to stop them from trembling. She drew a fortifying breath and held it until she'd completed her task with success. Air whooshed from her lungs on a sigh of relief when she set the pot back on the table, only realizing then that she'd done what she'd tried to avoid by not spilling and drawn unwanted attention anyway.

"Do try to relax," the dowager duchess said as she spooned some sugar into her cup and added a touch of milk. "We are all friends here, I hope, so you need not throw yourself into a tizzy on any account. My son and I are here to help you, Lady Amelia and Lady Juliette, as is Lady Everly. Is that not so?" Raising her cup to her lips, she glanced at the dowager countess and Coventry in turn before taking a long sip.

"Most assuredly," Coventry agreed. He'd leaned back against the sofa on which he and his mother were sitting and had stretched out his legs in a relaxed pose that suggested satisfied comfort.

Amelia couldn't help but envy him. She considered her teacup, wondering if she might attempt a sip without rattling the china, but then dismissed the idea and folded her hands in her lap instead. Perhaps if she could remain still she'd be able to present herself as a lady with greater ease than if she moved.

"As it is, you have both made a lot of progress," Lady Everly said. "To think you are the same young women I met in your brother's study right after he'd claimed the title is nothing short of astounding."

Amelia cringed as she recalled the incident—the manner in which they'd slouched and their horrendous use of the English language.

"That is not to say there is no room for improvement," Lady Everly continued, "and since I would like nothing better than for both of you to make the sort of match that would make the most sought after debutantes green with envy, I recommend we strive for nothing less than excellence while we continue your lessons."

"Oh . . . I . . ." Amelia glanced around at everyone's expectant gazes. "Must we?" She already felt as though she'd been stretched and squeezed in an effort to fit a particular box that Society had designed for her. With Raphe and Gabriella away, she'd rather been looking forward to a reprieve and to focusing her time on a new venture—one she hoped would be a success, not just for her own satisfaction, but for the people of St. Giles, as well.

"Your brother specifically asked that we make your search for a husband a priority," Coventry said. His dark eyes found hers, producing a flutter deep in her belly.

"Well, ye needn't trouble yerselves on my account, since I've no desire to venture down that particular path." Fidgeting with her gown, Amelia dropped her gaze to the carpet and wondered if she might be able to slide underneath it. Perhaps then those present would ignore the unflattering diction she'd used on account of the flustered state she was presently in.

"My dear," the dowager duchess said with a

sigh. It was the sort one might use with a very naive child, though Amelia felt it was kindly meant on account of the smile that accompanied it. "Might I inquire about your age?"

Hesitating, Amelia became acutely aware of a nearby clock ticking away the seconds. "Two and twenty," she eventually said.

The dowager duchess tilted her head in a sympathetic gesture that filled Amelia with a sudden feeling of inadequacy. "There are many who will consider you unmarriageable by this time next year. Is that what you wish?"

Amelia stared back at the dowager duchess for a long moment while considering the life she would lead as a spinster. She couldn't imagine not having a family of her own one day—of not having children. Especially since the thought of being alone terrified her.

Additionally, the idea of having to live off her brother forever disagreed with her immensely. She absolutely hated relying on others for help. In St. Giles, things had been different. Raphe had earned their keep while she had tended the house and ensured they had food to put in their hungry bellies. But now that his status had changed and he'd married, she had nothing to offer him in return except for additional expenses and worry.

"No," she said. "Of course not."

Lady Everly nodded with satisfaction. "Which is why I have taken the liberty of drawing up a list."

"A list?" Juliette asked.

Without saying another word, the dowager countess went to collect a sheet of paper from a nearby side table. She offered it to the dowager duchess, who peered at it for an insufferable moment before narrowing her gaze on both Amelia and Juliette. "Indeed, I believe these gentlemen will do very nicely."

"What gentlemen?" Coventry asked. He took the paper from his mother's hand and scanned the text. His eyebrows rose. "This is quite an impressive collection of suitors."

When Lady Everly nodded and the dowager duchess smiled with delight, Amelia knew her fate had been sealed with nine-inch nails. The next few weeks would obviously be a matchmaking expedition with her at the center of it. And in that moment, she missed Gabriella enormously, because whatever her sister-in-law had put her through in the name of improving her comport, it couldn't possibly be worse than being presented to a long list of gentlemen while the only man who held her interest supported the effort.

Chapter 2

When the dowager duchess came to call the following day, she did so without Coventry, for which Amelia was extremely grateful. She'd spent the better part of the night convincing herself she'd said all the wrong things the previous day, and that accidentally spilling her tea in a nervous moment of despair had proven she lacked the sophistication required to even hope for a man as refined as Coventry to consider taking her as a wife.

So she'd scarcely slept, which had only added to her annoyance. Especially after taking a look at herself in the mirror. She'd washed her face with cold water, which had had a rejuvenating effect, though not enough for her to feel remotely attractive. Not that feeling so had been a typical occurrence lately. Not after overhearing the remarks made by a few young ladies at her brother's ball.

It had been her debut, and she'd just danced with Coventry for the first and only time. It had promised to be such a magical evening, until she'd headed toward the ladies' retiring room, which had taken her past a salon where the door had stood slightly ajar. Laughter had drifted toward her in such an enticing manner she had been tempted to enter the room and join in the fun. But the words that had followed had stayed her progress and stopped her from doing so.

"Can you believe those girls are actually going to try to snatch up a title?" a high-pitched voice had asked.

"It should be forbidden," a gentler voice had said.

"On account of their background alone," a third voice had added, "not to mention their ridiculous attempts at pretending they actually belong to our set. The gall of it!"

"I completely agree with you, Susanne," the high-pitched voice had said. "It is obvious to anyone with eyes and ears that they lack any form of education."

"Becaws thay speak loik this?"

The laughter that had followed had pushed Amelia's heart into her belly, leaving plenty of room for a slow ache to fill up her chest. She'd spent a great deal of time since that evening wondering if she would ever belong to this world, if she and her sister would ever be good enough to demand respect.

Raphe could garner it with his power. He'd also had the good fortune to strike up a friendship with Coventry and marry Gabriella. Both had given him a foothold while Amelia often felt as though she was sliding away from an unpleasant past and straight toward an equally unpleasant future. Taking control had since become a necessity for her. She needed something she could command on her own without any interference from others—a project to lift her spirits and give her the sense of accomplishment that was otherwise denied her with every move she made.

"Will the duke not be joining us?" Lady Everly asked as the four women readied themselves to go out.

Placing her bonnet on her head, Amelia fiddled with the ribbon in an effort to make the sort of plump bow her sister had recently managed to master. Eyeing Juliette, she saw that hers was indeed perfectly tied at just the right angle. Exasperated by her own efforts, Amelia blew out a breath, undid the bow she'd just tied and made another attempt.

"My son had a busy schedule this morning," the dowager duchess explained. Standing by the front door, she waited for her companions to ready themselves, her eyes catching Amelia's before she added, "Being the responsible man that he is, he never misses a session in parliament."

Her gaze lowered to somewhere in the vicinity of Amelia's chin, which only caused Amelia to fumble even more with the silk ribbon she was trying to control. The dowager duchess came toward her, paused for a second and then raised her gloved hands to complete the bow Amelia had made a mess of once again.

"It is important to get it right the first time," the dowager duchess told her gently. "The ribbon will be too crumpled otherwise, though I do believe we have managed to salvage this one." She turned to address Juliette and Lady Everly. "Are you ready?"

"Absolutely," Juliette said. She was already heading through the door.

They arrived at a dressmaker's shop fifteen minutes later to the sound of a tinkling bell as they filed inside. Stepping further into the well-organized space, Amelia admired the rich display of color all rolled up into bolts of exquisite fabric. She'd never seen anything like it before. A dressmaker had been called to Huntley House when she and her siblings had first arrived so she'd had no need to visit a modiste shop. Standing here now, she couldn't help but marvel at the vibrancy. It stood in stark contrast to the dull browns and grays that dressed the people of St. Giles.

"Mesdames!" The animated voice that sang through the air belonged to an older woman whose slender figure suggested she took great care with what she ate. "Vot a lovely surprise! It 'as been far too long since you've graced me viz your presence."

Her accent reminded Amelia of a woman she'd rather forget, the French undertones pulling her back to a place filled with nothing but sorrow and neglect as her mother had cast her family aside in favor of seeking wealth and adventure. Shuddering in response to the unwanted memories that threatened, she made a stoic effort to push them all back by focusing her attention on a lovely display of lace laid out to her right.

"May I introduce the Duke of Huntley's sisters?" Lady Everly said. "They will be requiring evening gowns for some upcoming balls and soirees. At least ten, I should think."

Amelia spun toward the dowager countess. "Ten? But we have only received three invitations!"

"Yes, but a lady ought to have more than one gown to choose from, not to mention that more invitations may arrive, some possibly lacking the notice that would be required in order to request something new." Lady Everly broke off her explanation for a moment so she could ask the dressmaker to fetch a selection of pattern plates for them. She then continued in a sensible tone. "You are the sisters of a duke, and as such, you must look the part, which means you must outshine all other young ladies. Especially if you are to make matches befitting your status. And since I know your brother can afford the expense and that his deepest wish is for both of you to excel, I believe we should think of this as an investment rather than some unnecessary exercise in excess for you to feel guilty about."

"Indeed, you must not feel guilty," the dowager duchess said. "An outing such as this is meant to be relished and enjoyed."

Feeling as though every argument she might have presented had just been dismantled, Amelia found herself at a loss for words as the dressmaker waved them toward a seating arrangement surrounding a table on which a large pile of designs and swatches had been put on display. "These arrived from Paris last week," the woman explained. "Please, take your time to go through them while I select some suggestions for trim."

Hesitating, Amelia watched as the other ladies

reached for some of the sketches and began leafing through them. Torn between the instinct she had to save money rather than throw it away on unnecessary fripperies, and the tempting extravagance of wrapping herself in exquisite luxury, Amelia carefully picked up a handful of fashion plates and allowed herself to study them closely. Each design seemed to outshine the other, overwhelming Amelia with an indecisiveness she'd never thought to experience before. Lord help her, how was she to choose between all of these glorious dresses? She couldn't imagine.

But as the minutes ticked by and she made her way through the remaining possibilities, a few of the gowns began to stand out. "I really like these," she said as she held up five designs for the rest to see.

"Ah *oui*," the dressmaker said, materializing next to Amelia's shoulder. "And viz your generous bosom, ze drape vill be *merveilleux*."

Heat rose to Amelia's cheeks as she lowered the sketches and turned them over in her lap, as if doing so would discourage the scrutiny with which she was now being regarded by Lady Everly and the dowager duchess. Juliette, thank God, was too distracted by her own perusal of various designs to have paid much attention to the dressmaker's comment.

"Allow me to take a look," Lady Everly said. She held her hand toward Amelia and waited.

Wishing she could escape somehow, Amelia cast a longing glance at the door before reluctantly handing over the fashion plates to the dowager countess.

The lady considered them each in turn. Pointing to one, she spoke to the dressmaker. "Perhaps we can lower this neckline a little and trim it with lace?"

"An excellent recommendation," the dressmaker said. She quickly produced a length of pretty trim. "And if ve bead it viz crystals, ze gentlemen vill find it impossible not to admire ze young lady's charms."

Oh, if only a hole would open up in the floor and swallow her whole, Amelia thought while another blush swept up the back of her neck.

"Perfect," the dowager duchess declared. "Just as long as she does not look vulgar."

"I assure you zat everyzing vill be in good taste, though I vould like to suggest a bold contrast for ze trim—especially where Lady Amelia is concerned, since I feel her complexion will allow for it vizout issue."

By the time they returned home after further visits to a cobbler and milliner, Amelia was on the edge of exhaustion. The idea of taking a lengthy nap and resting her feet was an impossible one to realize, however, since Lady Everly invited the dowager duchess to come inside for refreshments.

"Pierson, can you please ask a maid to bring up some lemonade and sandwiches?" the dowager countess asked while parcels containing their shopping were handed over to a couple of footmen. "We will take it in the ballroom."

Alerted by the unusual request, Amelia couldn't help but dread what would happen next as she followed the older women through to the grandest room of the house. "They don't look the least bit tired," Juliette whispered. "Why don't they look tired?"

"I suspect they've been raised to withstand the most trying endeavors without any hint of fatigue."

Juliette sighed. "I was really looking forward to settling down with a book in the library after our busy morning."

"Chin up, Julie," Amelia muttered. "At least you were allowed to select modest gowns while I am destined to make my next public appearance breasts first."

Her sister's chuckle was cut short when they stepped into the ballroom where a couple of maids were already preparing a table while a footman set up some chairs. Amelia stared. The fact that Pierson had managed to convey orders to these servants so swiftly was truly remarkable.

"We will take half an hour's rest," the dowager duchess announced. She gave Amelia and Juliette a once-over. "And then the two of you are going to practice your dance steps so we can be sure they are up to par for the Elmwood ball on Friday."

Having risen early, Thomas had gone over his accounts with his secretary that morning before discussing the raises he had in mind for a couple of particularly diligent servants. He'd then considered the expenses required to fix the roofs for some of his tenants in Cornwall. With autumn looming around the corner, it would be best to take care of it now while the weather remained agreeable, so he'd penned a letter to his caretaker approving the work.

Once this had been accomplished, he'd taken his carriage from his residence on Weymouth and Wimpole streets directly to White Hall. There he spent the better part of three hours hoping the bill he'd suggested might be brought to attention by the current prime minister, the Earl of Liverpool. When it became clear it would not, he made a mental note to address the man personally at his first available opportunity.

For now, however, he had to collect his mother from Huntley House, a task he rather looked forward to since seeing Lady Amelia and Lady Juliette would undoubtedly offer a welcome distraction from his other affairs.

It wasn't until he arrived at Huntley House and followed Pierson into the ballroom that he realized just how much of a distraction they would actually prove to be. Because there they were, moving about as if trying to dance a minuet while his mother clapped a beat that echoed through the silence. She looked his way the moment he entered, and the clapping immediately ceased.

"Oh good," she said, coming toward him. "You are finally here."

His arm was suddenly linked with hers as she drew him toward Huntley's sisters. Both looked apprehensive. To one side, he registered a hint of amusement about Lady Everly's face while she watched whatever this was that was happening.

"Perhaps you can help?" his mother added. "It appears the dance instructor Lady Amelia and Lady Juliette have been using has focused most of his energy on teaching their brother. There are steps that must be mastered before the ball on Friday. If you can lead, it will be easier for the young ladies to learn."

Thomas noted Lady Juliette's shy appreciation but not without spotting the dread that widened Lady Amelia's eyes. For a fleeting second, she looked terrified, which was slightly odd since he wouldn't have thought her to be so self-conscious that letting him witness any possible missteps would cause her concern. They were friends after all and had danced together before without incident. But perhaps she was still embarrassed about her faux pas in the garden and worried about him witnessing another. Sympathizing, he held his hand toward Lady Juliette, allowing Lady Amelia a little more time to adjust to the idea of dancing together.

"I would be delighted," he said with a smile.

"Excellent." His mother turned toward Lady Amelia. "Perhaps you would like to rest your feet for a while?"

Lady Amelia dipped her head. "Of course."

Thomas watched her join Lady Everly in a corner of the room, his eyes lingering on the back of her exposed neck for a second before focusing his attention on his dance partner. "Shall we?"

Lady Juliette proved to be surprisingly light on her feet, only faltering twice during the course of five dances.

"You see," his mother said as she applauded Lady Juliette's efforts. "I knew you would do better with a partner." She turned toward Lady Amelia and gestured with her hand. "Come, my dear. It is your turn now."

Thomas didn't miss the sharp look in Lady Amelia's eyes as she rose from the chair on which she'd been sitting. There was a definite alertness to her that set her apart from anyone else he'd ever known, and when she made her approach, she did not move with the fluidity inherent to Society ladies, but with a crispness uniquely her own. Perhaps it came from her fifteen years in St. Giles amid cutthroats and thieves, her instinct to stay on guard so innate she could not shed it, not even for a dance.

Not that he minded.

On the contrary, he found her to be extremely refreshing—a view that reflected his opinion of Huntley and Lady Juliette, as well.

But with Lady Amelia, there was something else. If he thought about it, he supposed it boiled down to a massive amount of respect. Because knowing her past, the struggle she'd been through and how she'd embraced the role fate had forced her way at the young age of seven, was something he had to admire. According to Huntley, she'd scavenged for food, kept their home neat and clean, cooked to the best of her ability and nursed her siblings through various ailments. She'd stepped into a role their mother had abandoned, an endeavor that must have taken tremendous resourcefulness and courage.

Which was probably why it bothered him to see the uncertainty with which she now stood before him, no doubt worrying over her dance moves.

Because if everything Huntley had told him about her was true, Thomas imagined Lady Amelia to have not only nerves of steel, but a spine built on years of defiance, even if he had yet to catch a glimpse of either.

"My lady," he said, offering her his hand. She glanced down, took a deep breath as if in need of fortification before placing her palm in his. "You need not be nervous. Nobody here is going to judge you. We are your friends, and as such, it is our duty to help you succeed. I hope you realize that."

Her face turned more fully toward him, allowing him to see the firm set of her jaw. She pressed her lips together, but her eyes betrayed whatever determinedness she was trying so hard to convey. The varying shades of green and brown swirled together in a hazel mixture of distress so acute he felt his heart squeeze with compassion.

But rather than dwell on her riotous emotions, she jerked her chin with a definitive nod. "Thank you."

Confounded by her staunch ability to overcome whatever obstacle lay in her path for the sake of doing what had to be done, Thomas led her in a cotillion while his mother clapped the beat once again. The reel followed, then a country dance and the minuet, which had to be repeated three times since Lady Amelia continued to falter. But rather than show any sign of defeat, her posture grew increasingly rigid until making further mistakes became almost inevitable.

"You must try to relax," he told her gently while he guided her forward.

She was silent for a moment as they made a few complicated steps, before quietly saying, "It is difficult to do so when I have to concentrate on my every move." As if to accentuate the point, she made a mistake, prompting her to mutter something Thomas chose to pretend he hadn't heard.

"What you need is—"

"Shh!"

He blinked. "Did you just shush me?"

"I need to focus," she said without any effort to hide her irritation.

Choosing to accommodate her wishes, Thomas kept quiet for the remainder of the dance, which he had to concede was concluded without further issue.

"And now for the waltz," his mother said from her position next to the dance floor.

Attempting it with Lady Juliette had been a delight since she'd practically floated across the floor with effortless grace. Studying Lady Amelia, who appeared to have grown increasingly stiff during the last five minutes, he wondered how they would even manage to make a full turn without him looking as though he was dragging her across the floor. Somehow, she would have to loosen her posture a little.

Bracing himself, he chose to do something impulsive—something that would hopefully serve to distract her from what she was doing. Without warning, he grabbed her hand and spun her swiftly toward him, not pausing for a second as he swept her away in his arms, leaving her feet with little choice but to follow.

There was no denying the stunned look in her eyes. Her lips parted on a squeal of surprise. Thomas almost laughed with the pleasure of seeing her so bewildered, the rigid composure with which she held herself utterly dismantled in a heartbeat.

"What are you doing?" she asked when he spun her around to ensure that she wouldn't predict his next move.

"Teaching you that dancing can be fun and that you have to stop overthinking it. You already know the steps. What you need to do now is let them come naturally."

"You make it sound so simple." Her face began to tighten with that familiar look of concentration, so he quickly managed a lift, catching her off guard once more.

This time, her squeal was followed by a laugh and a distinct sparkle to her eyes. Gone was the earlier resolve, replaced instead by amusement. It made him feel curiously lighter, as though his happiness in that moment depended on hers. Fanciful thought.

"Besides," he added when they were once again gliding in a wide arc, "your gowns are long enough to conceal your feet, so even if you were to misstep at the ball, I honestly doubt anyone will notice."

"Truly?"

The hopefulness with which she spoke made him want to reassure her, so he gave her a nod while he squeezed her hand, not missing the blush that rose to her cheeks. It was probably caused by exertion. And yet, it did something to him—made him long for her laughter once more—so he lifted her again while spinning her about, not caring how inappropriate he was being. He was simply glad to watch her take pleasure in something for once. The fact that he'd been the cause of her joy filled him with no small amount of pride, even if it did result in a stern look from his mother.

"That will be all for today," she said once the dance had ended. "It is getting late, Coventry, and there are matters at home for us to attend to."

The comment served as a sobering reminder of his duties—duties he'd somehow managed to forget while he'd waltzed with Lady Amelia. "Of course."

The guilt that assailed him was acute. How could he have forgotten about Jeremy? The answer came to him swiftly when he recalled the abandon with which Lady Amelia had laughed—how brilliantly her eyes had sparkled while he'd held her in his arms. She'd looked . . . shockingly beautiful in that moment, he decided, which was something of an odd acknowledgment since he'd never really considered her looks before.

"It is settled then," Lady Everly was saying.

Thomas started. "I beg your pardon? What is settled?"

"The tea party tomorrow at Dorset House." His mother stared at him for a few seconds before producing a sigh. "It is scheduled for three in the afternoon. I have just assured Lady Everly that you and I will join her and Lady Amelia and Lady Juliette. Unless of course you have other plans?"

He shook his head, astonished he'd missed so much of the conversation, but he'd been dwelling on . . . "Right." He would not allow Lady Amelia to distract him again. The fact that she'd managed to do so once was something of a conundrum. "We will come to collect you at half-past two then."

He and his mother departed a few minutes later after assuring Lady Amelia and Lady Juliette that they had both made great progress with their dancing.

"I cannot imagine what you were thinking," his mother said once the two of them were seated across from each other in their carriage. "A gentleman does not spin a lady about in such a . . . a . . . careless manner. It is not proper!"

"She needed to forget herself for a while, Mama. I am sorry if you disapprove of the method with which I achieved that."

"Humph!" She folded her hands in her lap as though trying her best to remain the chastising parent. The twitch of her lips betrayed her, however, and soon she was smiling at him with warmth in her eyes. "I suppose I should thank you. I was actually at my wits' end before you arrived. What you managed to accomplish today with Lady Amelia . . . I cannot say I have ever seen her so animated before. It was really quite lovely to watch."

Settling back against the squabs, Thomas stretched out his legs and allowed himself to relax. "Thank

Chapter 3

Avoiding a tea party wasn't something Amelia had planned on doing, but it would be a necessity if she was going to keep the appointment she'd made for later that day. So she deliberately remained in bed for another two hours after waking, until Juliette eventually came to knock on her door.

"Are you all right?" she asked, popping her head in the room.

Amelia groaned from beneath the comforter she'd pulled up over her head. "I have the most dreadful megrim."

"Oh dear." Juliette stepped further into the room and carefully closed the door behind her. "Perhaps some chamomile tea will help? I can ask a maid to bring some up along with a breakfast tray."

"Thank you. That would be lovely."

Amelia ate the food as soon as it arrived and finished her tea while Juliette sat in a nearby chair and kept her company. "How do you feel now?" she asked when Amelia pushed the tray aside and leaned back against the pillows propping her up.

"As though three angry little men are hammering away on my skull right here, here and here." She pointed to the sides of her head and to the top.

"Would you like me to send for the doctor?"

Amelia forced a weak smile. "I'm not so sure there's a lot he can do. This will eventually go away on its own and without the expense of a doctor."

Juliette chuckled. "It's not as though we can't afford it now, and I'm sure Raphe wouldn't mind."

"That isn't the point, Julie." Wincing, she started massaging her temples for effect. "I wouldn't mind spending the money if I thought a doctor would help, but I doubt he would do anything besides telling me to get some rest. And if he were to suggest bloodletting—"

"Doctor Florian doesn't advocate that practice, Amelia."

Struck by her sister's unusually sharp tone and the defensiveness it conveyed, Amelia couldn't help but ask, "How do you know?"

With a shrug, Juliette gave her attention to her skirt, which apparently needed picking at that precise moment. "He mentioned it when I was sick with the measles."

Her illness five weeks earlier had been a terrifying experience for all of them. Raphe's secretary, Richardson, had recommended the young doctor on account of his broadmindedness and the keen interest he supposedly had for unconventional methods, but in the end, it had been Gabriella and Raphe who'd helped Juliette through the illness since there had been little else for them to do but make her comfortable.

"If you'll recall, Doctor Florian initially suspected influenza. It wasn't until his follow-up visit that he realized I had the measles. When Raphe asked him if there was something he could do to help me, Florian launched into a lengthy denouncement of purging, bloodletting and something else that I fail to recall at this moment. He insisted it does more harm than good."

"You speak of him with great respect."

"It is nothing more than what his profession and intellect demand."

Amelia wondered how much of the man's intellect her sister could possibly have been subjected to during their brief acquaintance. As far as she knew, the two had met only twice and that had been while Juliette had been racked by fever and feeling miserable. To suppose they might have enjoyed a philosophical discourse, or shared their political views or anything else that might have led Juliette to form an accurate opinion of his mental prowess was highly unlikely. Which made the whole thing all the more intriguing since it did suggest that her sister might be fostering a greater interest in the doctor, even if she had yet to be made aware of it herself.

"What time is it?" Amelia asked, deciding to drop the subject.

Crossing to the chest of drawers on which the clock sat, Juliette studied the time. "Eleven thirty. We're supposed to leave in about three hours."

Amelia pushed out a breath. "I dread it already."

"Perhaps you should stay home."

"Do you think Lady Everly would agree to let me do that? She is taking her responsibility as our sponsor far more seriously than I would ever have imagined, what with the list of suitors she presented and all the events she plans on taking us to."

"It does appear as though Raphe's concerns about her suitability were grossly misplaced, though I must confess I'm enjoying the dowager duchess's company, as well."

"As am I," Amelia admitted. The lady was far more approachable than she would have imagined a woman of her standing to be.

"Not to mention that it gives you plenty of opportunity to spend some more time with her son." Juliette grinned. "Honestly, Raphe couldn't have planned this any better if he'd known about your affection for Coventry."

Amelia crossed her arms with a shake of her head. "There's nothing to it."

"Of course there isn't." But Juliette's smile suggested she didn't buy that lie for a second. Thankfully, she chose not to pursue it, saying instead, "Leave Lady Everly to me, Amelia. I'll see to it that she doesn't press you about going out today." Rising, Juliette leaned forward and pressed a kiss to Amelia's cheek. "Try to sleep a bit more. You won't feel the pain if you do."

To do so was of course out of the question. Especially since Amelia felt perfectly fine and remarkably awake. She longed to get out of bed and proceed with her day, but knew she could not risk doing so if she were to truly convince Lady Everly of her need to stay home. So she stared up at the ceiling and waited for the hours to tick by. They did so with infernal slowness, allowing her plenty of time in which to consider the dances she'd shared with Coventry the day before.

He'd been perfectly gallant, of course, and considerate of her apprehension. She still hoped he hadn't suspected the cause of it—that he'd simply supposed it stemmed from her inexperience with the steps, which it might have done if her partner had been anyone else but him. But it hadn't been, and because of that, her heart had launched itself into her throat the moment he'd arrived and his mother had asked him to help. She could still feel the heat of his hand burning her skin, her stomach once again aflutter at the memory of his smile directed at her as he'd led her about.

And rather than portraying refined elegance, she'd been as light on her feet as an ox plowing a muddy field would have been if it were also dragging a cartload of stone behind it. Flinging her arm across her face she let out a groan. Why did he have to divest her of her senses so? She was having a hard enough time recalling correct etiquette, posture and speech without him constantly muddling her brain.

She knew she tended to tense up in her effort to overcome it, which invariably resulted in more mistakes than she'd otherwise make if he weren't present. And then there was the self-awareness she now harbored on account of a few cruel words—the knowledge that she could never hope to win a man like him. Everything combined to make dancing with him the sweetest kind of torture.

And yet, he'd miraculously managed to put her at ease during the waltz, a feat she would not have thought possible until it had been accomplished. His hands had found her waist—something that would have made her stop breathing if he hadn't lifted her up in the air. She'd been so shocked by the unexpectedness of it that all tension had fled her body, replaced by nothing but utter delight at the weightlessness she'd experienced. For a moment, she'd imagined what birds must feel like without gravity anchoring them to the ground. She remembered laughing too, because if something like that didn't warrant laughter, she really didn't know what might.

It had been incredible; a welcome distraction from her thoughts. And it had made her relax just as Coventry had wanted her to, if only for a moment. But while the whole experience had left her feeling breathless and more enamored than ever before, she knew better than to suppose he might hold a similar regard for her. The man was simply being helpful and kind. That was all there was to it and all there would ever be since she was not at all the sort of woman a man like him would consider marrying. Not for a fleeting second.

With this in mind, Amelia set her fantasies of Coventry aside and considered the task that had kept her at home today. Waiting until the front door closed with a thud, she went to the window and gave her attention to the street below where Coventry, having come to collect Juliette and Lady Everly as promised, assisted them into his carriage. Amelia watched with an ache in her chest until he'd climbed in as well and the conveyance had driven away. Expelling a sigh of relief, she then pondered her next dilemma, which would of course be leaving the house unnoticed, especially by Pierson. Well, there was nothing for it but to try. The man she intended to meet would not wait more than ten minutes for her at most, which meant she had to get going if she was to make her appointment.

Crossing to her wardrobe, she pushed aside all her pretty new dresses and pulled out the one she'd been wearing the day she'd arrived here. Fashioned from coarse brown wool, it itched in a way she hadn't noticed until she'd tried wearing fine muslin and silk. But considering where she was heading, anonymity would be a priority. Any sign of finery would likely get her robbed.

She stared at herself in the mirror once she was finished, studying her simple hairstyle, the lack of embellishment and the unappealing cut of her dress, which was further enhanced by the shapeless bonnet she'd put on her head. Raphe had bought it for her years ago as a gift for her birthday, an extravagance she'd found upsetting back then, even though she'd been pleased by his kindness. The brim had lost its stiffness some time ago, prompting it to sag in the middle. Compared with the ones she now owned, some might say it was a tragic catastrophe—certainly not the sort of thing the sister of a duke would ever consider wearing. Which was just perfect since it would hopefully prevent anyone from suspecting who she was as she made her way toward Bainbridge and High streets where the slums of St. Giles began.

Oddly, Thomas felt a distinct twinge of disappointment when Lady Everly told him that Lady Amelia would not be joining them. Although he wasn't planning to attend the tea party himself but to merely escort the women there, he'd looked forward to spending a little time with her on the ride over. "I do hope she feels better soon," he said as they plodded along Piccadilly.

"I'm sure she will since she isn't very prone to megrims." Juliette's brow knit in thought. "In fact, I don't recall her having one before. I'm usually the one feeling ill."

This statement had him sitting up straighter. "Do you suppose it might be a symptom of something more serious? Perhaps you ought to return home just in case she starts feeling worse."

"We won't be gone long as it is—just a couple of hours," Lady Everly said, "and according to Juliette, Amelia plans to sleep during that time, so I hardly think our presence, or lack thereof, will make an ounce of difference."

"I rather agree," Thomas heard his mother say from her spot beside him. "Megrims are a common enough ailment, unpleasant as they may be."

Relenting to their argument, Thomas kept quiet for the remainder of their journey while the ladies discussed the peeresses whose company they were about to keep.

"I intend to run a few errands while you take your tea," he said when they pulled up in front of Dorset House a few minutes later. "What time should I come to collect you?"

"Shall we say half-past four?" his mother suggested.

Agreeing, Thomas escorted the ladies to the front door and waited until they were all safely inside the building before returning to his carriage and continuing on his way. He'd promised Jeremy some new paints and was happy to oblige, not only because he could see that the boy took pleasure in mixing the colors and spreading them out on his canvases, but because it was clear that he was developing a talent.

Having instructed his driver about their destination, Thomas sat back and looked out the window. Unfortunately, the shop was located at the farthest end of Oxford Street, which would place him right on the fringe of St. Giles. Granted, one had to venture farther north or south to really notice the drastic contrast to Mayfair, but encountering the occasional street urchin or beggar would still be possible, which was why he usually sent a footman to manage the task. But since he was already out and not too far, he'd decided to see to it himself for the sake of efficiency.

Outside the carriage, he could see a varying array of architectural styles sitting wall to wall with each other. Some were angular in shape, lacking any form of embellishments whatsoever, while others were decorated with swirling filigree moldings and decorative columns. He'd been inside several of these homes over the years, and knew therefore that to judge them on their exterior appearances alone would be a mistake since some of the simplest looking ones contained the most lavish interiors.

Turning up Princess Street, the carriage made its way toward Soho Square. A light drizzle started up, the fine little droplets dotting the windowpane and prompting the pedestrians to bow their heads as they walked. He considered them—the ladies in their finery and the gentlemen wearing top hats—and thought of how strange and exotic this world must appear to Huntley and his sisters. Yes, they'd lived an aristocratic life as children, but they'd all been so young when they'd lost their parents that he wondered how much of it they could remember.

For a second, he tried to imagine what it must have been like for them to lose everything, suffering through years of hardship only to be forced back into a society that would happily reject them at the first available opportunity. He shook his head, unable to fathom their ability to persevere in the face of such constant opposition. Perhaps . . .

Straightening himself, he stared at the people out in the street. One person stood apart from the rest on account of her clothing. Not even a scullery maid would dare to dress like that, and there was something about the way in which she walked— something familiar. As his carriage drove past her, he turned to look at her face. It was slightly concealed beneath the ugliest bonnet he'd ever seen and tilted in such a way that he only caught sight of the lower part of her profile. But it was enough. There was no doubt in his mind that the woman out there was Lady Amelia, hurrying off to only God knew where with an urgency that replaced the immediate anger he felt because of her scheming with a mixture of curiosity and alarm.

Where the devil did she think she was going? The carriage moved on and he lost sight of her. Waiting a moment, he knocked on the carriage roof, signaling for the driver to pull over and stop. The second he did so, Thomas jumped out, keeping the carriage between himself and the pavement so Lady Amelia wouldn't see him.

"Wait for me here," he told his coachman before edging his way along the street until he caught sight of Lady Amelia once more. She'd passed him in the short time it had taken him to alight, allowing him to cross the street and pursue her unnoticed.

Instinct tempted him to call out in greeting. He'd take some savage satisfaction in her startled expression when he asked her what the bloody hell she was up to. Damn, but the little twit hadn't even thought to bring along a chaperone! And if something happened to her, it would be on his head. Huntley would murder him where he stood and rightfully so.

Christ, he was going to wring her neck when he caught up with her, but not before figuring out what harebrained insanity might have prompted her to feign sickness so she could meander about Town in such scruffy attire. One thing was certain—he was more likely to find out if he followed her than if he stopped her and asked. So he kept his distance as they wove their way toward High Street.

Keeping several yards between them, he watched her cross the street. Drawing a staggering breath, he felt his heart clench. Dear God, she was heading straight for Seven Dials, and he would have to go after her in order to ensure her safety. Only he wasn't dressed to blend in, but rather as a prime candidate for a mugging. Steeling himself, he started across the street while pondering all the ways in which he'd like to throttle her for being so reckless. She obviously had no regard for her own safety, never mind the fact that he would likely return to Dorset House smelling of sewage. Already, the putrid stench of filth was drifting toward him, not the least bit dampened by the rain.

But rather than head up Bainbridge as he'd expected, she stopped in front of a large building that would have been handsome had it not been so neglected, and knocked. The paint peeled, and from where he stood a short distance away, he could see that several roof tiles were missing. The windows were also in bad shape. Some were only cracked, but several had holes in them while one had been boarded up where the glass had gone missing. Keeping his eyes fixed on Lady Amelia, he watched with interest as the front door opened and an older gentleman with thick white hair and bushy whiskers came into view. He greeted Lady Amelia and waved her inside. The door was promptly shut, leaving Thomas to wonder how on earth she might be acquainted with Mr. Gorrell and what business a woman like her could possibly have with one of London's most notorious solicitors.

Chapter 4

The damp smell of wood provided the air with a thick mustiness that was hard to inhale. Coughing, Amelia watched tiny drops of water cling to a stain on the ceiling. One by one, they spilled into the puddle that sat on the floor.

"The recent rain we've been having has not been very helpful," Mr. Gorrell said, following her gaze. "Perhaps you are starting to reconsider?"

Amelia shook her head. "Not at all."

"You ought to know that that is not the only leak." Scraping the heels of his shoes across the unvarnished wood planking, he walked past a staircase that looked too fragile to carry anyone up it.

Amelia followed him into the adjoining room that would once have been used as a parlor. The paint on the walls was now chipped and peeling. Cracks stretched like veins across the plaster while the parts of the molding that had not gone missing sagged with exhaustion. To think this place—this house—had once been as grand as her own, that the wealthy had come here for tea and dinner and perhaps even the occasional ball, was both sad and wonderful all at once.

Turning toward a grimy window, she glanced out at the London scenery beyond. It was unusually bright and inviting now that it stood in contrast to this pitiable interior, which seemed to have been drained of all color. With a sigh, she went to the table where Mr. Gorrell waited and took a seat on the closest chair.

"I am not easily put off," she told the solicitor, "at least not once I've set my mind to something."

"Perhaps this list of necessary work will change your mind." He handed her a piece of paper. "Since our previous meeting, I thought it prudent to ask a few laborers to give an assessment of the damage and what might be required in order to make the house habitable."

"Thank you." Amelia scanned the bold letters and the long column of words they formed. "The entire roof must be replaced?"

"You cannot be surprised by that, surely?"

Biting her lip, she returned her attention to the necessary repairs, which included broken marble in the ballroom, a hole in the dining-room wall, missing floor planks throughout and three blocked chimneys. "Do you know how much of the wood has rotted?"

"Enough for it to be a bother."

Lifting her gaze, Amelia gave Mr. Gorrell the same assessing gaze she'd used on street vendors in St. Giles whenever she'd felt they were trying to get the best of her. "That isn't a very useful answer."

Mr. Gorrell shrugged. "What do you want me to say? You can see for yourself how run-down it looks. Frankly I can't comprehend your interest in the place. If it were up to me, I'd probably have it torn down."

"That would be a pity."

Leaning forward, Mr. Gorrell crossed his arms on the table and gave Amelia the sort of hard look that might have unnerved a more timid woman. Influenced by a harsh past, she remained unaffected and stared straight back into his narrowed eyes.

"What can you possibly want with it?" he asked.

"If you don't mind, I would like to keep my intentions pertaining to the property private." She slid the piece of paper back to him. "These repairs are not enough to deter me. On the contrary, I am prepared to pay the full price for it today as long as you have the necessary papers for me to sign."

"I did bring them with me," he said, "but I'm afraid the three thousand pounds we discussed will no longer be sufficient."

A cold chill swept over Amelia's shoulders while her stomach pinched itself together with the feeling that he was taking advantage of her. Well, he was about to discover that where this matter was concerned, he would not be dealing with a duke's mild-mannered sister, but with a woman accustomed to bargaining with thieves.

"When last we spoke, you told me that was the price for the building, and you assured me you would sell it to me if I was able to gather the funds. Well, I have done so, and I am ready to pay."

"Unfortunately, there has been some development since then."

"What development?"

He shrugged as though her interest in the property no longer mattered, which was quite a change from the eagerness with which he'd greeted her the first time she'd come to inquire about the building. As she understood it, the owner had been an old heiress who'd been driven into poverty by a series of lovers on whom she'd squandered her fortune. Forgotten and impoverished, she'd died alone in a part of town that none of the people she'd known in her youth had cared to visit. With no heirs, the house had been handed over to her solicitor, who was now trying to sell it for profit.

"As it turns out," Mr. Gorrell said, "you are not the only interested party."

She caught that thought and held it for a moment while considering its significance. "Who am I competing against?"

"Well. I cannot possibly tell you that without getting myself into a fair bit of trouble."

"Very well." She sat back and crossed her arms. "What is this other person's counteroffer?"

Mr. Gorrell smiled at that point with the sort of glee that made the fine hair at the back of Amelia's neck stand on end. "Five thousand."

Maintaining a blank expression proved difficult. She stared back at the greedy solicitor with dumbfounded shock and blinked. "I beg your pardon, but did you just say *five* thousand?"

"I am as stunned as you, I assure you. I even

thought three thousand might have been a stretch but this is proving to be quite a sought-after address." He followed that comment with a chuckle.

"Right." Amelia balled her hands into fists and straightened her spine. "Have you accepted the offer yet?"

Mr. Gorrell shook his head. "No, my lady. You were the first potential buyer to show an interest, so I thought it only fair to inform you of the development before moving ahead with someone else— give you a chance to counter, even though I'm sure you'd rather not."

"Well, Mr. Gorrell, that is where you are wrong." She had no idea where she would find the extra money, but acquiring this building was so essential to her plan she would have to figure it out somehow. "I will give you five thousand five hundred for it, but only if we sign the papers today."

Mr. Gorrell's eyes widened. "You cannot possibly have brought that much blunt with you."

"Of course not. But I can give you the three thousand pounds we initially agreed upon as security. You'll have to give me a week in which to come up with the rest."

The way he pinched his lips together proved he wasn't in favor of the idea, but eventually the promise of making an additional five hundred pounds must have convinced him, because he stuck his hand out across the table and waited for her to shake it. She did so with the awful feeling she'd just been hoodwinked, but at least the house would finally be hers, even if she didn't have a clue as to how she was going to pay for it.

"Here we are then." Mr. Gorrell pulled a collection of papers from his portmanteau. An inkwell and a quill were placed on the table beside them. Amelia watched as he dipped the quill in the ink and proceeded to add what appeared to be the date and his signature. "Sign here please," he said. He handed her the quill and pushed the papers toward her, pointing to a spot right beneath his own handwriting.

"Perhaps we should note that the sum will not be paid in full today?" she asked, adding her own signature to the proof of sale. She handed the quill back to Gorrell.

Once this was done, she retrieved the staggering amount of money she'd brought along with her and placed it on the table between them.

Gorrell's fingers snatched up the notes, his lips twitching slightly while he proceeded to count them. "I shall give you a receipt," Gorrell said. He reached for another piece of paper, scribbled a few sentences and then handed it over to Amelia before saying, "I'm also going to write up a promise note and have it delivered to your house." All signs of pleasure vanishing from his features, he gave her a stern look. "You understand the consequence of not making good on the money you now owe me, I hope?"

Swallowing, Amelia tried not to be unnerved by the situation she was now in. "A debt collector will come to call on me."

When he nodded, she felt her skin tighten around

her shoulders. Raphe would have to be informed of her predicament, which wasn't as awful as it might have been if he hadn't known about her interest in the building. But he had already forwarded her an entire year's allowance so she would be able to pay for the project and all of the renovations it would entail. The idea of asking him for more did not sit well with her at all. Besides, doing so would be impossible, since he would not be back from Paris in time to help her. Not to mention the fact that he thought she was looking to invest in a Mayfair home. This particular building would likely shock him.

"Interest will be added," Mr. Gorrell said. He returned his things to his bag, rose, and gave her a solemn look. "So I hope you know what you're doing."

"Thank you, sir. You needn't worry about getting paid." With that promise, she walked him out into the drafty foyer. "If you don't mind, I would like to remain here a little and take a closer look at the various issues."

Without arguing, he handed her the keys. "Just be sure to lock the door when you leave, or you'll have squatters living here by the end of the day. I've a spare set at my office, which I'll hand over to you when you make the last payment."

Thanking him for his advice, she bid him a good day and waited for him to leave. The house was almost hers, and nothing in the world had ever felt more satisfying than that. Not even the missing wall paneling in the library could put a damper on the good mood she was now in. Unfortunately, not a single book remained on the shelves. They'd probably been sold along with the furniture and other items; an entire life's worth of thoughtful purchases broken up into parts.

Moving on to the dining room, she noticed damp spots on the walls. The floor warped beneath her feet, and beyond the three tall windows she could see a tangle of untamed shrubs and weeds.

When she started up the main stairs and felt the railing give way against rot, she wondered if she'd been a fool not to walk away. "Five thousand five hundred pounds." The sum ghosted through the dank space, preceding her onto the landing. "I must be mad." At three thousand, she might have been able to sell the place and turn a profit if her project failed and she was forced to do so.

Expelling a breath, she stepped over a puddle and went to look out one of the bedroom windows. The rain was picking up, and people on the street below were moving faster. She would have to join them soon if she was to get home before Juliette and Lady Everly returned. And since there was no point in lingering here, she decided to head back out now before it really started to pour.

With that in mind, she turned to leave the room but was halted when a loud thud shook the walls. It almost sounded like the front door slamming, which could only mean that someone else was now in the house with her. Stopping to listen, she held her breath for so long she almost managed to convince herself she must have imagined the whole thing. Until footsteps began tapping a slow and torturous beat.

Amelia felt her heart thump with discomfort, then chastised herself for being so silly. It was probably just Mr. Gorrell, who'd forgotten to tell her something. But wouldn't he call out to her then? Looking around, she spotted a piece of dislodged planking. It wasn't exactly her weapon of choice, but it would have to do.

So she grabbed it with both hands, then tiptoed back out onto the landing. There, she squared her shoulders and forced herself to stay calm. She was not some helpless woman. Her brother had showed her how to defend herself against men who might threaten her.

With this in mind, she started down the stairs, pausing every now and again in order to listen. Nothing. She continued forward, stepping onto the floor below without making a sound. Again she listened, this time hearing the scraping of heels against wood. Her stomach tightened, as did her hold on the board she carried. Glancing across at the front door, she considered making a run for it. But then what? She'd lock up the house with a stranger inside?

Another noise came from the hallway, and Amelia swung toward it. She was now determined to get rid of whoever it was who had chosen to enter without permission. Rounding a corner, she watched as a shadow slid across the floor and disappeared into the study. Her mouth went dry, but she didn't let that put an end to her hunt. She was chasing him, not the other way around, which meant she had the element of—

A tall broad-shouldered figure stepped out, and Amelia screamed as she swung the plank straight at the intruder. Except the hallway's width did not allow for her to make a full rotation. Instead, she struck the wall with a bang that sent tremors shooting through her hands. She dropped the plank and, finding herself unarmed, curled her fingers into a fist and proceeded to strike.

A large hand grabbed hold of her wrist before she delivered the blow. So she tried with the other until this too was trapped by her attacker, which left her with only one choice. Swinging her leg back, she prepared to kick as hard as she could.

"Stop!"

The voice that spoke froze her in place more effectively than anything else would have. It prompted her heart to thump out a much faster rhythm. Beneath her woolen dress she could feel her skin prick with a flush of mortified heat. Pulling breaths into her lungs, she forced herself to look up and acknowledge the fact that the man who held her was worse than a stranger. And as her eyes met Coventry's from beneath her dark lashes, she knew what it meant to be truly afraid, because she had never in all of her life seen a man look back at her with such intense fury.

Chapter 5

"Wh-what are you doing here?"

His eyes darkened as he stared down at her up-turned face. "I should be asking you that question." The familiar pleasantness with which he usually spoke had been replaced by a chilling austerity. Feet planted slightly apart, his solid stance afforded him a commanding look that stretched up his long legs to a broad torso and shoulders that now appeared wider than ever before.

Tiny shivers rose up her spine, sinking beneath her skin in an icy cluster of dread. He was no longer the kind and jovial man she'd fallen in love with, but someone else entirely—someone she'd never met before. "Please. You're—"

"Tell me," he demanded. The words rushed past his teeth in a dangerous whisper.

Drawing back, Amelia tugged on the wrists he still held while doing her best to stay calm. He remained immovable, his strength much greater than hers, and although she knew he would not hurt her, she couldn't help the panic that claimed her in the face of such dominating power.

"Let me go."

Confusion widened his eyes until he dropped his gaze to where he held her. Something painful came alive in his gaze, and without warning he released her as swiftly as he had grabbed her, then took a few steps back. There he stood now, scowling at her, while his chest rose and fell with strenuous movements. The pain she'd caught sight of had vanished, banked beneath layers of harsher emotions.

"You lied to us about being unwell." There was nothing accusatory about the way in which he spoke. He was just stating a fact, and yet the manner in which he said it shrouded her in guilt.

"I'm sorry, but I had to come here."

"Without escort?" Straightening his posture, he flexed his fingers and started moving toward her once more. He didn't stop until he was just a handbreadth away, and it took every ounce of self-control Amelia possessed not to flee from his angry advance. "What the bloody hell were you thinking?"

The force of his voice struck her like blow. It tore through her insides, shredding her composure in a way that made her feel small and vulnerable. Never in her life, not even when she and her siblings had faced starvation, had anyone made her feel quite so wretched. And she hated him for it in a way that sent blood pumping through her veins at an alarming speed. It heated her insides to boiling point until there was nothing to do but release her anger just as he had. "Don't yell at me!"

His eyes flashed but he didn't retreat. "I suppose I should give you a prize instead? For excellence in devious behavior?"

"How dare you?"

Towering over her, he leaned in closer. "I dare because I am in the right. You, however, are a schemer, and if there's one thing I cannot abide, that is it."

"What a coincidence since me taste fer pompous men is equally lacking." *Oh bother!* He'd riled her so much she'd lost her cultured tongue.

"You insult me even though you are the one who lied about your whereabouts and then proceeded to traipse around London without a chaperone dressed in whatever that is?" He made a wild gesture with his hands. "Only to come to this godforsaken place which, by the way, happens to be located right next to one of London's most dangerous neighborhoods."

Well . . . when he put it like that, she supposed he might have a little reason to be upset. Still, his tone of voice was not to her liking. Nor was the way he was looking at her, as if she'd just murdered someone and he'd found her standing over the corpse with a bloody knife in her hand.

"What business did you have with Mr. Gorrell?"

He asked the question more calmly than he had the previous ones, but rather than make her wary, it prompted her to think of the whole situation with greater awareness.

"Were you spying on me?" She hadn't had time

to think about how he'd arrived here yet because of how shocked she'd been.

The anger that had followed had been an equally large distraction. But now? What she felt was . . . well, she wasn't really sure what it was, to be exact. Of course she understood his outburst, but she also resented him for not giving her a chance to explain. And to think he'd been following her, watching and waiting without bothering to make his presence known, just so he could have this moment in which to catch her in the wrong, made her start to wonder about what she'd ever seen in him in the first place.

"I prefer to think of it as keeping an eye on you, Lady Amelia."

"So that would be a yes."

A vein began to tick at the corner of his right eye while air pushed itself in and out of his nose with each heavy breath. Turning away, he thrust his hands through his hair, which was darker inside the dimly lit house, before circling around to face her once more.

"Do not try to deflect." When she raised her eyebrows, he muttered a curse. "I promised your brother that I would protect you. Figuring out what you might be up to seemed like the right approach. The only approach. Because what if something had happened to you during this little outing of yours? What if it hadn't been me who'd walked through the door and discovered you here on your own, but a ruthless cutthroat instead?"

Amelia's confidence wavered once more as he

came up behind her to quietly murmur, "Your plank of wood and your fists would have been just as useless on such an individual as they were on me."

Shuddering, she closed her eyes against the grim reality of which he spoke. "I should have locked the door after Mr. Gorrell left."

His breath seemed to cease. And then, "You never should have come here in the first place." Remaining at her back, he stood like a solid threat against all of her hopes and aspirations. "You should have gone to Dorset House for tea. And you should not have lied."

"I'm sorry," she repeated. She'd regretted the lie from the very beginning, but had found it necessary.

"Because what if . . ."

His breath vibrated against the side of her neck, as if speaking had become more difficult. Holding herself very still, Amelia tamped down the strange displeasure she felt at his nearness. It was so apart from how warm it had been just yesterday when they'd danced.

"What if I'd had to inform your brother that you'd been hurt?" A chill curled around her spine as he let those words sink in. "The risk was there, Lady Amelia, by your own design."

Gasping, she stepped forward, away from him, and took a deep breath before letting herself address him. "I am not a helpless female." Balling her hands into fists by her sides, she turned to stare at him, waiting for him to react.

"No. You are far worse than that," he said, surprising her with his comment. "You are the sort of woman who thinks herself immune to danger. After all, you used to roam about St. Giles without incident, so you think you can go on doing so—or at the very least thwart your attackers by some ingenious means that won't leave you beaten or violated."

The harsh words struck her like a whiplash licking at her chest. Still, she refused to cower. "I see your point," she said with a calmness she'd thought had long since deserted her. "But now it is time for you to see mine."

"By all means. Convince me that coming here as you did was not the most reckless thing in the world."

Steeling herself, she met his gaze. "It seemed like the most appropriate place for me to meet with Mr. Gorrell."

"And why is that?" he asked with a sigh of exasperation while raising his eyes to the ceiling.

"Because it made it easier for us to discuss this building." She drew a deep breath and then added, "I am in the process of purchasing it from Mr. Gorrell."

Surprise flooded his features, filling Amelia with a sense of victory for as long as it took him to digest what she'd said. It dwindled as soon as he'd grown accustomed to the idea and chose to ask her, "For how much?"

"I don't see why that might be relevant."

The vein next to his eye began twitching again. He clenched his jaw, and Amelia instinctively took a step back. "Mr. Gorrell's services do not come cheap. He is in fact quite likely to fleece his clients unless they know how to handle him. So if I were to imagine how your negotiations went, I would suppose he mentioned a reasonable price that you then accepted. Later, he probably told you there was another interested party who wished to offer more. My question to you is whether or not you've agreed to pay the final asking price."

Since her heart had dropped to her feet, Amelia could no longer feel it beating inside her chest. Instead, she felt hollow inside. She'd been conned. Dear God, how could she not have seen it? Her eagerness to finalize the purchase had made her stupid, and now, Coventry was about to realize just how foolish she'd truly been.

Oh, if only her mind had not been filled with ideas of helping people. But she was who she was, and now that she could afford it, she wanted to make a difference in the world. Except there was little chance of that happening if she continued to be blinded by her ultimate goal. And now . . . Her throat worked against the awful threat of hot tears. No! She would not be reduced to a weeping female. Not as long as Coventry was watching. Hell, she'd rather die than let that happen.

"Well?" he prompted.

Bracing herself against the critical stare that was sure to follow, Amelia raised her chin and told him plainly, "I've paid three thousand for it."

Contemplation kept him silent for a couple of seconds before he spoke again. "Considering the size and state it is in along with the location, three thousand is not as bad as I had feared. In fact, I might have invested that sum myself had I known the house was on the market."

"That is not the full sum."

His brow knit in a frown, his shoulders bunching slightly as he leaned toward her. "Then what is it?"

Focusing on a point to his right, she forced out the words that had to be said. "You were right. Mr. Gorrell did precisely as you have described. He asked for three thousand, which I brought with me today."

"I won't even begin to wonder at how you procured such a large sum."

"Huntley gave it to me." Coventry's mouth dropped open. He clearly hadn't expected this. "It is an advance on my allowance."

"So then your brother . . ." He shook his head before leveling her with a frank stare. "Huntley knows about all of this?"

"In a manner of speaking." Unfortunately, she failed to keep her voice level.

Coventry was quick to notice. "And what manner would that be?" he asked while raising an eyebrow.

Knowing she'd probably already lost whatever respect he had for her, Amelia blew out a breath and confessed. "He knows I came across an investment opportunity—one that would likely be gone by the time he returns from Paris."

"He never said a word of it to me."

"Perhaps because he and I didn't speak of it until the day before he was leaving? It was all quite hectic amid the packing. You know, he did try to convince me to wait, but when I told him how serious I am about this venture and how certain I am of its profitability, he allowed me to pursue it since I will be spending my own money and the only person who stands to lose is me."

"Then why sneak about?" Coventry asked. "If your brother knows about this, why hide it from me?"

"Because you aren't like him." The words flew from her with a biting undertone that seemed to drain all the air from the room. Regretting the way in which she'd said it, Amelia tried to explain. "You're from a world that doesn't allow women any kind of independence. Had you known, you would have insisted on coming with me, of hovering over my shoulder while I spoke to Mr. Gorrell. Worse, you would probably have taken over the negotiations and denied me any chance of seeing to this project on my own."

"Considering how things turned out, that would probably have been an excellent thing."

"No, it wouldn't have!" How could she make him understand when he was so bent on seeing the worst? "As I said, your suspicions about Mr. Gorrell were correct. He mentioned another offer at five thousand and I countered at five thousand five hundred."

"Christ! What the hell were you—"

"Let me finish, will you?" His glower conveyed his reluctance for her to do so, but he jerked his chin in agreement nonetheless. "Ever since moving to Mayfair, I have felt . . . lost. I don't belong with the aristocracy, and I don't believe that I ever will, no matter how much I try." The words spoken behind her back at her brother's ball mocked her once more. "But there are some benefits to my new situation and the wealth that has come with it. I'm now in a position to do something constructive with my life, something meaningful and . . . I would so much rather spend my money on buying this house and renovating it than on jewels and dresses. I've no need for those, but after fifteen years of being able to move about freely, of feeling as though I was in charge of my destiny, however dismal that destiny might have been, I need to do something of my own; something that's only mine and that nobody else will interfere with."

"You're seeking power and control."

She hadn't really thought of it like that, but perhaps he was right. "I will make mistakes. I know that. But they will be my mistakes and—"

"Your mistakes so far have not only been costly but completely unnecessary." He considered her with a blank expression that made her insides squirm. "What troubles me the most, however, is your dishonesty. Frankly, I thought you were better than that."

"I . . ." If he'd told her he hated her, it wouldn't have hurt more than the disappointment that showed on his face. "I wasn't sure how to explain all of this to you or your mother or Lady Everly. Chances were that one of you, if not all, would have tried to stop me from coming here today." Pouring every bit of remorse she felt into her gaze, she whispered, "I couldn't let that happen."

Inhaling sharply, he expelled his breath on a nod. "Very well then."

"Very well?"

"I will try to think of the best way in which to accommodate the desire you have to make something useful of this broken-down building. In the meantime, we need to leave. I am supposed to be back at Dorset House in twenty minutes and I think it might be best if we get you home first."

Agreeing, Amelia followed him outside where she locked the door before accompanying him to where his carriage waited on a side street. Helping her in, he claimed the opposite seat and proceeded to look anywhere but at her, feeding her guilt until she felt so rotten about her handling of the situation that sitting still became difficult. She clutched at her seat cushion in order to keep her hands from fidgeting.

"I want you to come to me from now on," he said, his voice landing on the windowpane as he stared out at the rain-streaked buildings they were passing.

"But I—"

His head swung around so his eyes could drill into her. "No buts." His lips pressed tightly together to form a severe line across his otherwise handsome face. "You betrayed my trust today, and that is something I will not allow you to do again. Is that understood?"

Amelia knew she'd placed herself at his mercy. He had the power to crush her dreams now that Raphe wasn't here to step in. So she nodded and said, "Of course," adding the formal, "Your Grace," to underscore his authority.

He held her gaze for a while, the rich brown irises darkening to near black. "When are you supposed to pay Mr. Gorrell the money you owe him?"

"One week from today."

"Good. I will escort you. And when I do, I trust you will be dressed in a more appropriate manner, because *that*, what you are wearing . . ." He shook his head. "What if someone had recognized you?"

"That was why I wore it. To avoid recognition." When he frowned, she explained, "No aristocrat is going to look too closely at a woman who's dressed like this. They'll cross to the other side of the street first."

"And yet I spotted you because you were the only visible anomaly." Crossing his arms, he leaned back and closed his eyes, blocking her from his view. "Why do young women always have to seek out adventure? It leads to nothing but trouble and . . ." His features hardened on the unspoken words. The low gravelly tenor of his voice vibrated through her, stealing into her chest and squeezing her heart with such fierceness she gasped.

It was then that she realized his anger had to be based on more than her actions alone. There was something more complicated than that at play—a manifestation of more than one singular emotion. She felt it so profoundly that whatever the cause, it ran deeper than anything she could have said or done on her own.

Unsure of how to soothe him, she reached out

her hand and paused. She wasn't supposed to touch him. It wasn't considered appropriate behavior even though her instinct might be to offer comfort. She'd always done so for her siblings, but this was different. Coventry wasn't a relation. He was a man for whom she'd felt nothing but love and adoration until he'd shown her his wrath. Now she didn't know what she felt besides frustration and heartache. What should have been an enjoyable project was turning into a nightmare. The excitement she'd felt for it had vanished during the course of the last hour, leaving her with an emptiness inside that she did not care for.

So she withdrew her hand and leaned back against her side of the carriage while wondering if she would ever understand his reaction today. Because although she knew she'd disappointed him, she did not think she warranted some of the harsh words he'd spoken or the menacing way in which he'd delivered them. Which made her wonder if she'd really known him at all, or if the smitten state she'd been in had made her ignore his true character.

Chapter 6

Sipping her tea, Amelia tried to focus on what the dowager duchess was saying. The lady had arrived half an hour earlier and was now seated on the opposite sofa next to Lady Everly while Juliette occupied an adjacent armchair. The subject of discussion was a bit of gossip that had been picked up during yesterday's tea party, but Amelia was having some trouble following the line of conversation. Her thoughts kept drifting to other issues.

For one thing, it had now been twenty-four hours since she'd seen Coventry last. She'd spent most of that time going over their conversation while simultaneously trying to figure out how to acquire the money she now owed Mr. Gorrell. Both contemplations had kept her awake for most of the night until she'd had to acknowledge that Coventry had been right. She had behaved recklessly and with no consideration for anyone else but herself. Achieving her goal had been so important to her she'd failed to consider the ramifications of her actions.

There was no doubt in her mind that Coventry

was an honorable man. If he'd promised Raphe he would look out for her during his absence, then Coventry would take his duty to do so seriously. She also had to remember that he'd been raised with Society rules dictating his every move while circumstance had not required her to have an escort whenever she went out alone. Raphe had worked and boxed most days, so she'd had to see to the errands outside of the house as well, like shopping for food, buying wood for the fireplace and selling their old clothes to rag-collectors. She'd had to deal with some questionable individuals over the years, but Mr. Gorrell was the first to get the better of her. Perhaps because his station had made her less suspicious—a mistake that would not be repeated.

Once her annoyance with herself and Coventry had abated a little, she'd had to acknowledge he'd made some valid arguments. What if someone *had* recognized her? The possibility had existed the moment she'd stepped out into the street. Would she be able to forgive herself for the negative effect such an incident might have on Juliette? And what about Raphe? He'd agreed to give her the funds she'd asked for, but he'd also trusted her to use them wisely.

With a sigh, she watched Lady Everly speak to the dowager duchess about a Mr. Somethingorother. Not caring, she chose to continue her pondering. She would have to come up with an additional twenty-five hundred pounds now. It seemed like an impossible task. Especially when her time was being monopolized by dress fittings, dance lessons, social calls, balls and whatever else Lady Everly and the dowager duchess had in mind.

"So what do you think?" Lady Everly asked.

Amelia blinked at the realization that the question was being directed at her. "About what?"

"About our thoughts on your potential suitors," the dowager duchess clarified. She pointed toward the paper that lay on the table. It was the same one Lady Everly had produced two days earlier but with a few additional names penned across the bottom.

Picking it up, Amelia glanced at the long list of names. "I don't believe I'm acquainted with most of these gentlemen," she said. Noting a number next to each one, she asked, "What is this?"

"Their annual income," Lady Everly said with a smile. "We do not know what all of them are yet, but we will figure it out soon enough."

Amelia nodded while she glanced at the single digits. "So . . . Lord Yates makes . . . three *thousand* pounds?"

Lady Everly chuckled. "Might I suggest you add a zero to that number?"

"A title and a fortune? What a fine catch," Juliette muttered.

Her dry tone made Amelia laugh, which in turn made Lady Everly roll her eyes while the dowager duchess watched with a sympathetic smile.

"In case you are wondering," Lady Everly said, "I favor love matches, but one has to start somewhere when seeking a husband, and this seemed like as good a place as any."

"And there is no harm in falling in love with a rich

man," the dowager duchess added. "If anything, I should think that doing so would be simpler."

"As long as he reciprocates the sentiment," Amelia said without thinking. She immediately regretted the words when everyone paused to stare at her. "It would only lead to heartache if he didn't," she added with a shrug. Not that she knew anything about that since she was as out of love with Coventry as she'd been before she'd met him.

He would never make her happy. Yesterday's argument had confirmed how ill-suited they were for each other. Which was just as well since he no doubt had some duchess-in-training to court at some point or other.

"I suppose that is true," Lady Everly agreed. "But I can assure you that the worst thing of all would be for him to share your affection and then marry someone else."

"Why on earth would such a thing happen?" Juliette asked. "I mean, if he were from a good family and you—"

"A family feud could be the cause." A bitter note had entered the dowager countess's voice. "One might be surprised by how scheming parents can be and the negative impact it can have on their children."

"Which is why we all wish to do what is in your best interest," the dowager duchess hastily added.

"My brother doesn't insist we marry nobility though," Amelia said, "so I don't think we need to limit our choices to titled gentlemen alone." She'd actually felt bad about doing so even before she'd overheard those women at the ball. Because what right did she and her sister actually have to breeze into Society as if they were just as deserving of an earl or viscount or . . . whatever . . . as the ladies who'd been raised to marry such men since birth? The fact that their parents had been gentry was hardly enough when considering their lack of education and accomplishments. Until recently, they hadn't even known that a fish knife existed.

"Of course you needn't," the dowager duchess said. She shifted her gaze to Amelia, eyes bursting with kindness. "But what harm is there in aspiring for greatness? Granted, you must pick a man who you like, one with whom you feel a certain . . . compatibility. The more you have in common, the easier it will be for the two of you to enjoy each other's company, to become friends and, in time, grow to love one another. That is how it happened for me and my husband, and we were tremendously happy."

"In that case, we might be in need of more paper," Amelia said. She sipped her tea until she had everyone's full attention. "Names and fortunes are clearly not enough for my sister and I to form a proper opinion of these potential suitors. We shall need to list their interests and characteristics, as well."

"What about looks?" Juliette asked.

Amelia felt her lips lift at the corners as she glanced toward her. "While they may matter in order to hold a visual interest, they are the least important when it comes to marital bliss. You only need to think of Mama in order to know how true that is."

"Agreed." Juliette stood. "I'll fetch the writing materials so we can start adding additional information."

They spent the next hour jotting down each gentleman's preferred pastime activities, the locations of their various estates and whatever else Lady Everly and the dowager duchess were able to recollect. Amelia was just jotting down Mr. Lowell's skill at whist when Pierson came to knock on the door. "The Duke of Coventry is here," he announced right before the duke entered the parlor.

His hair was more tame than when Amelia had last seen him, his clothes impeccably tailored to fit around his powerful body. He was every bit the dashing aristocrat he was supposed to be, and for a moment, she forgot how he'd chastised her yesterday and the chagrin she'd felt immediately after. But then his eyes bore down on hers and the edges of his jaw transformed into rigid planes. He had not forgotten their argument, and just like that, the memory of it and all the feelings that had since been evoked tumbled through her on an avalanche.

"Ladies," he said, following his greeting with a bow. "How lovely you look."

At least Amelia could agree with him there. Indeed, her appearance was much improved today since she'd chosen to put on a white gown sewn from the finest muslin. It had pretty puff sleeves and a blue silk ribbon tied right beneath her breasts. Determined to make a better impression, she kept her back straight and held her hands neatly folded in her lap. But her heart shook with every step he took in her direction, and it occurred to her then that the only remaining seat was the one immediately next to her on the sofa.

Lowering himself onto it while eels swam around inside her belly, he leaned back, waited a few seconds and then looked straight at her with eyes that demanded her attention. "May I please have some tea?"

She sucked in those words on a deep inhalation. This was her home, and with Gabriella away, her position as the elder sister made pouring tea for a gentleman caller her responsibility. The edge of Coventry's mouth twitched, no doubt because he'd seen the flush now heating her cheeks. Did he mean to punish her by making a study of all her mistakes?

Swallowing a groan, she picked up the teapot and poured with an elegant turn of the wrist that pleased her. It must have surprised him as well, for he thanked her as if he'd expected her to spill it. Instead, she felt the edge of her own mouth twitch when she handed him his cup. She'd learned long ago that even the smallest of victories ought to be savored, and so she did exactly that.

"We were just about to decide on the most eligible suitors for Lady Amelia and Lady Juliette to pursue," the dowager duchess explained.

"Ah," Coventry said with a grin. "I have arrived at a hunting party. Will you be bringing out the hounds, I wonder?"

"They shan't be needed." Picking up the list of names, Lady Everly waved it in the air. "When these young men see Lady Amelia and Lady Juliette at

Elmwood House on Friday, they will flock to them on their own accord. Mark my word."

The slight puckering of Coventry's forehead suggested he wasn't convinced, but if that were the case, he failed to mention it. Instead he asked, "So then . . ." He reached across the table, accepting the list from Lady Everly's outstretched hand. "Which of these is your main mark?"

"You needn't speak of them as though they're going to get shot at," Amelia muttered.

"Does Cupid not wield a bow and arrow?"

Puffing out a breath, she crossed her arms, then remembered that she was supposed to keep her hands folded in her lap, and lowered them once more. She couldn't say why Coventry was grating on her today for he'd been nothing but courteous so far. But there was something . . . perhaps the way he looked at her now, as if to say, *I know your secret, and I will hold it over you forever.* The worst part wasn't even the fact that she only had herself to blame, it was the realization that he might be the only person capable of helping her. But to ask him to do so . . . Ugh! She'd almost rather swallow a slug.

Almost.

"We have advised Lady Amelia to consider Mr. Lowell first," the dowager duchess said. She'd obviously decided to ignore the comment about Cupid.

Coventry gave a thoughtful nod while he studied the paper. "His grandfather is the Earl of Scranton, so there will be a title there one day. Presently,

however, I doubt that few would think it inappropriate for him to marry a viscount's granddaughter,
regardless of her upbringing."

Amelia flinched at the factual way in which he
was talking. Not a hint of emotion seeped into
his words as he continued to speak in favor of the
potential match. By the time he was done, she felt
raw inside. He'd even said he would happily make
the necessary introduction, which could only mean
he was pleased with the idea of her marrying Mr.
Lowell. Perhaps he believed a courtship would
give her something else to think of besides lying
to him in order to buy an overpriced ruin. She still
couldn't help but shudder with the thought of him
knowing how thoroughly she'd been duped.

But a part of her had hoped against all odds that
he might not have been quite so eager to see her form
an attachment to another man. Foolish woman that
she was. He had never viewed her as anything other
than his friend's sister, and he never would.

Tightening her stomach around the pain slicing through it, she reminded herself that she didn't
care. He was not as kind as she'd thought him to
be but in possession of a brutal streak she'd rather
avoid from now on. Still, she ought to make a
better effort at offering him an apology. Perhaps
then they could at least return to some sort of
friendship where she didn't feel as though he was
constantly judging her.

"He will inherit a large estate one day," Lady
Everly said, still speaking of Mr. Lowell. "In the

meantime, the twenty thousand pounds he makes per annum is a respectable sum. If I recall, he even enjoys a good game of croquet."

"Really?" Amelia asked with interest. She'd only recently been introduced to the sport a couple of weeks ago, but had taken to it with pleasure right from the start.

"Why does that seem to please you?" Coventry asked. "Do you like to play?"

"On occasion," she said with a bit of a shrug. Looking at him then, she added, "There can be something very rewarding about hitting a ball with a mallet."

He looked dubious, but still ended up saying, "In that case, I would suggest trying golf, but that game requires more finesse than one would be able to garner from wielding a cumbersome bit of wood."

His implication wasn't lost on her, which prompted her to respond in kind. "My only regret is when I miss."

"I believe golf is played at a club just north of London," the dowager duchess said, seemingly unaware of the veiled argument taking place. "I can look into it if you would like to learn."

Amelia forced a smile. "Thank you, but that won't be necessary. I believe I shall stick to croquet for now. Especially if that is what Mr. Lowell enjoys playing."

"I believe he is fond of shuttlecock too," Lady Everly said. "In fact, he enjoys playing a wide variety of games."

"Excellent." Amelia reached for her teacup and

took another sip. "We shan't be bored then when we're together. What a relief."

Beside her, Coventry made a sound that sounded a bit like a choked cough. So she glanced toward him and saw he was actually smiling. Or doing his best not to and failing miserably. It lasted only until he found her watching, at which point his lips tightened to accommodate the stern look that followed.

With a shake of her head, Amelia turned away and decided that she would have one of the tempting biscuits that sat on the table just waiting to be devoured. Picking one up, she bit into the flaky treat, enjoying the flavor of ginger and spice as it nipped at her tongue.

"Shall we resume your dance lessons then?" the dowager duchess asked.

Amelia froze with the remainder of her biscuit still poised in midair.

"I think the ladies did very well last time," Coventry said. On the table before him, his tea remained untouched, prompting Amelia to wonder if he'd requested it only to unnerve her. "They need not go over the dances again."

"I disagree," Lady Everly said. "Amelia made several mistakes, so I would like to ensure she can manage to refrain from doing so when Society is watching."

With a sigh, Amelia accepted the fact that she was once again the center of unwanted attention. She set down her biscuit and glanced at Coventry, whose posture remained as stiff as ever. Still, the dances would allow them a chance to speak more privately, which might not be such a bad thing if she truly wished to convey her regrets with sincerity.

Well, it was rather like swallowing cod-liver oil, wasn't it? One did it because one had to, not because one wanted to. But in this case, it would be the right thing to do, which left her with little choice but to get it over with.

"Perhaps you are right," Coventry said. "It would be unfortunate if anyone thought her to be anything less than the lady she truly is." Getting up, he turned to offer her his hand with a meaningful look.

The fact that her insides collapsed beneath his regard did not prevent her from forcing elegance into her limbs and rising as if she floated on air. Her chin came up and her eyes met his with defiance. "I can assure you that that will not happen, Your Grace." She settled her hand carefully over his, just as Gabriella had taught her, and followed the gesture with a smile. "Shall we proceed?"

A flicker of uncertainty entered his gaze, and for a second he simply stood there, staring back at her. But then he collected himself and nodded. "Certainly." He glanced at his mother. "I trust you will be counting the beats again?"

"Of course."

Coventry led Amelia across to the parlor door and out into the hallway. "Then by all means, let us get on with it," he murmured, leaving no illusion about his desire to partner with her this afternoon. It was just as lacking as hers was.

Chapter 7

Feeling irritable on account of the sleepless night he'd passed, Thomas led Lady Amelia through to the ballroom while the rest of their small party followed behind. She did not glance at him once while they walked, her eyes stubbornly trained on their destination. A weaker woman would no doubt have shied away from him after the way he'd treated her yesterday, but not Lady Amelia. Her posture was more correct than he'd ever seen it before, her determinedness to safeguard her pride so astute it gifted her with a regal bearing. She was not going to let his angry words bring her down. On the contrary, she would thwart them with her head held high.

There was something to be said about that. For one thing, he respected her for it. For another, he couldn't help but be a little bit proud of her for standing up to him with as much resolve as she had. Most young ladies would have backed away. Then again, most young ladies would not have lied about their whereabouts and then proceeded to traipse through the streets of London dressed like a beggar in order to rendezvous with a man at a questionable location. The memory of it still infuriated him and yet . . . as convinced as he'd been of her wrongdoing last night, he'd since concluded that she might have been right about a couple of things and that she deserved an apology for his aggressive behavior.

"We will start with a typical country dance," his mother announced once he and Amelia had stepped into the center of the ballroom. A beat began and he held out his hand. She placed hers over it and it occurred to him she was making a particular effort to touch him as little as possible, the point of contact so light it was barely there at all.

Annoyed for some reason he couldn't explain, he led her through the paces at a leisurely speed, turning, stepping aside and moving forward with precise movements. Today, she had no difficulty with her steps. Even the reel and cotillion were executed with success. It was almost as if her annoyance with him lent an element of focus she'd been denied before. Which seemed absurd. If anything, he would have thought it would have been the other way around.

"And now for the waltz," his mother said. "If you manage that as well as the previous dances, Lady Amelia, you are bound to become a remarkable success."

Thomas took his position across from her. She still refused to meet his gaze, her eyes trained on a spot right next to his shoulder. The effect of her standoffishness—the contrast it held to the last time they'd danced—was such that he felt compelled to force a reaction from her. Any reaction would do at this point. So he stepped toward her the moment his mother began to clap and pulled her into his arms.

A gasp flew from between Lady Amelia's lips as he swept her into the dance a second earlier than she'd expected. Her eyes were brightened with amusement before she banked the emotion with a glare that pushed at his chest. "What are you doing?"

"What does it look like?" Tightening his hold, he leaned in and whispered, "I am dancing, Lady Amelia, that is all."

They were close, not quite inappropriately so, but enough for him to notice the way her tendons worked in her neck, straining against the rapid beat of her pulse. He'd unnerved her again, and if her hitched breath had not been enough to confirm this, her sudden missteps did.

"Damn you, Coventry." Fire burned in her eyes, swallowing the brown and leaving nothing but dazzling green.

He clutched her tighter in order to steady her pace, and perhaps for another reason as well, though he chose not to think of what that might be. Those eyes, however. Hell, he couldn't stop looking at them no matter how much they conveyed her annoyance with him.

But he wasn't going to admit the effect they had on him either, how they seemed to steal his breath and shake his heart. So he chose to tell her a truth—one he never shared with anyone. He wouldn't have mentioned it now if she hadn't given it power. But since she had, he told her gently, "I have been damned for the last five years, my lady. A curse from you can hardly make matters worse."

Color drained from her face, leaving her pale and with a startled expression that almost bordered on pity. Hating it, he spun them around, leading her in a series of wide circles that quickened their pace until they were both breathing harder. Would they ever resolve this tension between them? he wondered. It had risen like a brick wall, and Thomas wasn't entirely sure of how to knock it back down or if doing so would even be possible. He hoped it would be, for he rather missed the smiles Lady Amelia had always bestowed upon him. They'd been so full of genuine happiness they made him want to smile too, no matter how rotten his day might be.

But she didn't appear to be in any mood for reconciliation at the moment, and he had to admit that his most recent remark didn't make it seem as though he might be either. Except he was. As disappointed as he was in her, especially for lying, he desperately wanted to put their dispute behind them and get back to their amicable repartee. He continued to ponder that thought until his mother clapped the final beat and he drew Lady Amelia to a stop. Perhaps if they could have a chance to speak privately?

"Mama," he said as he led Lady Amelia toward the spot where his mother was standing beside

Lady Everly and Lady Juliette. "The dances have exhausted us. Do you mind if we take a turn in the garden and get some fresh air before I continue with Lady Juliette?"

His mother considered the request for a moment. She glanced toward the French doors leading out onto the terrace, then returned her gaze to him. "I see no harm in it as long as you remain within view."

As if disappearing from view was an option on the stretch of green that sat between the house and the park. "Thank you," he said without pointing that out. "We won't be very long."

Whatever Lady Amelia's thoughts were on his attempt to whisk her away from the others, she didn't voice them. Rather, she accompanied him in complete silence and with renewed stiffness to her stride.

"I must confess this hostility between us is beginning to grate on me," he said, leading her out to the terrace.

"Then you obviously have no patience for combat since it has only been little more than twenty-four hours since our falling-out."

He gave her a humorless smile. "Is this how you wish to continue? With each of us throwing sharp rejoinders at the other until we eventually say the one thing that will ruin our friendship forever?"

"No." She sighed. "Of course not. But you are obviously still angry with me and I . . . well, to be honest, I thought my irritation with you had subsided until you arrived this afternoon."

Not knowing what to say to that exactly, he

drew her toward the steps leading down to the lawn. A couple of trees stood in one corner close to the hedge that hugged the fence. Beneath them sat a stone bench, partially shaded by overhanging branches. It was a much finer day today than it had been yesterday. The sun had turned the cloudless sky a bright shade of blue, the golden rays enhancing the colors around them with an almost surreal vibrancy that shifted everything else to the background. It was just him and her now, secluded from the outside world in this tiny piece of heaven the garden had to offer.

They reached the bench and he motioned for her to sit, which she did while he remained standing. "I am not the sort of man who stubbornly insists on being right. While I do strive to avoid mistakes, I am not without fallibility." Raising her gaze, she looked at him in a different way than she had done since his arrival. Her eyes were more studious now, more attentive and somehow more alert. It prompted him to continue. "With this in mind, I have assessed our conversation yesterday at great length and found . . ." It was vital he chose his next words wisely in order to avoid making matters worse. "The way in which I responded to your behavior was unacceptable. Please accept my apology with the assurance that I will never insult you in such a way again."

"Thank you, but my behavior, as you put it, was deserving of your wrath. I acted carelessly because I wanted to accomplish my goal. The obstacles in my path didn't matter—I was too intent on thwarting them by whatever means necessary."

Pressing her lips together, she appeared to be suddenly lost and uncertain, and the innate need that followed, to sit down beside her and pull her into his arms, was quick and powerful. He resisted it only because of his strict upbringing, and then immediately wondered what on earth had come over him.

Her next words chased his fragile ponderings away. "You're not the only one who needs to apologize, Coventry. What I did was reckless, just as you said, for numerous reasons. Lying to you only made matters worse and I . . . I now fear it will influence the opinion you have of my character. Which is why I must assure you that I don't make a habit of being dishonest. But I felt it was necessary at the time, though I was wrong to do so, and for that I am sincerely sorry."

Her features softened until nothing but genuine remorse remained. It shone from her eyes and traced the curve of her lips in a desperate plea for forgiveness. "It occurs to me that I never asked you about your reasoning." Stepping closer, he allowed himself to sit down beside her while keeping a respectable amount of distance between them. "Why did you do it, Lady Amelia? Why is acquiring that house so important to you that you would risk so much in order to obtain it?"

It took a while for her to speak. In fact, he'd begun to think she wouldn't answer, her gaze fixed on a flower bed filled with a lovely collection of roses. The sweet scent permeated the air while bees buzzed to and fro in their lively search for nectar.

"One of the hardest things about moving into this grand house and being dressed like a princess, besides knowing I'll never truly fit in and that some will always question my suitability, is remembering the people I left behind—especially the children." She swallowed and then clenched her jaw before looking at him with liquid-green pools of emotion. "I cannot stand the idea of having so much when they have so little, that some improbable stroke of luck has elevated me to this, and for what? Unless I put my wealth to good use and do something meaningful with it, what point does it have?"

"I cannot say, besides offering you a comfortable life that you would have been denied if your brother had not inherited the title."

"And just look at the series of events that had to take place in order for that to happen." She shook her head and produced a weak laugh. "For years I've accepted my fate, believing that if I was lucky I might one day marry a blacksmith. Instead, I find myself pursuing some of the wealthiest men in England."

"Your birthright makes you worthy of them."

"It shouldn't."

He found her blunt statement a little unsettling. "Your lineage is—"

"There ought to be more to it than that—a proper education at the very least."

"You are wrong if you think you are lacking in

that regard. From what little I have managed to gather about you and your sister, your proficiency in math and science surpasses that of most young ladies, who tend to receive only basic training in such areas. They are raised to marry well and produce the next heir. It is rare that their skill with numbers goes beyond the ability to keep the necessary housekeeping records, while you . . . Your brother mentioned you have all studied numerous texts on the subject and that you also have a sound knowledge of history, geography and politics."

"Books were our only source of entertainment. We'd brought a few with us when we left our home and after having read them all repeatedly, Raphe began exchanging them for others. He kept insisting that knowledge was power, and that it was something no one could ever take away from us."

Touched by the sadness with which she spoke, Thomas raised his hand with the intention of reaching for hers. Blinking, he acknowledged how wrong such a gesture would be, the numerous ways in which she might misjudge it. So he lowered it once more, settling it back in his lap. "Your brother was right. He did well by you and your sister."

"Yes. I believe he did." A smile lifted the corners of her mouth. "And if I can do well by others, then my conscience might find some peace."

"How do you mean?"

Her smile widened with the sort of pleasure that poured from every part of her. It produced a glow that warmed his skin in a way the sun failed to do, and for a moment, he was awestruck by her beauty. It was rare and unique, the kind that revealed itself slowly until it was so overpowering it could no longer be denied. And as she leaned closer and he managed to catch a glimpse of perfection in the thick dark lashes that shaded her eyes, he felt something ease inside him. It was almost as though she were able to pull out his knotted insides and replace them with rippling waves of calm.

"My intention is to open a school."

The words were so soft he almost missed them. Without thinking, he dropped his gaze to her mouth as if seeing some movement there would confirm she'd spoken. Instead, he found himself studying the subtle dip of her lower lip and how carefully her upper lip hovered over it. It left him feeling slightly unsettled, if not completely confused about the sudden interest he seemed to be having in that particular part of her face.

And then the weight of her comment struck him and his eyes snapped back to hers. "A school?"

She gave an enthusiastic nod. It was almost as if the strain that had existed between them had been completely undone and tossed aside. "Precisely." Her eyes gleamed with the sort of pleasure one might find in shocking someone with a bit of juicy gossip. Except this was so much more substantial, it fairly boggled his mind. "What I'm planning is to renovate that house and then offer the children of St. Giles a proper education, free of charge."

"Free of charge," he repeated like the dumbfounded fool he'd been reduced to in the face of her startling attempt at charity. Shaking himself, he straightened his spine and tried to focus on the implications of her idea. It would certainly be welcomed by the poor, but the cost would be staggering. "How will you fund it?"

"I'm not entirely sure," she confessed. "If you must know, this has all been a bit of a hasty decision on my part."

He raised an eyebrow. "You don't say."

"There's no need to mock me," she chastised. "I'll figure it out one way or another. There simply has to be a way."

"Your tenacity will no doubt reveal the answer."

"Yes well . . . there is one small issue I thought I might ask for your assistance with." She was suddenly on her feet, which forced him to rise, as well. He watched as she began to pace while making all sorts of agitated gestures with her hands. "Now that we are friends again . . ."

Oh hell. This was not going to end well.

"Yes?" he prompted when her attention seemed to drift toward a couple of birds now perching on a branch.

She spun toward him as if he'd startled her. "Well . . . I . . . you see, the thing is . . ."

"What?"

Stopping right in front of him, she seemed to deflate on an exhalation of breath. "I think you're going to be very angry with me when I tell you this, but the truth is, I can think of no one else to turn to for help."

Balling his fingers into fists, he forced down the rising panic her words evoked. "Tell me," he said, since knowing was better than not doing so.

With a sigh, she crossed her arms in that manner he now recognized as a sign of defensiveness. "As it turns out, I don't have the money I owe Mr. Gorrell."

Thomas's entire body went rigid and he did his best not to mutter an unpleasant curse. "Did you ever have it?"

"No."

Biting his tongue, he took a moment to force some sense of calm into the words he would speak next. "Then why"—*the bloody hell*—"did you bid as high as you did?"

"Because if I hadn't, I would have lost the building. I'm certain of it."

"To whom?" His words came out louder than he'd intended because of his frustration, so he drew a fortifying breath and ran his hand through his hair before addressing her once again. "I do not believe Mr. Gorrell had another buyer. He tricked you, Lady Amelia, forcing you to pay much more than that hovel is worth."

"It is not a hovel," she said with a glare. "It is an opportunity to do something more important than parade about in silk gowns and dance at balls." Her hands were suddenly clasping his. "Don't you see? This is a chance to do something significant."

As he gazed down into her upturned face, he could feel her energy seeping from her hands and straight into his. It flowed up his arms and filled his chest with a new awareness, as if he'd lived in a world of grays and whites and she had shown him the color. Disturbed by the powerful effect she was having, he snatched his hands away and stepped back quickly. What was she thinking to touch him with such familiarity? Had it even occurred to her she'd done so or had she merely been propelled by the fire that blazed in her eyes? Surely, it must have affected her soul.

With a glance toward the terrace, he ensured no one had noticed the gesture, and breathed a sigh of relief. The last thing he needed right now was for his mother to suspect his interest in Lady Amelia went beyond his duty toward Huntley. Which it didn't. To suppose such a thing would be madness, even if he might be able to lose himself in her eyes and her mouth made him think of ripe strawberries served on a hot afternoon.

"Very well," he said, if for no other reason than to stop thinking about her in tantalizing terms. "What do you propose?"

Her lips parted and she stared straight back at him with no small degree of stupefaction. "What do I propose?"

"Yes."

She stared at him some more, then gathered herself and asked, "Will you give me a loan?"

He should have expected the question, all things considered. Later that day, he would certainly wonder why he hadn't. For now, he simply tried to process her request. "You want to borrow two thousand five hundred pounds from me?"

"I don't know who else to ask. Raphe—I mean, Huntley—won't be back in time to help me, and if I don't pay what is owed, Mr. Gorrell will call a debt collector."

"Such a man can be turned away for a while, perhaps long enough to allow for Huntley's return." Inhaling deeply, he pushed air back out through his nose. "There's no guarantee that Mr. Gorrell will not use such a delay against you, however. All he would have to do is let everyone know you broke your promise—that you cannot be trusted—that Huntley's sister cannot make good on her word—and the scandal will ruin any chance you have of finding a husband."

Closing her eyes against the harsh reality he painted, she bowed her head. "Then help me. Please."

"Give me a couple of days in which to think about it, and I will let you know what I decide." It was the best he could do at the moment, at least if he was to use his common sense, that was. Because the alternative would be to make a hasty decision based solely on some new, inexplicable desire he had to save her from the mess she'd created. And that was something he simply couldn't allow himself to do.

Chapter 8

"I feel as though I'm caught in a dream," Amelia whispered to her sister when they climbed the steps to Elmwood House Friday evening. A long parade of carriages pulled by magnificent horses rolled by behind them in the street. "Being a guest and arriving with all of this showiness is something of an experience."

"I'm just glad our gowns managed to arrive on time," Juliette said. "It's nice to enjoy the evening with something new to wear."

Amelia chose not to mention that her sister had several other gowns in her wardrobe that she'd never worn before. At least two of them would have been appropriate for this evening's event. Still, she had to concede that she was a bit pleased with the prospect herself. After taking a close look at each of the gowns the dressmaker had delivered, she'd settled on a pretty creation of gold silk gauze. It had been meticulously stitched in layers of breezy skirts that billowed behind her as she walked. The bodice, cut lower than she'd expected, was accentuated with a pretty row of shimmering beads while a wide satin sash cut beneath her breasts to tie at the back in a bow.

Arriving at the entrance, she felt her stomach tighten with anticipation, because although she'd decided to forget about trying to win Coventry's affection—not that she wanted it any longer since she'd fallen out of love with him—she couldn't help but hope for him to be a bit taken with her this evening. It was an innate longing for him to be drawn to her femininity, to look at her with masculine appreciation glowing in his eyes and . . . Well, she simply wanted him to find her attractive. What harm was there in that?

Lady Everly introduced her and Juliette to their host and hostess, the Earl and Countess of Elmwood. Amelia managed to complete an acceptable curtsey before continuing through to the dazzling display of light reflecting off three crystal chandeliers and countless gemstones.

Accompanying her chaperones, she made brief and polite conversation with those who approached and asked for introductions. Her dance card was pulled from her reticule and soon contained the names of three partners with whom she would be dancing. She recalled two of the names from the list prepared by Lady Everly, but couldn't remember the third, though she believed he was a baron. His title had been lost amid all the compliments he'd been bestowing.

"Ladies . . ."

The deep timbre of Coventry's voice drew her attention as he came up behind them.

With her heart pattering so rapidly against her chest that she started to fear for her stays, Amelia took a deep breath and turned slowly toward him, catching him right in the middle of his elegant bow. Their eyes met and for a second he seemed to go utterly still. Blinking, he straightened to his full height and allowed his gaze to wander from Amelia to Juliette to Lady Everly and then back to Amelia once more before saying, "You must be the loveliest ladies here, besides my own mother."

From her position to his right, the dowager duchess chuckled before moving toward Lady Everly and whispering something in her ear. The countess nodded and replied with an equally incoherent answer. Coventry turned toward Juliette. "I was hoping to dance with you if your card has not yet been filled."

Juliette grinned. "Indeed it has not been. I'd be delighted to partner with you this evening, Your Grace." She handed him her card and Amelia watched while he scribbled his name.

He turned to her next and for one fleeting second— just long enough for her skin to grow hot beneath the intensity of his regard—he lowered his gaze to the wide expanse of skin her gown revealed. "And you, my lady?" he inquired, his eyes meeting hers once again. "Would you be kind enough to partner with me, as well?"

Unable to get a single word past the dryness in

her throat, Amelia nodded and handed him her card. He studied it so long she began to grow anxious. A frown appeared on the bridge of his nose. Looking up, he gave her an assessing look, considered the card once more and proceeded to write.

Amelia almost snatched the card from between his fingers when he finally held it toward her, her eyes flying across the various names until she encountered his. "The waltz?" She raised her head with a jerk and stared at him in confusion.

"Since your brother did task me with protecting you, I think I ought to prevent another gentleman from claiming it."

"But . . ." She looked at her sister, whose eyes kept shifting from Amelia to Coventry and back again. "What about Juliette?"

His lips widened to form an accommodating smile. "I believe Lord Yates will be more than happy to step in. She will be fine."

"But . . ."

Stepping back, he sketched a quick bow. "You must excuse me now. I have a bit of business to attend to. Mama?" He drew the dowager duchess's attention. "I trust you and Lady Everly will keep a vigilant eye on Lady Amelia and Lady Juliette for the next hour or so?"

"Of course." Both matrons were suddenly leading Amelia and Juliette away from Coventry while the dowager duchess craned her neck and scanned the room. "Let us find Mr. Lowell," she said. "He must be here somewhere."

Resisting the urge to tug on his cravat, Thomas strode toward the gaming room and approached the sideboard where a selection of bottles and carafes had been put on display. He poured himself a brandy, downing the spicy liquor in one swift gulp before pouring himself another. What in God's name was Lady Amelia wearing? He tried to recall, but his mind remained blank, save for a vision of creamy skin rising from beneath a blur of gold trimmings. And her breasts! How the hell had he failed to notice the impeccable shape of them before? They were like a pair of treats encased in smooth deliciousness just begging to be sampled.

Damnation!

He'd have to have a strict word with his mother and Lady Everly about this. Not that there was anything inappropriate about Lady Amelia's choice of gown per se—especially not if its purpose was to cause her dance partner to falter—but he'd been so accustomed to seeing her more modestly attired that this new vision she presented was like a kick in the shin.

Refraining from fetching a shawl or some other large piece of fabric and demanding she cover herself had been bloody difficult. In fact, he'd been tempted to stick to her side and ensure that every gentleman she entertained would be looking at her face instead of a few inches lower. But the fact was he'd come here for more than one reason, and since he'd no desire to ruin Lady Amelia's evening, he'd chosen to remove himself from her company and leave her in his mother's and Lady Everly's capable hands before he said something regrettable.

Savoring his next sip of brandy, he scanned the room until he located Lord Liverpool. The prime minister was finishing up a game of faro so Thomas strode forward, slicing his way across the carpet until he stood at the man's shoulder. Leaning down, he whispered close to his ear, "I was wondering if I might have a word."

"Your Grace," Liverpool said, turning his head and looking up. He didn't seem too pleased with the interruption, but excused himself to his companions anyway before shoving himself to his feet and following Thomas to a private corner. "How may I be of service?"

"It is about my bill," Thomas began.

Liverpool raised a knowing eyebrow. He rocked back on his heels before saying, "I am sorry, Coventry, but I do not see a positive outcome for it."

"Why not?" This bill meant everything to him. "Have you even tried to convince others of its importance?"

Lord Liverpool blew out a breath and quietly nodded. "It is not that we do not think children ought to be protected, but forcing men to acknowledge by-blows and then creating a law that allows these offspring the same rights as legitimate children is unwise. There are women who would happily take advantage of such a law. And what then? Would you insist that every earl who cavorts with his mistress should give the product of his indiscretion the right to inherit?"

Thomas leaned forward and met the earl's unrelenting gaze. "I would have men take responsibility for their actions. And I should like for each of them to have the opportunity to make their offspring heir, if that is what they wish to do." Tempering his tone, he softly added, "It is what *I* would like to do."

Liverpool stared at him for a long moment before saying, "Although I sympathize with your . . . situation, your bill is too personal, Coventry, and far too preposterous to even consider. No one else can relate to it, so I would suggest you think of something else—a different proposal with greater appeal. Like a way in which to reduce crime or create better working conditions for the lower classes. That is something even the House of Commons can get behind."

Tightening his hold on his glass, Thomas acknowledged Liverpool's dismissal. It was a blow, mostly because of the effect it would have on Jeremy's future. The very thought of it turned his stomach, but there was little he could do. Passing a bill was difficult work, and he'd known he'd faced an impossible battle. Unwilling to reveal the extent of his disappointment, he gave the prime minister a swift nod. "I will think about it," he said. Wishing Liverpool a continued good evening, he took his leave and returned to the ballroom where a minuet was presently underway.

Several ladies smiled and batted their eyelids in his direction. He greeted them all with a noncommittal nod—one that would hopefully dissuade them from thinking they might have a chance at snatching him up. Marriage wasn't something he planned to consider—not as long as he had Jeremy to look after. The boy's well-being, his education and care, were his prime concern. Everything else seemed somewhat insignificant by comparison.

Although . . .

Stepping past a pillar, he was suddenly afforded an unhindered view of the dance floor where at least two dozen ladies and gentlemen were twisting and turning in time to the music that rose from the orchestra's five violins. Only one face captivated his interest, however. Lady Amelia. She was radiant right now with the blush of exertion painting her cheeks in a pretty shade of pink. And her smile. It was enough to make even the most stalwart bachelor want to propose. She was clearly enjoying herself and the attention Mr. Lowell was giving her in the form of winks and privately spoken words. There was an intimacy between them that for some unknown reason made Thomas want to march out onto the dance floor and pull her away from the man's hungry gaze.

Drawing a breath, he forced back the unwelcome darkness materializing in his gut. It was only a dance. That was all. Not to mention that Mr. Lowell would make her a wonderful match. Thomas knew the man well—considered him a friend. He'd be a fool if he ruined things between Mr. Lowell and Lady Amelia by acting like a jealous suitor. Which he wasn't. Not in the least.

"She has turned out well."

Glancing at the man who'd spoken, Thomas greeted another of his friends, Baron Hawthorne. "It does appear that way, does it not?"

Hawthorne moved so he and Thomas stood shoulder to shoulder while watching the dance. "Her sister has too, by the way. Shall we wager on how long it will take for each of them to marry?"

Thomas took a sip of his brandy before tossing a look at his friend. "I'd rather not. The ladies are under my protection until Huntley returns. It would not be right."

"Understood. But I will still offer my opinion on the matter, if you like." When Thomas said nothing, Hawthorne added, "I expect they will both have gentleman callers tomorrow. Lowell there is certainly smitten."

Frowning, Thomas considered the way the man's eyes followed Lady Amelia's every move. He wouldn't care about her past in the least. If anything, he would welcome the idea of marrying a duke's sister and the connection such a match implied. "How long until he proposes?" In Thomas's mind, it was no longer a matter of *if* but of *when*.

"I cannot say. Perhaps a week?"

Thomas's head snapped to the side, his eyes coming to rest on his friend's somber face. "That soon?"

Hawthorne shrugged. "Like I said, I cannot say,

but that would be my guess. He will want to seal the deal before someone else tries to do so. And they will. That much, I *can* guarantee you."

Unsure of how he felt about that, Thomas returned his attention to the dance, which was presently coming to an end. Lady Amelia accepted Lowell's arm and allowed him to escort her off the floor, steering her toward Thomas and Hawthorne.

"Coventry," Lowell said as he and Lady Amelia came to stand before them. "You are looking well this evening."

"As are you," Thomas said. Unable to help himself, he glanced at Lady Amelia before meeting Lowell's gaze once more. "I never realized you were such a skilled dancer."

"One must make a particular effort when partnering with a woman as lovely as Lady Amelia." Dropping a besotted look in Lady Amelia's direction, Lowell said, "I believe she has woven a spell with her charm. I am quite taken, no doubt about that."

Lady Amelia turned a becoming shade of pink. Her lashes lowered ever so slightly, in an innocent sort of way, and the smile that followed held an element of shyness to it that could have slayed an attacking army.

Holding himself completely still for fear he might say or do something uncharacteristic and rash, Thomas took another sip of his brandy, realizing then that his glass was empty. He glanced around quickly, eager to locate a footman on whom he could count for a refill. Except Lowell was now talking again, praising Lady Amelia's grace and beauty to a point where Thomas was tempted to grab the man by his lapels and give him a sound thrashing for no other reason than that he'd noticed. That, and the fact that Thomas was well enough acquainted with the man to know of his appreciation for the female form. There was no doubt in Thomas's mind that Lowell had noticed how well Lady Amelia's bodice hugged her breasts or how that enticing display of skin swelled against her décolletage with every breath she took.

Christ!

"Are you all right?" The question was spoken by Hawthorne, who was studying him in a quizzical sort of way.

Thomas blinked. "Yes. Of course." Except his throat had gone dry and he couldn't seem to gather his thoughts in any coherent way.

It made no sense whatsoever, but it did remind him to have a private word with Lady Amelia and let her know that she should be careful when keeping a man's company, no matter how well-mannered or honorable that man happened to be. So he looked at her—at the sweet innocence glowing in her eyes. It was so apart from the fierceness with which she'd confronted him earlier in the week and the anxious resolve that had overcome her two days ago when she'd spoken of her plan for the school.

The feistiness was gone, replaced by a feminine softness that did peculiar things to his stomach. Not that the feistiness hadn't affected him in its own way, because it had certainly forced him to pay attention to her, but this . . . this purity she was emitting was where her true power lay. Doubting she was aware of it, he pinned her with his gaze. "My lady, I was hoping to have a private word with you. If you will permit?"

All hint of calm evaporated from her features, replaced by a flash of concern. "Certainly, Your Grace." She turned to Lowell. "Thank you for the dance."

"I hope it will be our first of many," he murmured as he gave a slight bow.

Hawthorne received a smile from her while he in turn wished her a continued good evening. Thomas offered her his arm and began leading her toward the French doors that would take them out onto the terrace.

"You danced well with him," he said while steering her past a cluster of guests and toward a quieter corner.

"I had a good partner with whom to practice." Her voice was light, underlining the compliment.

He smiled in response. The soothing effect of her words warmed his heart. "Thank you, my lady." Drawing them to a halt, he moved so he faced her directly. Wondering how to proceed from this point, he decided to simply address his concerns. "I would like to caution you, however."

"Oh?"

He absorbed the way her lips parted around that word and was instantly assailed by a series of unforgivable imaginings involving the two of them in a way that sent blood roaring through his veins.

What the hell? He balled his hands into fists and dug his nails into his palms in an effort to focus on what he needed to say. Thinking of her in a state of undress . . . gloriously naked and with her hair tumbling down over her back and those breasts . . .

"I understand you are enjoying the attention men like Lowell are giving you." He could barely speak on account of the tightness that surged through his limbs, the quickening of his pulse and the low inhalations of his breath. Combined, they produced a sense of panic and guilt so acute he was tempted to flee. It took every bit of self-control he possessed to thwart the instinct and remain where he was. "However . . ." He forced the words out. "I feel it is my duty to warn you against encouraging any man too much."

"How do you mean?"

She seemed genuinely curious while he was beginning to feel completely out of his depth on this one. "Your gown." He indicated the garment with a wave of his hand, hoping this would be enough of an explanation.

"Is there something wrong with it?" She sounded truly concerned.

"Well . . ." Squeezing his eyes shut for a moment, he wondered how best to explain and decided there was nothing for it but to be completely honest. "It is a bit risqué."

"Ah." Pressing her lips together, she crossed her arms as if trying to ward off his critical assessment.

And then the worst possible thing happened. She turned away from him, but not before he caught a glimpse of wetness clinging to her lashes. "Lady Amelia?"

"It wasn't my idea, you know, to cut it so low. I should have known you wouldn't approve since you never . . ." Her hand came up, swiping at her face. Shaking her head, she turned back to face him with a look of renewed strength he hadn't expected. "For some reason, you always find me doing the wrong thing, whether it's falling from a tree, tripping during a dance or undergoing a questionable business venture. Tonight, I was actually hoping for your approval, only to realize I've worn the wrong gown."

"My lady, I meant what I said to you kindly."

"I know you did. I have nothing but my own foolish expectations to blame for the way in which I feel right now."

"And how is that?" He'd meant to advise her in the best way possible. Instead, he'd hurt her.

The knowledge did not sit well with him. Indeed, it made him want to pull her close and whisper comforting words in her ear, which would probably be the worst idea ever since they were in public and he'd no desire for a swift engagement, not to mention what she might think of such an intimate gesture. The last thing he wanted was for her to assume his interest in her went beyond the bounds of friendship. Which it didn't.

"It doesn't matter." She smiled in spite of the pain that welled in her eyes. "Perhaps we ought to go back inside and enjoy the rest of the evening?"

"There is something else." He simply had to

make this right. So although he knew it was probably a terrible idea and had only intended to help her with her financial problem by suggesting she host a charitable fund-raising event, he found himself saying, "I won't lend you the necessary funds you require in order to pay Mr. Gorrell, but I *will* offer it to you as a donation."

Her expression froze for a second before transforming into a visage of wary jubilation. "Truly?"

There was no going back now, so he nodded. "A few conditions will apply." He might be making the most generous offer of his life at the moment, but he wasn't going to do so without some certainty that she would be fully invested in this project.

"Name it. Anything at all."

He could think of a few things he'd like in return, but going there would be stupid and dangerous, so he bit his tongue and focused on practicality. "First, I expect you to draw up a viable business plan so I can assess your understanding of the costs and logistics involved in this endeavor." She opened her mouth to speak, but he held up his hand. "Next, you must tell my mother and Lady Everly about this project and your involvement in it, and finally, you must acquire their approval."

Amelia stared at him. Her legs shook beneath her skirts while a series of wild little flurries rushed through her. What he'd said about her gown earlier had upset her more than it should have. Worst of all, he'd seen the devastation she'd felt in response to his censure. Consequently, he'd regarded her in a way she'd rather forget as fast as she could—with pity. But even as she'd wished herself a world away from him, he'd surprised her with this incredible offer.

"I understand." Telling the dowager duchess and Lady Everly would not be easy. Indeed she dreaded it already. But she was prepared to do as he asked in order to achieve her goal. "Why don't you stop by my house tomorrow afternoon? I'll have a business plan ready, *and* I'll tell your mother and Lady Everly everything, as well."

"You cannot possibly have a plan ready so soon." He looked her carefully in the eye. "These things take weeks, months even, to prepare."

"I don't have that kind of time." She knew she faced a challenge, but he was also underestimating her if he didn't think she'd made any calculations before approaching Mr. Gorrell in the first place. "Trust me, Your Grace. I will put the plan together by tomorrow afternoon."

He still didn't look convinced, but at least he didn't argue. Fortunately, his expression had also returned to normal, which was quite a relief. She hadn't really known what to make of the way in which he'd been studying her earlier. It was as if his eyes had glazed over when he'd mentioned her gown. She'd almost expected him to grab her as he had done at the house and reprimand her for daring to wear a fashionable French design.

Apparently, he did *not* like the daringly low neckline, a fact that had made her confidence dwindle until she'd felt anything but beautiful and sophisticated. Rather, his remark had made her feel stupid for ever supposing a mere gown could make a difference—that it would miraculously alter his perception of her. Not that she'd expected him to fall on his knees in reverence, but a bit of masculine appreciation on his part would have been nice.

"Regarding my earlier comment," he began, as if reading her mind, "I am sorry for the effect my words had on you, but as your friend, I feel it is my duty to be honest with you."

"I understand. About the house—" She simply had to escape this topic.

"I wasn't though. Honest, that is. Not completely."

Stunned, she stared back up at his face, watching shadows spill across the angular planes. "What do you mean?"

He stared at her, his eyes holding hers for so long her knees began to grow weak. "You are stunning," he finally murmured, so low she barely heard him. "I know I may have suggested the opposite, and for that I apologize. It is just . . ." His nostrils flared as he puffed out a breath. "Men are primitive scoundrels at their core, not because they want to be, but because it is in their nature. Here in Society, they are taught to suppress their instincts. And they do, for the most part, but that does not mean you should not be careful."

"You worry a man might see me like this and be overcome by lust?" She couldn't help but laugh. "I think that's absurd."

His hand struck out swiftly to clutch at her

wrist. Fire lit in his eyes. "Do not underestimate the power you wield." His hold on her tightened. "You have been put on display tonight by my mother and Lady Everly. The only problem is most men will see you as a treat to be whisked away and devoured. They will know marriage is likely to follow, but they will not care, because their desire to possess what you offer will override their common sense."

The harshness with which he spoke sent a spike of fear up her spine. And yet, she kept her head up and tried not to let him affect her, which was futile since no man had ever affected her more. No, they weren't right for each other and she would do well to consider any other gentleman but him, but as much as she tried, she couldn't deny her attraction to him. Not even when he was hurting her wrist and saying the most unbelievable things.

"Are you suggesting that I would allow myself to get ruined?"

That seemed to sober him. Releasing his hold, he ran his hands through his hair and muttered an oath. "No. Yes. I do not know." He stared at her as if she presented a puzzle that he was having a damnable time solving. "Your brother has asked me to protect you during his absence, and I would be remiss in my duty toward him if I did not tell you these things."

At least he was being truthful, so perhaps she should be, as well. "You're right. The dress is too much. I knew it when the dressmaker was asked to lower the neckline another inch, but your mother and Lady Everly insisted on such an alteration being to my advantage. I don't know enough about the ways of the *ton* yet to argue on such a point when they're both doing so much in order to help."

His face relaxed into a visage of quiet relief. "Then you will wear something a little more modest in the future?"

"Yes."

With a nod to confirm their agreement, he offered her his arm. "I believe the waltz will be starting up soon," he said. She placed her hand upon the firm muscle that lay beneath the sleeve of his evening jacket. "Let us go back inside so we don't risk missing it."

Saying nothing, Amelia allowed him to guide her back into the ballroom. She'd looked forward to the dance all evening, and their recent conversation was not going to change that. It would simply serve as yet another reminder of why he would never in a million years consider making her his duchess.

Chapter 9

Watching the red wooden ball roll heavily along the ground, Amelia quietly nudged it along with her mind. Just a few more inches . . . It stopped short of the wicket toward which it had been heading.

"Is it my turn now?" Juliette asked. She was standing a few paces away next to Mr. Lowell and Mr. Burton, who'd both come to call for the third day in a row. Hoping to avoid the monotony of more pleasantries served with a cup of tea, Amelia had suggested they all enjoy the fine weather with a game of croquet.

"I believe so," Mr. Burton, a gentleman farmer with a very impressive income and a joyful expression, said.

Stepping aside, Amelia watched her sister take her position and swing her mallet toward her target. The ball flew across the grass in the right direction, but missed the wickets along the way.

"Allow me to help," Mr. Burton called, marching off in Juliette's direction. He and Lowell had been showing up every day since the Elmwood ball.

Which had apparently kept Coventry away. He'd come to call as planned but had not been shown in. Instead, he'd left a note with Pierson stating that he would return some other time when she was not busy entertaining other guests.

This had repeated on Sunday, prompting her to inform Pierson this morning that if Coventry and his mother happened to call, they were to be shown in immediately. No matter what. After all, she had only one more day remaining before she would have to meet with Mr. Gorrell again, so it was imperative that she convince Coventry to make the donation he'd offered.

"Perhaps we can go for a ride tomorrow," Lowell suggested, moving a bit closer to her. His dark brown hair held a fussy appeal on account of the breeze that continued to disturb it. He was an attractive man without question, and Amelia knew she was fortunate to have gained his notice. She could certainly do a lot worse. And Burton wasn't bad either. He wasn't classically handsome the way Lowell was, but there was a kindness to him—an element of generosity and pleasantness—that held great appeal.

"We may have to consider another day," she said. "Perhaps later in the week?"

He gave her a somber look. "Just as long as I know you are not trying to set me aside."

"Of course not." She gave him a smile that would hopefully put him at ease. "You know I enjoy your company." Which was true. For one thing, she found his appreciation for games appealing. For another, he was doing an excellent job of distracting her from the yearnings of her heart. If they were to marry, she supposed she would be content even if passion would probably be lacking. He simply didn't seem to have it in him to stir such emotion in her. Nor did Burton.

Indeed, only one man was capable of accomplishing that and he . . . She blinked as she stared toward the stairs leading down to the lawn. Because there he was now, striding toward her at a leisurely pace that made butterflies flitter about in her belly.

Dressed in a green jacket and gray breeches with boots that gleamed in the afternoon sun, he carried himself with a casual ease that belied the penetrating glower in his eyes. For some peculiar reason, he did not look the least bit pleased, though he did seem to make some effort to hide the fact behind a strained smile.

"My lady," he said by way of greeting once he'd managed to circumvent the croquet course. He tipped his hat toward Lowell and Burton, who'd rejoined them after helping Juliette. "Gentlemen." Glancing toward Juliette, he said, "It looks as though you are having a great deal of fun here."

"Lady Amelia and Lady Juliette are extremely hospitable and much more interesting company than most young ladies of our acquaintance," Mr. Burton remarked.

"He is right," Lowell said. His eyes met Amelia's. "I cannot tell you how happy I was when you suggested we play this game. Most ladies would never think to do so when receiving callers."

"Oh." Amelia briefly wondered if she might have made a faux pas but then dismissed the idea since Lady Everly had sanctioned the game. "I simply thought it might be a refreshing change from contemplating the weather."

A smile lifted Mr. Burton's lips. "How right you are, my lady."

Coventry didn't seem to agree. "The thing of it is, however, my mother and I have been trying to speak with you for three days now, and whenever we come to call, you are otherwise occupied." He shot a meaningful look at Lowell and Burton.

"I'm sorry" was all she could think to say since she obviously wanted to speak with him as well, but she could hardly turn her callers away either. That would be rude.

"No, we are the ones who ought to apologize," Mr. Lowell said. "We have been monopolizing your time, Lady Amelia, but it is difficult not to do so when you are as lovely and diverting as you are."

"You're too kind," she said while doing her best not to blush. The curious thing was that it wasn't the compliment as much as it was Coventry's gaze boring into her that made her feel hot and unbalanced.

"We will take our leave now," Mr. Burton said.

Mr. Lowell nodded. "Indeed we shall."

Amelia and Coventry escorted them to the front door where Pierson handed the pair their hats and gloves. Mr. Burton bid everyone a good day and headed out.

"Shall I bring my curricle on Thursday then?" Mr. Lowell asked before leaving the house.

"Yes. I think that would suit." Amelia was keenly aware of Coventry's hovering figure standing close behind her in the foyer. "What time did you have in mind?"

"Eleven o'clock?"

"Perfect."

She waited until Pierson had closed the front door and disappeared into a nearby hallway before she addressed Coventry. "You look as though you are in a snit again." She headed on through to the parlor where Lady Everly and the dowager duchess awaited.

"If so, it is only because getting an audience with you has become more difficult than getting one with the king."

She couldn't help but grin in response to his grumpy tone. "Perhaps a cup of coffee will help."

"Not tea?"

"You don't especially . . ." *Like tea*. She stopped herself quickly, aware she'd been about to reveal how well she'd been paying attention to his every like and dislike. "Coffee's more fortifying, I think. Unless of course you'd prefer a glass of brandy."

"Thank you, but coffee sounds splendid right now."

Entering the parlor, Amelia greeted the dowager duchess before ringing for a maid who arrived soon after. Their orders were placed and the maid departed, closing the door behind her.

"Perhaps I should fetch Juliette," Amelia said.

"She asked if she might take advantage of the weather and try to do some painting," Lady Everly explained.

"I see." Amelia folded her hands in her lap. She was not unaware of the fact that Coventry was looking at her with keen anticipation. So she blew out a breath and readied herself for the battle that probably lay ahead of her and said, "There's something I must confess."

Silence. It was as if all sound had attached itself to her comment. Amelia looked at Lady Everly and the dowager duchess. Both were now giving her their full attention, and since there was nothing else for it if she wanted Coventry to help her, she didn't hesitate for another second, plunging head-first into the subject at hand.

"I have purchased a house."

Lady Everly blinked while the dowager duchess stared back at Amelia with obvious confusion. "A house?" she asked.

Amelia nodded. "That is, I still need to make one more payment, but once I do, it will be mine."

"I do not understand," Lady Everly remarked. "A house is not something one happens to buy when one goes shopping."

"Most young ladies would settle for ribbons," the dowager duchess murmured, upon which Coventry coughed.

Amelia darted a look in his direction and saw he was smirking. Actually, he looked as though he was trying not to, which resulted in an odd twist of his mouth and a puckering of his cheek, but there was no denying the smirk nonetheless. It was there.

"I saw it advertised in the *Mayfair Chronicle,* so I went to visit Mr. Gorrell, the solicitor in charge of the sale," Amelia explained. "The building was inherited by a spinster who died earlier this year. She had no one to leave it to, so she told Mr. Gorrell to do with it as he pleased, and he elected to sell it."

"Mr. Gorrell, you say?" The dowager duchess glanced at her son. "Isn't he the cunning sort?"

"Yes," Coventry said without commenting further.

But that one word was enough to unsettle Amelia and make her feel stupid for not inquiring about Mr. Gorrell before entering into a business arrangement with him. Perhaps then she might have avoided getting cheated.

"Where is this house of yours located then?" Lady Everly asked.

"At the end of High Street. Right where it intersects with Bainbridge."

"But that is in St. Giles!" Lady Everly's face had morphed into a stricken expression of absolute shock.

"Almost," Amelia said, "but not quite."

Lady Everly stared at her. "I would say it is close enough." She leaned forward in her seat. "Does your brother know about this?"

"In a manner of speaking."

"What exactly does that mean?" Coventry asked in a dry tone that suggested she'd best come clean right away. "You told me he gave you an advance on your allowance, so I naturally assumed he was fully informed about every detail."

"Well . . ." Amelia did her best not to lower her gaze or fidget while she sat there, the subject of three inquisitive gazes. "He knows I planned to purchase a house in need of a few minor repairs."

"A few minor repairs?" Coventry asked in stunned disbelief.

"I told him it was a good investment opportunity, and since he knows how . . . unfulfilled I've felt since moving here, he agreed to support me in this endeavor."

"Because he probably thinks you were looking to buy one of the older houses in Mayfair, do a few touch-ups and sell it for profit."

Amelia couldn't deny Coventry's accusation. The fact was, she hadn't been completely honest with Raphe for the simple reason she'd wanted to work this out on her own. The less he knew about it, the less he'd interfere or deny her.

"I never mentioned its exact location." She'd told him it was on High Street, just not where.

The maid entered at that exact moment, bustling about as she set down the tray and distributed cups and saucers. When she'd left the room again, Amelia reached for the teapot, happy to have something with which to distract herself for a moment. She poured coffee for Coventry next and then offered them all a biscuit.

"Amelia," Lady Everly said. She picked up her teacup and cradled the delicate china between her hands. "I would like to know what you plan to do next. From what I have been able to gather from this surprising conversation, you still owe Mr. Gorrell some money and the house you have purchased is not in a particularly good state. Correct?"

"Yes, my lady. I have yet to give Mr. Gorrell another two thousand five hundred pounds."

"Good heavens," the dowager duchess breathed.

"Since Lady Amelia finds herself a little short on money," Coventry said, "I have offered to supply the necessary funds."

"As a loan, I hope," the dowager duchess said.

Coventry leaned back in his chair and stretched out his legs. "As a donation."

His mother stared at him. "You are as cracked in the head as she is! One does not donate such a large sum of money, no matter how wealthy one might be, unless it is to support a viable cause."

"And I believe this may well be such a cause."

For the first time since this conversation had begun, Amelia felt supported and understood, which in turn eased her nerves, producing a state of calm that would surely see her through this. Her appreciation for Coventry's assistance in that moment could not have been greater.

"I cannot wait to hear how," Lady Everly said.

Coventry met Amelia's gaze and gave a quick nod. "Go ahead. Explain it."

"What I wish to do is create a school." She then spoke of her own experiences growing up in that part of town and how difficult it had been, of how little education the poor children received and how this limited their chances of ever making more of their lives and escaping the poverty they were born into. "It's an unfair world, but if I can do this, then there might be a little bit of hope for a tiny corner of it."

"There is no denying the goodness of your heart, Lady Amelia," the dowager duchess said. "I can think of no other young lady who would go through so much trouble in order to accomplish something like this for others."

"It is an important project," Coventry added. "That is the reason for my donation, Mama, although it does come with a few conditions—one of them being that Lady Amelia had to tell the two of you about it."

"You were wise to make her do so," Lady Everly said. "With our support, I have no doubt this school will have the beginning it deserves, though I do think it might be prudent to discuss the financial aspects of such a project and the specifics of eventually running a business like this."

"Which leads us to my second condition." Meeting Amelia's gaze, Coventry quietly asked, "Is your business plan ready?"

Unable to hide her enthusiasm, Amelia excused herself in order to go and fetch it. She'd barely slept a wink the night after the ball since she'd expected to make her presentation the following day. When that hadn't happened, she'd used the extra time to put a bit more work into the plan, adding a few sketches and floor plans for visual effect. "Here it is," she said when she returned to the parlor.

Coventry's mouth fell open as he watched her enter the room with rolls of paper bundled under her arms and three folders clutched between her hands. He quickly rose to help her, gathering a few of the items when they began to fall to the floor.

"As you can see, I have quite a few things to show you." She was pleased to see their surprised expressions and hoped they'd soon come to realize she hadn't bought the house without thinking a few things through.

Resuming her seat, she picked up one of the folders and opened it. Inside were the papers she'd received from Mr. Gorrell—information on the year in which the house had been built, its size, the number of rooms and other features, along with the previous owner's tax payments and overall cost of running the home. These numbers had been neatly listed on a thick stack of paper compiled over the course of three decades.

"Having these accounts has been useful," Amelia said, handing the folder to Coventry. "It has made my calculations easier since I have no experience otherwise with running a house this size. Naturally, the teachers' salaries will be a bit higher than a maid's—more on par with that of the housekeeper, I should think."

"That will probably depend on each teacher's qualifications," Lady Everly pointed out.

Agreeing with her, Amelia picked up the second folder.

"After seeing the house for the first time a couple of weeks ago, I decided to work out an estimate for the cost of repairs." Coventry looked up from the papers he was leafing through with eyes that brightened with interest. "So I went to visit a roofer, a glazier, two carpenters and a few laborers."

Lady Everly shook her head in dismay. "When on earth did you find the time?"

Amelia shrugged. "It wasn't so hard to do. A

great deal can be achieved if one rises early enough in the morning." When nobody commented on that, Amelia picked up a folder. "Their offers are listed here, complete with descriptions of each item requiring attention." She passed the folder to Coventry, whose expression turned to one of surprise as he studied the information she'd gathered. "The cheapest estimate I could come up with," Amelia continued, "is three hundred pounds. The most expensive would be roughly eight. It all depends on the quality of the materials used and which laborers we hire."

"You figured all of this out in just a couple of weeks?" Coventry asked.

Amelia shrugged. "I do not lack determination."

"Indeed you do not," Lady Everly said with a sly smile that suggested she might be very impressed by Amelia's accomplishment thus far.

The dowager duchess seemed to share her opinion. "You would make a fantastic secretary." A touch of humor sparkled in her eyes.

"And here," Amelia said, because she wasn't anywhere near being done yet, "are my notes on how I plan to finish each room with the individual cost marked down. There's a list of the teachers who will have to be hired along with an outline of the courses I'd like the school to provide. Mathematics and English will be primary subjects along with history, geography and science. Additionally, I would like to include basic French, some art and an introduction to philosophy and logic. The students will be mixed—boys with girls for the sake of efficiency—though gender specific classes like woodwork and cooking will be taught separately."

"This is quite an innovative plan," Coventry said. Head lowered over the papers still resting in his lap, he picked up a biscuit and bit into it before looking up at Amelia. "I don't believe there will be another school like it."

"If you pull off this vision of yours, my dear," Lady Everly said, "the aristocracy might even be hoping to send their children there."

Smiling, Amelia shook her head. "It is not for them, I'm afraid. I will not allow wealthy children who can afford to attend Harrow or Eton to steal spots from the poor. And besides, I doubt they will want to share a class with someone who is not of their own social standing."

The dowager duchess frowned. "I suspect you might be right about that."

Agreeing, Lady Everly said, "Let us talk about how you intend to acquire the necessary funds to run this place. If you want it to be free, as I imagine you do, you will need more than Coventry's donation."

"I've actually given this matter a bit of thought myself," Coventry said, surprising Amelia with his level of interest. "St. Agatha's Hospital is run entirely on charitable donations and fund-raising events. Perhaps that would work for this school, as well."

"It is not a bad idea," the dowager duchess remarked. "Quite the contrary."

Amelia agreed. "We could host a garden party

while the weather is good—include a raffle of some sort."

Tilting his head, Coventry met her gaze, his eyes lingering on hers for an extended moment until he finally said, "I like that idea."

Elation shot up inside her, buzzing through her veins until she felt slightly lightheaded. Not only was her plan being accepted, but Coventry actually approved of the way in which she was handling it. More than that, the easy smile he wore and the spark that lit up his eyes suggested he was rather impressed.

"I was also thinking of offering paid evening classes for adults," she said. "I'm not sure how successful it would be, but there could be painting, needlework, French . . . some of the same classes offered to children but maybe just one or two days a week."

"That would require the teachers working late, which they might not wish to do," Coventry pointed out.

"Of course. But their earnings would also be higher, so it all depends on how driven they are. In any case, it's just something I thought I'd ask them about when I interview them for their position. And here . . . before we forget . . . are some sketches I've made along with a couple of floor plans." Picking up the rolls of paper, she undid the ribbons that tied them, pushed aside the plate of biscuits on the table and spread out the first sketch.

Everyone leaned forward in their seats and stared down at it.

"You made this?" Coventry asked. His finger traced the outline of the dining room.

Amelia nodded. "You'll see I've divided a few of the really large spaces, like the ballroom, in order to allow for an extra class there."

"Talented, smart and creative," the dowager duchess murmured. "Woe to he who underestimates *you*, my lady."

Appreciating the compliment and the attention they were all paying to her restoration plan and the value the building would have on the community, Amelia answered the rest of their questions with pleasure.

"I'll escort you to Mr. Gorrell's office tomorrow and help you with the final payment," Coventry told her once all the papers had been neatly put away again.

Thanking him, she found it impossible not to smile in response to the warmth emanating from his eyes, for there was something else too—some hint of wonder, as though he were seeing her for the very first time and found her to be . . . something more than before.

"You did well today," Lady Everly said once the duke and his mother had taken their leave. "It is about time he sees your true worth which, if I may be honest, is so much greater than even I could have imagined. This idea of yours and your ability to follow through when women aren't generally regarded as being capable of much more than marrying and producing children, is remarkable. Coventry noticed it too."

"The important thing is I managed to convince him to help after his initial disapproval."

"Of course that is the most important thing," Lady Everly said dryly. "Your personal interest in him is completely inconsequential."

Amelia froze. "My personal interest?"

A sympathetic smile materialized on Lady Everly's lips. "My dear, I can see that you follow him with your gaze wherever he goes and . . . the look in your eyes when the two of you dance is so . . . full of longing and desire that one would have to be blind not to see you have feelings for him."

"Oh God." A shiver raked across her shoulders. "Do you think his mother might know?" An even more awful prospect occurred. "Do you think *he* does?"

"His mother is a wise lady. I have no doubt she has figured it out." The dowager countess paused for one awful second while Amelia held her breath in anticipation. "Her son, however, is in my opinion completely ignorant of the fact. Which is probably just as well since you now have the opportunity to court him without him being the wiser."

"Court him?" Amelia stared at the middle-aged woman who stood before her with sparkling eyes of mischief. "A woman cannot court a man."

"Why not? This project has presented you with the perfect opportunity, Amelia. It is a chance for you to spend more time with him, for him to see how valuable you are."

"Please stop." She wasn't so sure she could stand the thought of pinning her hopes on such a dream.

"I don't believe I would care to marry him even if he asked."

Lady Everly's eyes widened before narrowing into a pair of slits. "What did he do?"

"It's more a question of what I did." She shook her head while thinking back on her encounter with him at the house. "He was furious with me when he realized I'd lied about having a headache so I could go and see Mr. Gorrell instead. I've never seen anything like it. It was so unlike him and so very . . . terrifying, in a way. Not because I feared *him* as such. It was rather his sanity that concerned me."

Sighing, Lady Everly nodded. "There is no doubt in my mind that you should have been honest and that you should not have gone to that part of town on your own without proper escort."

"But Coventry's reaction—"

"Was out of proportion, perhaps, but he is a man of principle, Amelia. Surely you must know this. So if he swore to protect you and you deliberately thwarted this attempt, you cannot be overly surprised by his anger with you." Reaching out, she clasped Amelia's hand and gave it a gentle squeeze before releasing it once more. "The important thing is that you are able to prove to him now that you did what you did for a very good reason. Mark my word, you bamboozled him today and as long as you can continue to do so, he will have no choice but to fall in love with you."

Confounded by her prediction, Amelia said nothing

in response. But as she followed Lady Everly back into the parlor to collect her papers, she couldn't deny the thrill sweeping up her spine. Perhaps there was a chance after all to win Coventry's heart. It was probably a slim chance, but it was a chance nonetheless, and she'd be a fool not to take it.

Chapter 10

After worrying over what to wear since going to bed the previous evening, Amelia eventually selected a white gown with dark blue embroidery on the sleeves and hem. The bodice was modestly cut, and embellished with a pretty silk ribbon that encircled her torso and hung down her back. So when Coventry finally arrived to escort her, she was satisfied that she looked her best. He, of course, was nothing short of outstanding, dressed in a navy blue jacket and beige-colored breeches. His boots, which were likely newly polished, accentuated the length and sturdiness of his legs in not just a fashionable way, but in a masculine one too.

"Allow me," he said once they'd taken their leave of Lady Everly and Juliette and descended the outside steps to where his carriage awaited. Amelia's maid, Heather, had chosen to sit outside with the driver, for which Amelia was grateful since she enjoyed being able to speak with Coventry in private.

He held out his hand and she paused, struck by the way the sun washed over his hair to highlight streaks of golden honey. His face was clean shaven, the planes of his cheeks so smooth she was tempted to reach up and test the surface with her fingers. Anticipation lingered in the confines of his bold brown eyes while his lips curved a little to the left—a slight tilt that spoke of an amused sort of pleasure.

One of his eyebrows drew up in expectation, and she chose not to linger any longer, her hand settling neatly in his before she stepped up into their conveyance. He climbed in behind her and claimed the opposite seat.

"You look lovely today." His comment was spoken as the carriage rolled into motion and began its meandering progress toward Piccadilly.

"Thank you, Your Grace."

He pressed his lips together and studied her. "Do you think it might be possible to avoid saying Your Grace? I would prefer for you to call me Coventry."

"I do call you Coventry," she reminded him.

"Yes, but you also say Your Grace a lot, and frankly, I don't much care for it."

"Oh." She considered that bit of information. "I thought I was supposed to use the honorific as much as possible, so I do so whenever I remember to."

Chuckling, he leaned back into his seat to portray a pose of complete relaxation. "That rule mostly applies to when you are not well acquainted with the peer in question, but you and I are friends. We have certainly known each other long enough for you to be slightly more at ease around me."

"But no given name."

He gave her an odd sort of look. "No. That wouldn't really be done when even my mother insists on using my title."

Amelia sighed. "Forgive me, but I find that terribly strange and difficult to adjust to. I still call my brother Raphe. Huntley doesn't come naturally."

"I suppose it is a matter of what you have been used to." He glanced out the window for a second before returning his attention to her. "For the *ton*, addressing a gentleman by his title denotes respect. Only a very close friend one has known since childhood would ever consider forgoing the use of it."

"Surely wives are also permitted to do so."

"Hmm . . . opinions on this vary. Some probably do address their husbands by their given names when in private."

"Will you do so when you marry?" The question slipped out without her even thinking.

He stared at her before shifting a little as if with discomfort, then told her plainly, "I do not know. It is not something I have really considered since I have no immediate plan to snatch up a wife."

Fearing she might have touched a nerve on account of his brusqueness, she pulled back a bit and considered an issue that truly puzzled her. "What I cannot figure out, is how to address a group of ladies who all hold the same title."

"How do you mean?"

"Well, let's say there are ten duchesses in a room and—"

"An unlikely scenario since there are only five dukes in all of England and four of them are married." He flashed her a smile that bore a teasing element to it.

Amelia allowed the effect of it to tighten her stomach before saying, "Very well, let's say there are *four* duchesses in a room."

He nodded, but that teasing smile of his lingered. It kept her feeling slightly unsteady and incredibly aware of his mouth. Trying not to look at it directly, she settled her gaze on his eyes and immediately regretted doing so, because the look there made heat pour through her in waves. There was something predatory about it that spoke to a secret yearning deep down inside. Not that she thought the look was the product of anything other than a bit of mischief on his part. He was just having some fun with her, that was all.

So she gathered her composure and continued with her question. "How does one distinguish between them when they are all to be addressed as Your Grace?"

"I suppose one would look at the duchess to whom one was speaking."

Amelia shook her head in disagreement. "Using their names would be so much simpler. Can you imagine a conversation they might have between themselves? I think it would become rather confusing."

"Once again, the scenario is unlikely to occur since two of the duchesses never visit Town anymore on account of their age."

"But surely—"

"Just use the appropriate titles, my lady. You cannot go wrong with doing that."

Amelia wasn't sure she agreed. She could think of at least one way in which *she* could make it go wrong, but since the carriage was pulling to a stop and Coventry had turned his attention toward the door, she decided to drop it.

They entered the town house where Mr. Gorrell had his place of business, waiting no more than five minutes in the reception room before he came to greet them. "Your Grace," the man said without so much as a glance in Amelia's direction. "What a delightful surprise!" He led the way through to his office and gestured toward a chair. "Please have a seat and tell me how I might be of service."

Still standing, Coventry gave the man a solid perusal before pausing on his face. "You may begin by greeting Lady Amelia properly."

It was as if she'd remained invisible until that point and the act of Coventry mentioning her name had made her materialize in the room. Mr. Gorrell's eyes widened. Giving Amelia his attention, he then spoke a series of hasty apologies while keeping a wary eye on the duke. "I take it this is about the house you are interested in?" he finally asked.

"Yes." Moving forward, Amelia went to sit down. "I'm here to pay the remainder of what I owe you."

"You owe me nothing, lady." Mr. Gorrell went to claim his seat behind his desk.

Coventry remained standing, hovering close to Amelia's chair. She liked that—the solid feel of him at her back. It gave her strength and courage. "You're mistaken," she said. "Our agreement was for me to give you an additional two thousand five hundred pounds."

Spreading his arms with a shrug that irked her, Mr. Gorrell leaned back against the squeaky leather of his seat and said, "I'm afraid that deal fell through when the other interested party made a higher offer."

"No." She could feel her stomach collapsing in a tumultuous roil of uneasiness. This couldn't be happening. It simply could not. "You signed the sales contract. We both did. With the understanding that you wouldn't sell the property to anyone else. I gave you three thousand pounds in order to ensure this!"

Mr. Gorrell looked at her with confusion. "Not as far as I recall. The way I remember it, you said the price was too high and that you could no longer afford it."

"That's not true!" Panic overcame her, sharpening her voice into something loud and shrill that she hated but couldn't do anything about.

Mr. Gorrell crossed his arms over his stomach. "What proof do you have, my lady? The sales contract perhaps?"

"You took that because you said you needed it in order to finalize the sale. But you did give me this." Reaching into her reticule, she pulled out a piece of paper and placed it on the table.

Coventry stepped forward to look at it. "This is a receipt signed by you, Mr. Gorrell."

The solicitor picked up the paper and studied it.

"No," he said. "That's not my signature." He then pulled out a stack of papers from a drawer and placed them on top of his desk. Spreading them out, he pointed to each document in turn. "*That* is my signature. It looks entirely different."

Picking up some of the documents, Coventry studied each one against the receipt. He looked at Amelia with a steady gaze that did little to comfort her at the moment. "They do indeed."

"But . . ." She could feel herself shrinking beneath the weight of her own stupidity.

"So you see," Mr. Gorrell said, "there is no agreement between us."

Coventry stared at the man for a long uncomfortable moment until Mr. Gorrell averted his gaze and shifted with a hint of unease. The papers the duke held in his hand crumpled between his fingers, and he was suddenly standing on the opposite side of the desk, leaning over Mr. Gorrell's cowering form. "I do not know what game you are playing at, Mr. Gorrell, but I would suggest you stop trying to cheat Lady Amelia out of her money before I decide to take offense to your tone. Meeting me at dawn would *not* be in your best interest, sir."

Amelia stared. Had Coventry really just threatened to challenge Mr. Gorrell to a duel? It seemed absurd and yet somehow so very heroic. Still, she couldn't allow him to shoot the man or worse, get shot while trying to do what she'd failed to do herself in protecting her best interest.

"Coventry," she began, not knowing precisely how to continue.

He cut her a hard look that warned her to stay silent. "What I would like to know," he said before she could manage to find her tongue, "is if another party actually exists or whether Mr. Gorrell here has simply chosen to steal from you."

"Your Grace," the solicitor muttered. "I'll return the three thousand pounds to her ladyship if that will settle the dispute."

"So you admit that I paid you," Amelia said with disgust. "I don't want the money back, however. What I want is the house you said you would sell to me."

"Who else did you make a deal with?" Coventry asked in a low and terrifying tone.

Mr. Gorrell shook his head. "I cannot say. You have to believe me."

"Unfortunately, I do not," Coventry told him. He leaned back and straightened himself to his full height. "Which is why you will accept the final payment we are going to make today. If you do not, I will personally see to it that charges are brought against you, and in case you are wondering, I have an excellent barrister who will no doubt make certain you enjoy a lovely retreat in Newgate Prison."

The solicitor was visibly trembling beneath Coventry's gaze. "I t-tried to dissuade her from making the purchase. Had I succeeded, n-none of this would have happened." Swallowing, he shifted his wary eyes between Coventry and Amelia. "I'm a *good* solicitor."

"You're a thief," Coventry told him sharply. "Now see to it that the sale is finalized or God help me, I'll—"

"Very well." Mr. Gorrell hastily relented. With shaking fingers, he produced some papers that he proceeded to fill out and sign. A seal was added, and the document was handed over to Amelia for her signature, as well. She read the document carefully and then looked up at Coventry who gave her a nod of approval before she wrote down her name.

"And here is the rest of the money," Coventry said, placing a bundle wrapped in brown paper and string upon the desk.

Mr. Gorrell quickly unwrapped it to reveal a thick stack of crisp bank notes. "Thank you, Your Grace." His expression was not as pleased as Amelia would have expected it to be. After all, the man had just received more money than the house was worth and had also avoided a duel. He ought to look more elated.

Pulling a set of keys from his jacket pocket, he offered them to Amelia. "Here is the second set I promised you."

She held out her hand, and he dropped the keys into her palm with a jangle.

"If that is all," Coventry said, stepping toward the door, "her ladyship and I would like to wish you a good day."

Nodding, Amelia curled her fingers around the precious metal she now held and rose to her feet. "You're a very dishonest individual, Mr. Gorrell. I can only hope our paths never cross again."

With that, she turned on her heel and exited the office with the full intention of putting the despicable man from her mind. She now had a house to renovate after all, and that thought alone was enough to banish the bitterness Mr. Gorrell had instilled in her earlier, replacing it with a thrilling sense of excitement instead.

"**T**he laborers I spoke with when I was considering the cost of repairs said it would probably take four months to complete," Amelia told Coventry as they stepped into the dilapidated ballroom. After leaving Mr. Gorrell, they'd gone to take a look at the house since Coventry had not had the chance to consider the promises it held when he'd last been inside it.

"I believe it may take longer than that," Coventry said. He crouched and studied the floor. "We are facing extensive work, my lady. As it is, I am not even sure the house is safe for us to visit." Standing, he faced her.

"I think the place looks very promising," she said.

She would not allow disappointment to show. Not when he'd been so incredibly helpful. She shot a look at him and he shook his head with a boyish grin that immediately turned her insides to goo. Lord, the man had a way of affecting her most feminine side, of heating her blood and making her want things that . . . No. She wouldn't think of that. Not when doing so would only lead to misery. Lowell would make a far better subject for her attention.

With that in mind, she strolled toward the dining room only to find herself pulled to a halt by a firm set of fingers curling around her arm. Her breath hitched and she instinctively spun around, almost staggering beneath the dark gaze that now beheld her.

The edge of Coventry's mouth lifted. "Forgive me if I startled you. That was not my intention." He stepped back a little, but his hand remained where it was, emitting waves of heat that rippled up her arm, spreading its way through her torso and making her clamor for more distinct contact.

Lord help her, she wanted his hands not only on her arm, but on her shoulders and back as well. She wanted him touching her waist, her legs and even her ankles. But most specifically, she longed to feel him in other places—places she dared not even think of. And yet, as he stood there staring down at her with darkness hovering at the back of his eyes, she felt a wanton heat begin to pool and a tightness start to form. It was both uncomfortable and pleasant and so unlike any sensation she'd ever had before. It made her want to press up against him and savor his strength in a way that was both illuminating and frightening at the same time.

Because until that moment, she'd loved him and then not loved him. Now she felt herself falling for him all over again. Except it was different this time, because whereas before she'd been struck with a girlish fancy for a dashing man who'd kindly helped her and her family, she'd since met a darker, more powerful side to his character, and as much as that side had made her wonder about her feelings for him, it was also this side that had pulled her back, though in a different way than she'd ever imagined.

Because somehow, in an odd turn of events, it was the anger she'd seen and the dangerous glint in his eyes when Mr. Gorrell had threatened to take advantage again that had called to a far more basic need inside her. It had awakened an awareness of her own elemental desires—desires she'd never fully considered until this exact moment when all her awareness was centered on his masculinity and how she longed to explore it further.

"My lady?"

She blinked. "Yes?"

His eyes slid away from hers for a second to study another part of her face. Looking back up, his hand dropped, leaving a cold patch in its place. "Which classroom do you plan on having in here?"

Startled by the question, Amelia took a deep breath and gathered her thoughts. Yes, they were here to discuss the renovations, not for her to have a lust-induced fantasy while undergoing some sort of feminine awakening.

"The light spilling in from these windows over here would make this an excellent room for art. We can put a partition over here, perhaps one that can easily be removed at a later date if necessary. It doesn't have to be made from brick."

"You are thinking of a wooden one?"

"It would be faster and have less of an impact on the structure of the building, I should think."

He studied the spot she'd indicated on the floor. "If you move it a little bit further to the right, you may be able to have an extra window on this side. You will still get enough light for the art room, but it will prevent this room over here from being too dark."

It was something she'd been considering; she just hadn't wanted the art room to be too small since space would be required for easels. But perhaps that was a sacrifice she would have to make since the other classroom would need a decent amount of light as well—at least enough for the students to read and write. To use oil lamps or candles during the day would be ridiculous.

"You are right," she said. "Dividing the space like that does make more sense."

His gaze drove into hers. "You do not have to agree with me."

"I know." She turned to continue on through to the dining room as she'd initially planned, satisfied with the knowledge that she'd left him looking as unstable as she had felt a few moments earlier.

Keeping a moderate amount of distance, Thomas followed Lady Amelia while she made her tour of the house with her maid never more than a few paces away. That must have been Lady Everly's doing, for which he had to allow a degree of appreciation since he might otherwise have taken advantage several times already.

Arriving in the dining room, he studied the cracks in the plaster and the spots of rot in the flooring. The plaster would be easily repaired, the floor not so much. A lot of boards would have to be replaced and if Lady Amelia decided to match the wood, it would probably be expensive. But he would advise her to do so since it would at least restore the splendor of the house and make it easier for her to sell in case the school didn't work out.

Not that he didn't expect it to now that he'd gotten to know her better. She had a powerful will. It propelled her forward regardless of the obstacles placed in her path. And although he'd had to threaten Mr. Gorrell in order to conclude the business with him, Lady Amelia had not shied away from the scoundrel when he'd all but told her that he was taking her money and giving her nothing in return. Indeed, she'd faced him head-on, insisting she was in the right and he was in the wrong.

It wasn't until Mr. Gorrell had picked her argument apart with his lies that Thomas had chosen to step in and do what Lady Amelia did not have the power to do. And now, watching as she moved around this dilapidated place she owned with beatific joy sparkling in her eyes as she planned and plotted her next course of action, he found himself overcome by her enthusiasm. It was so infectious he'd felt compelled to reach out and touch her.

What had happened next had confounded him to his core. Because there was no denying the awareness that had come to life in her gaze when he'd let his hand linger upon her arm. It had been aglow with surprise, wonder, pleasure and then . . . most incredibly of all . . . raw, unrestrained desire. The effect had been so powerful it had almost knocked him completely off center—something she'd actually accomplished seconds later when she'd tossed him a sultry smile and murmured, "I know."

There had just been something about the expression—something that made him want to toss her over his shoulder and carry her off to only God knew where. He hadn't thought that part through before reminding himself of time and place and who the lady was that he was presently thinking such dastardly things about. Huntley's sister. Lady Amelia. An innocent debutante destined to make a prime catch this Season. He really couldn't afford to let himself lust after her. It had been bad enough in the carriage on the way to Mr. Gorrell's when she'd asked about using his given name. Hell, he could think of several scenarios now in which hearing her say it would be his undoing.

Glancing across at where she was presently standing in front of a large window with sunshine spilling in on her, he couldn't help but marvel at his own idiocy. How the hell had it taken so long for him to realize how lovely she was? And not only that, but smart too and stubborn as hell and a few more things that were getting under his skin. She was different from any other woman he'd ever known—completely unique—and he wanted her more and more with each passing second.

It was all because of that damnable dress she'd worn to the Elmwood ball. Although he had to admit she would have gotten his attention without it the moment she'd brought out her business plan. Because *that* was not something he'd been expecting. Not in the least. Indeed, it had positively stumped him that she had endeavored to put such a thing together and then proceeded to present it with such unequivocal professionalism. To say he was impressed would be an understatement. But to actually pursue her . . . He simply couldn't. Because doing so would involve marriage, and that was something he couldn't offer. Not when all of his attention had to be pinned on his responsibility and the boy who needed him. There was no room in his life for another person as long as Jeremy depended on his help.

With that in mind, he trained his features into something bland that he hoped would mask his true feelings. "Would you like me to interview the laborers you plan on hiring?" he asked when they returned to the foyer.

"If you don't mind, that would be helpful," she said. They stepped outside with her maid in tow, and he waited while Lady Amelia locked the door. "Perhaps we can have another outing tomorrow? I would like to decide on the windows since ordering them may take some time. The same can be said of the flooring."

His heart rolled over in his chest at the very idea of seeing her again so soon, but he reminded himself that it might be advisable not to—that a few days apart would be in the best interest of both of them. "I am afraid I have some other commitments that I must attend to for the next few days. Next week would work better."

With a nod that failed to convey what she was

thinking, she started toward the awaiting carriage with him by her side. "Very well," she told him plainly. A tight smile followed. "Next week it is then."

Arriving home, Thomas removed his gloves, discarded them on a table in the foyer and continued up the stairs to the nursery. "Hello," he said as he entered. He deliberately kept his voice quiet but cheerful.

Both his mother and the nurse looked his way. They offered greetings of their own with smiles to go with them. Jeremy, however, kept his eyes on the canvas before him, his concentration fixed on his paintbrush's circular movement.

"He is painting a carriage," his mother explained.

Thomas didn't comment. He crouched next to the child and studied what was meant to be a wheel. The carriage would probably be added later. "Has he finished his morning lessons?"

His mother and the nurse exchanged a look before his mother rose and gestured for him to follow. They retreated some distance and she quietly explained, "Miss Greyer has handed in her notice."

Thomas felt his jaw tighten. "Why?"

"She said she found Jeremy impossible to work with." Her eyes reflected the despair he knew she felt. "Jeremy didn't engage in conversation about any of the topics Miss Greyer tried to bring up in an effort to engage his interest, and after a while he just started repeating something, she said, over and over." Her brows knit with worry. "She called him a daft little idiot."

Thomas felt his temples begin to pound in response to the blood that rushed to the top of his head. Miss Greyer was fortunate to have taken her leave before he'd learned of this incident, or she might have gotten her neck wrung for spouting such insensitive cruelty.

Clenching and unclenching his fists, he told his mother tightly, "Thank you for letting me know." He glanced to where Jeremy sat and drew a deep breath. "No more governesses."

"But he needs to be taught and—"

"I will do it, Mama."

She shook her head as though not quite understanding him. "I do not see where you will find the time. Jeremy is not like other children. He requires a lot of attention."

"Yes," he told her sharply. "I am aware of that. And I realize I also have parliament and Huntley's sisters to attend to, but Jeremy is important. You know that as well as I."

She nodded. "Perhaps if you cut your parliamentarian session short this year and only attend the occasional meetings?"

"That will give me more time with Jeremy in the mornings." He considered the prospect. "It is a good plan since there is only a month left of the Season anyway. And as far as my bill is concerned—"

"Don't you think you ought to wait with that for a few more years and see how things develop?"

Thomas's vision darkened. "I thought you supported me in this."

"I support the principle, but I am not certain that pushing this bill would be in Jeremy's best interest."

"You believe he will not be capable of running a dukedom." The words sounded flat and angry to Thomas's ears—a perfect reflection of how he felt.

"He is only five years old, Coventry." The touch of her hand on his arm made him flinch. She let it fall away. "I think it is too soon to tell."

Feeling numb, betrayed and defeated, Thomas turned away from her and went to sit with Jeremy. "You may leave us," he told the nurse before leveling his mother with endless amounts of hurt. "You too."

"Coventry . . ."

He dropped his gaze to the painting. "Please go."

A moment passed and then the door to the room clicked shut. He expelled a deep breath and briefly closed his eyes, regretting he'd caused his mother pain. She was only looking out for Jeremy's best interests after all, whether he chose to agree with her opinion or not.

"That is a fine wheel," he said. Jeremy's hand didn't stop its circular motion. "If you paint another, you can set the carriage on top."

When there was still no response, he carefully moved to touch Jeremy's hand. The boy stilled, but never looked up as Thomas repositioned his hand where the next wheel should go. There was a slight hesitation—a moment of anticipation—and then

Jeremy returned his paintbrush to where it had been before and resumed the movement.

Thomas sighed. He had no idea of how to teach the boy or of how to advise and help him. He wasn't always this difficult to reach, but Thomas supposed the incident with Miss Greyer had had a particularly negative impact. So he chose not to press for a greater response. Instead, he kept Jeremy company with nothing more than his presence until finally, the boy stopped painting and quietly asked, "Can I have a story?"

Chapter 11

It had been two days since Amelia had seen Coventry, although his mother had come to visit each afternoon since. She and Lady Everly had continued to tutor Amelia and Juliette in a variety of things from proper table manners to how one ought to greet an acquaintance in the street. Having insisted numerous times that Gabriella had already given them such lessons and failing, Amelia had resigned herself to their instruction. By the time Wednesday rolled around, she regretted telling Mr. Lowell that she would be busy until the end of the week, and when she finally woke up on Thursday, she'd been thrilled with the idea of doing something besides walking in a straight line with a stack of books upon her head.

"Ladies," Mr. Lowell said when he and Mr. Burton, who'd been invited to join them, arrived at two o'clock that afternoon. "It feels like an eternity since I saw you last."

"He has lamented over the fact since Tuesday evening when I saw him at our club," Burton said. He reached for Amelia's hand first and then Juliette's, kissing the air above their knuckles. "And I must confess I share his opinion."

Their charm was undeniable. Juliette certainly seemed to appreciate it while Lady Everly praised both gentlemen for their kindness. But Amelia couldn't seem to feel anything but apathy toward them. It wasn't that she didn't like them, because she definitely did. But after discovering what passion felt like—what it meant to want a man with a desperation that bordered on insanity—she just wasn't as excited about the prospect of being courted by anyone other than Coventry.

Still, she was intent on enjoying her day since it did offer an enticing escape. She would also accept Mr. Lowell's and Mr. Burton's company in the future. Both men would probably be prepared to offer her a comfortable life while Coventry had no plan to do any such thing, in which case her desire for him would be utterly pointless as it would remain unexplored.

"Was it very difficult for you, growing up in St. Giles?" Mr. Burton asked her while they strolled along a path in Kew Gardens later. "I imagine it must have been."

"It certainly wasn't easy," Amelia told him. "No child should have to endure it."

"Could you not have chosen to live somewhere else?" Mr. Lowell asked. He was escorting Juliette while Lady Everly brought up the rear at a respectable distance.

"We couldn't afford anything else," Amelia told

him, making an effort to keep a level tone. She had to remind herself that the circumstances she'd faced with her siblings would be so foreign to these men it would be all but impossible for them to relate.

"But your parents were gentry." Mr. Lowell glanced across at her with a curious frown. "Are you saying they left nothing for you to inherit? Not even a penny?"

"Yes." She'd no desire to elaborate on how awful it had been to discover her father's body and to later realize why he'd taken his own life. "Shall we visit the Chinese pagoda? If the view from the top is as remarkable as I imagine it to be, I'd like a chance to see it."

"It makes you feel as though you're on top of the world," Mr. Burton said as they started heading toward it. After climbing a long flight of stairs, they stepped out onto a platform with a railing from which they could see far and wide. "Look," he added, pointing toward the horizon. "There is London in the distance."

"I see it," Amelia said. She stared out over the landscape below. Out there, in that cluster of minuscule buildings, was Coventry. She couldn't help but wonder what he might be doing—what sort of responsibility kept him so busy he had no time for her until the following week.

"I have not been able to stop myself from wondering about what you have been busying yourself with these past few days," Mr. Lowell said. He'd come to stand beside her. Juliette stood on Amelia's other side, between her and Mr. Burton.

Mr. Lowell leaned in closer and lowered his voice to a whisper. "The truth is you have captivated my awareness so acutely I can hardly concentrate on anything else."

She should at the very least have felt a faint flutter in her chest. Had it been Coventry who'd spoken such words, her heart would have pounded. But with Mr. Lowell, as attentive and charming as he was, she felt absolutely nothing. The same could be said of Mr. Burton or any other man who wasn't *him*—the center of her own private imaginings.

"You flatter me," she told Mr. Lowell politely since he deserved nothing less than respect. "The fact is I have purchased a building on the edge of St. Giles—the old house at the end of High Street. My intention is to bring it back to life and turn it into a school for the less fortunate children in the area."

Mr. Lowell's eyes widened. His lips parted as though he wished to say something but couldn't quite think of the right words.

Mr. Burton came to his rescue. "What a marvelous idea," he said. "The City could do with some quality education for the lower classes."

"I appreciate you saying so," Amelia told him with genuine feeling. "It won't be easy, but I think the reward will be worth it."

"Your expense must be quite significant," Mr. Lowell said once he'd gotten over his initial shock.

Amelia nodded. "More so than I would have imagined."

"You're doing an incredible thing, though," Juliette

said, offering her support. "I just hope I'll be able to leave an equally significant mark on the world one day."

A significant mark on the world. A legacy.

Amelia hadn't thought of it in those terms before, but she supposed it would be if everything worked out according to plan. "I intend to fund it with charitable fund-raising events and donations. It's the only chance I have of ensuring costs get covered since I've no plan to charge the students."

"Well then," Mr. Burton said. He met her gaze with that pleasant smile of his. "Allow me to offer five hundred pounds to your cause."

"Consider that one thousand with my five hundred added to it," Mr. Lowell said with a glimmer of satisfaction in his eyes.

Amelia could scarcely believe what they'd said. Her lungs expanded on a rush of air as she stared at each of them in turn. "Gentlemen, you are far too generous."

They chuckled while taking a last look at the view. "Indeed, we are more than happy to help," Mr. Burton muttered.

He drew her aside when they made their way back to the carriage after enjoying a few refreshments down by the lake. "May I invite you for a walk in the park tomorrow, my lady?"

With no other plans and the certainty that Mr. Burton would prove a better distraction from her yearning for Coventry than remaining at home with her sister and Lady Everly was likely to do, Amelia agreed to the outing without hesitation.

She was quickly rewarded with a happy grin in return. It didn't do much to her insides, but it did make her feel wanted in a way that Coventry had not yet managed to do.

Three days. That was how long it had been since he'd last seen her.

"So I will inform Mr. Stevenson that you would like to invest another thousand pounds in his work on the Stockton and Darlington railway?" Thomas's secretary, Mr. Bryant, said. He made a note on a piece of paper.

Thomas nodded. "Yes." It would likely be years before the route would be ready since opposition was hampering the progress. Already, the bill presented to parliament requesting the rail pass through the Earl of Eldon's estate and one of the Earl of Darlington's fox coverts had been defeated by thirteen votes. A new bill would be presented soon with the hope that Viscount Barrington might be more agreeable. Until then, Thomas intended to continue supporting the venture since Mr. Stevenson's invention of the steam locomotive had already proved the man's ability to accomplish his goals.

"Will there be anything else?" Mr. Bryant asked.

"Not today. Thank you." Thomas waited for Mr. Bryant to leave the room and close the door behind him. He then leaned back in his chair and closed his eyes.

Three days.

Christ. He'd hardly slept at all. Doing so had

been almost impossible when he continued to be assailed by images of Lady Amelia. Even now he envisioned her face, that laughing smile and those sparkling eyes framed by long dark lashes. When she was happy, that was.

But he now knew what she looked like when she was angry, as well. He had no regrets about being the cause of such impassioned emotion. How could he be when her fury had only served to enhance her beauty? Since seeing her thus, he'd discovered new aspects to her—a persistence unlike any he'd ever encountered before. She would not be held back by any means, and yet, he sensed the confidence with which she attacked this project of hers was hiding a different kind of insecurity—the sort that made her feel unworthy of her position.

Pondering this, he wondered if she realized how wrong she was to concern herself about that. Granted, there were people who took pleasure in being unnecessarily cruel and who would not readily accept her because of her background. But her beauty and kindness and her vivacious approach to life in general was such that Thomas had to admit she was without a doubt the most stunning woman he'd ever encountered.

With that thought came another, of her lying naked on his bed with her hair spread out around her in silky waves of chestnut perfection. He imagined a welcoming smile and that same seductive look she'd given him on Tuesday when they'd visited the house together. Curling his fingers against the armrest of his chair, he gripped the wood and imagined his hands caressing her body. Would she sigh or whimper or moan? He'd no idea and never would since such a fantasy could not be brought to life. Not unless he married her. Which he wouldn't.

Damn!

Perhaps a new mistress would have to be sought after all. He hadn't had one in years. Not since Jeremy's birth. And he really didn't look forward to the idea of sating his needs with a random woman who'd want to be dressed in silks and jewels in return. The thought disagreed with him. Especially since he knew he'd be imagining *her*—his desire for her was so intense he found himself in a constant state of irritation. Which his mother was not taking kindly to in the least. She'd left the house twice now because of some cutting remarks he'd made, for which he'd had to apologize to no end, which only made him all the more irritable. And so the cycle continued.

Expelling a breath, he got to his feet and marched across the floor. Jeremy had proven to be an excellent distraction. The boy had asked if he might take a closer look at one of the carriages, to which Thomas had readily agreed. Showing him how the vehicle worked had been fun. They'd had some lemonade together afterward, and for the very first time, Thomas had felt a connection. He'd since enjoyed teaching Jeremy basic sums and helping him with his penmanship. It was slow progress, but not as impossible as those awful governesses had made it seem.

But now that Jeremy was taking his nap and Thomas had completed his work with his secretary, his mind was once again assailed by unwelcome thoughts—thoughts that would lead to nothing but unfulfilled need and desire.

Deciding some fresh air would be the solution, he snatched his hat from the hallway, put on his gloves and went to the mews to collect his horse. He had no patience to wait for a groom to bring it around with the thought of Lady Amelia stirring his blood in a frantic way that tensed his muscles and hastened his pace.

Ten minutes later, he was riding toward Hyde Park and feeling not even a tiny bit better. How the devil had she managed it? She was stuck in his brain in a way that made him want to curse the day he'd agreed to look out for her during Huntley's absence. Everything had been fine up until that point. He'd made polite conversation with her the few times their paths had crossed, and that had been that. Now, she'd made him aware though—aware of her glorious figure, of her impressive ability to overcome anything she set her mind to, of a daring side that might not have served her well when she'd chosen to go to St. Giles on her own, but which would certainly be welcomed in the bedroom.

Damn it. There he went again.

Muttering another curse, he turned into the park and began making his way along Rotten Row. At least it was a beautiful day with scarcely a cloud in the sky. The air was pleasantly warm without being too hot, most likely because of a gentle breeze that occasionally rustled the leaves in the trees.

Thomas tipped his hat in greeting to a few acquaintances as he rode past them, not stopping to speak with any of them. He simply wasn't in the mood for inane conversation. In fact . . . A woman dressed in a dark pink gown and with a pretty straw bonnet perched upon a head of chestnut curls caught his attention. Even though she had her back to him, he was certain of who she was. Lady Amelia. And she was out strolling with a gentleman who appeared to be paying a great deal of attention to whatever it was she was saying.

Gripping the reins, Thomas fought the unpleasant wave of displeasure that rose inside him. He'd never been a jealous man—had had no reason to be—and yet what he felt now, this urge to get off his horse and shove Lady Amelia's companion aside so he could take his place, could not be described as anything else. It made him want to punch something, his muscles already flexing beneath his jacket in preparation for such a possibility. But somewhere in his brain where a small degree of sanity still survived, he knew he had to calm himself in order to avoid the scandal a violent outburst would incite.

Perhaps obtaining a mistress was not the right approach. Perhaps what he really needed was to fight someone. He hadn't boxed since Huntley's departure. The two of them always sparred together, and with him gone, Thomas had not been back to Gentleman Jackson's. If he could find someone willing enough to give as good as he got, it might work wonders for his state of mind. It was certainly something worth looking into.

In the meantime . . .

Nudging his horse forward, he trotted over to where Lady Amelia was walking. She and her companion looked up, and he saw now that it was Mr. Burton. The man was looking annoyingly satisfied with himself while she appeared to be very pleased with his company. Still, the wide smile she gave Thomas when he dismounted in front of her could not be denied. It was for him and him alone. His heart immediately doubled in size. Some of the tension left his shoulders, and he relaxed a little. Getting rid of Mr. Burton would probably make it disappear altogether, he thought wryly, tipping his hat in greeting to both of them.

"Mind if I join you?" he asked.

Mr. Burton did not look too eager but had no chance to deny him his company since Lady Amelia immediately said, "Of course. I'd be delighted to hear what you've been doing since the last time I saw you."

Fantasizing about you in the most scandalous ways possible.

They started walking, with him leading his horse by the reins. "I have been looking into some laborers for . . ." He glanced across at Mr. Burton before saying, "Something I am working on."

"Is it for the school?" she asked. "Mr. Burton

is well aware of the project and has even do-
nated five hundred pounds toward it. So has Mr.
Lowell, by the way. They've both been extremely
magnanimous."

Gritting his teeth, Thomas tried to look pleased.
"Indeed."

"I have the funds and decided they would be put
to better use if they went toward a school than if
they continued to sit in the bank," Mr. Burton said
with a jolly grin that Thomas instantly detested.

He would not lower himself to telling the man
that five hundred pounds was nothing compared
to his own two thousand five hundred. Instead, he
swallowed that bit of information and focused on
Lady Amelia.

"I also attended a couple of sessions in parliament,
took care of some necessary correspondence and met
with my secretary. My property in Cornwall is in
need of a few repairs, and after the housekeeper chose
to get herself married to a sea captain, I have had to
look into acquiring someone new for the position."

Squinting against the sunlight that caught her eyes,
she angled her head in order to catch his gaze. "So
you've been just as busy as you said you would be."

"Yes." They walked a few more paces. "And you?"

She turned her head in order to look straight
ahead, preventing him from seeing her face as fully
because of her bonnet. "Your mother and Lady
Everly have been busy ensuring that Juliette and I
were not bored."

"Mama did say something about developing your

cultural acumen. I believe a few operas and plays were mentioned."

Lady Amelia sighed. "I've been reciting Shakespeare with a pile of books on my head."

"You cannot be serious," Mr. Burton said with no attempt at hiding his shock.

Thomas, on the other hand, was finding it hard not to laugh at the image he had of her doing such a ridiculous thing. He pressed his lips together when she confirmed that it was indeed true.

"Apparently, I have a tendency to slouch when I am distracted. This was meant to be a lesson in avoiding such a terrible transgression."

Thomas couldn't help himself. He laughed, but since his mouth was still closed, the sound had nowhere to go except out his nose, which it did with a snort. "I am sorry," he muttered, "I regret that I missed it."

Lady Amelia's head swiveled toward him, allowing him to see the flush of pink that colored her cheeks and the slight embarrassment painting her eyes. "I'm not." She immediately averted her gaze once more. "It was a trying experience, but at least it was somewhat relieved by the pleasant excursion we had yesterday to Kew Gardens."

"Oh?"

"Mr. Lowell and Mr. Burton escorted my sister and I."

Thomas bristled. So she'd spent an entire afternoon with these men whose interest in her had been most apparent when he'd seen them fawning over her earlier in the week. The idea did not sit well with him in the least, though it ought to do so since both would be excellent matches for her. Still . . . Mr. Burton's presence and that adoring way in which he kept looking at her just grated.

"How good of them," he muttered.

"Lady Everly was there, as well," Mr. Burton said. "As chaperone."

"And where is her ladyship now?" Thomas asked. Perhaps he ought to have a word with her about accompanying Lady Amelia about when she went on walks with a gentleman. All things considered, they couldn't be too careful when it came to her reputation, no matter how respectable Mr. Burton might be or how appropriate it was for a young lady to walk with a gentleman unescorted when out in public.

"She is at home," Lady Amelia said, and Thomas noted that the statement was slightly clipped.

He decided to drop the matter for now in favor of addressing Mr. Burton. "So tell me, sir, how is your farm doing these days?"

The question achieved its purpose by getting Mr. Burton to launch into a long explanation about sheep and agriculture, preventing Thomas from having to say another word for the remainder of the walk, which in turn allowed him to simply enjoy Lady Amelia's closeness. There was also the added benefit that she might realize how dull a life with Mr. Burton would be, and thus refrain from showing any further interest in the man.

"Well," Mr. Burton said when they arrived at the entrance to Hyde Park. He turned an expectant gaze on Lady Amelia before glancing briefly at Thomas.

Lady Amelia smiled. She, too, looked at Thomas as if expecting him to take his leave. He refused, looking back at them instead as if he couldn't imagine what they might be thinking.

Eventually, Mr. Burton asked, "Shall I escort you back to Huntley House, my lady?"

"No need," Thomas said before she could manage a response. Mr. Burton's eyes widened. A frown appeared on his forehead, and then he took a hasty step back.

Whatever he'd seen in Thomas's expression, it had prompted him to retreat, which he did with an elegant bow and a quick, "Very well then." He tipped his hat toward Lady Amelia. "It has been a pleasure. I shall look forward to our next encounter." His eyes met Thomas's once more, and all joy seemed to drain from his face. "Good day, Your Grace."

"Good day, Mr. Burton."

And then he was gone, hurrying away as though he couldn't escape their company fast enough. Thomas turned to Lady Amelia and found her glaring at him. "*What* was that about?"

"What do you mean?" he asked as innocently as he could manage.

She planted her hands on her hips in a stance that did not look very ladylike at all. Her features hardened, and she was suddenly as foreboding as the fiery vision she'd presented twice before when

she'd been angry with him. Just as on those previous occasions, he found the experience incredibly
arousing and could only hope to God she wouldn't
notice the state he was suddenly in because of her
fiery gaze.

"Do not pretend innocence, Coventry. You have
been antagonistic toward Mr. Burton since the
moment you chose to join us for a private walk to
which you were not invited."

"You didn't tell me to go away."

"Of course not. I was happy to see you."

The admittance burned straight through him.
She was happy to see him. Warmth fanned out in
the confines of his chest. "So then?"

"But you obviously have an issue with him, in
which case you probably should have considered
avoiding us or riding off again after a brief greeting. Instead, you ruined what was actually a perfectly nice walk."

Sighing, he determined to make an attempt at an
apology. "I am sorry. That was not my intention.
But you cannot possibly be enamored with him, in
which case—"

"Oh? And why is that?"

"Because he talks about nothing but sheep!"

She actually stomped her foot in response to that
remark. "Only because you encouraged him to do
so. Until you arrived, we were actually having a
riveting discussion about hothouse roses."

He couldn't help but stop for a second. "You
have an interest in that?"

"No. Of course not. He brought me a bouquet,

and my enthusiasm with it sort of led to the subject in a roundabout way."

Noting that her anger had dissipated a little, he decided to take advantage. "Come," he said, offering her his arm. "I will escort you home."

She stared at him for a long second, then sighed as though expelling all of the hardships of the world with one single breath. Her hand slipped into place, and the two of them started forward, crossing Piccadilly and following one of the paths through Green Park toward the Huntley House garden gate.

"I've missed you, you know," she said after a while.

The comment completely threw him. "Really?" He couldn't help but glance at her. She was biting her lip in a way that made him want to sink his own teeth into that plump piece of flesh. Would she welcome such a wicked advance? Or would she protest and insist upon gentler caresses?

The wondering was going to see him committed in Bedlam.

"Not the arguing," she went on, "but the company. Mr. Lowell and Mr. Burton are both pleasant enough. I'm sure marrying either of them would result in a comfortable life. But . . ."

Her voice faded into the background, drowned out by his mind's fixation with that one sentence. It would mean that one of those men would have the right to bed her, that one of them would see her naked, have the privilege of touching her in the most intimate of ways possible, of bringing her pleasure, and worse—of having *her* bring *them* pleasure. Such a notion was not to be borne. It clawed at his brain and turned his blood to thick and sluggish gunk that made his entire body feel heavy with disgust.

"Coventry?"

He started at the urgent sound of her voice. "Hmm?"

"Did you hear what I said?"

Shaking his head, he tried to focus on her pretty features in the hope that doing so would banish the unsettling thoughts he'd just been having. "Forgive me, but I must have gotten distracted."

"By what?"

"A political issue," he lied, hoping such a subject would make her relent. To be certain of it, he followed it with a question of his own. "You were saying?"

"Nothing much besides how I enjoy your company." He now wished he'd paid better attention. "We might not always agree on everything, but I find that I rather like that."

"You do?" *That* he had not expected.

She shrugged. "There's something to be said for complete and utter honesty. It means I can appreciate your compliments more because I know you're saying what you truly think as opposed to what you're expected to say. In other words, you would never tell me I look lovely unless you actually believed it."

He couldn't help but smile in response to her

observation. "That is true. And since we are on the subject, you do look incredibly fetching today. Your hair is especially enticing."

"My hair?"

He had *not* meant to go quite that far, but since he had . . . "It is sometimes more riotous, but today the curls have settled in exactly the right way." When she blushed, he felt compelled to add, "I would be tempted to touch it if such a gesture were allowed."

Surprise sprang to life in her eyes, and he wondered if perhaps he'd revealed too much. But this concern was quickly forgotten beneath the thick haze of lust that followed when she quietly whispered, "Oh yes," for it bore with it not one but two revelations, the first one being that she wanted him just as much as he wanted her. The second was that he now sensed how she might respond when she came apart in his arms, and that alone was enough to jar his senses back to the proper time and place.

He'd started a dangerous game now—one from which he'd be wise to retreat unless he wanted to acquire a wife. Which he really didn't. His life was complicated enough without having to deal with a marriage, as well. Not to mention that Lady Amelia was the sort of woman who would want to be included in his affairs. He would have to explain things to her. Which was something he simply couldn't imagine doing, because what if she failed to understand? What if she failed to forgive him for lying? It wasn't a risk he was prepared to take. No matter what. Because if she failed to understand . . . if she failed to safeguard his secrets . . . His heart drummed an unsteady beat at the thought of such a thing coming to pass.

Taking her in, her now pondering gaze, he knew he ought to be able to trust her. After all, her loyalty toward her siblings was undeniable. But this wasn't just about him. It was about protecting his sister's reputation even in death and about safeguarding Jeremy's future. So he would have to forgo the temptation she offered and throw a few punches instead.

"Will you tell me how your meeting went with the laborers?" she now asked. The passionate gaze with which she'd assessed him moments earlier had retreated, banked by a look of pure practicality.

"It went well. I found one of the offers particularly interesting because of the terms." There was no denying her curiosity as he spoke. Her attention was now riveted on this new subject pertaining to the school. "They have agreed to a fixed fee as long as we buy all the materials ourselves, which should reduce the cost of labor while allowing us to negotiate with every supplier."

"I like that idea." She grew pensive for the next few paces, and he saw that they had almost reached her garden gate. "Are you still very busy?"

Not really.

"Yes." He forced a more serious expression. "There are still a few things I must see to tomorrow and perhaps even on Saturday."

"But you will come and collect me on Monday so we can visit the glazier?"

Being a man of his word and not liking the worry that spilled from her eyes, he deliberately put aside the concerns he had about keeping her company so often. Circumstance could not prevent it. Not when he'd now become her partner in this endeavor she was undertaking. He wasn't precisely sure how that had happened, though his need to see her succeed so he wouldn't get murdered by Huntley no doubt had something to do with it. It was the reason he'd offered to cover the costs and the reason he was now helping her procure the necessary people required to fix the house in a satisfying manner. That, and the fact that he had to keep an eye on her for his own peace of mind.

"Yes," he told her simply. "I will come and collect you on Monday morning at ten. We will make a day of it since I would also like to take you out to visit one of the lumber mills and stone masonries outside London."

"Oh. How fascinating!"

He couldn't help but grin. "Do you know, I don't believe I can think of another lady who would find it so."

"Perhaps because they have no use for the products such places supply. But *I* do. Which is why I cannot think of anything else I would rather do than shop for flooring." She gave him a wry smile. "I am fully invested in seeing this through to the end."

"I know you are." It was one of the things he admired about her, though he chose not to say so. Instead, he bid her a good day and waited until she was safely inside her garden with the gate securely closed behind her before mounting his horse and heading toward his club. From there he would continue on home before making his way to the Black Swan Inn. He'd visited the place, which sat in the pit of St. Giles, a few times with Huntley when they'd been looking for something a bit tougher than what Gentleman Jackson's was willing to allow.

The experience had been an exhilarating one. It had given Thomas the chance to shed his aristocratic shackles and to deny proper etiquette and protocol while engaging in a brutal fight that had served to exorcise his demons, if only for a moment.

There, in the Black Swan courtyard, with sweat soaking his shirt, his title hadn't mattered. He'd been his opponent's equal, and he'd taken a beating he now longed to experience again, if only to banish the lust that Lady Amelia provoked.

Tightening his grip on the reins, he directed his horse to St. James Street with strict self-censorship. He really had to pull himself together and stop thinking about her. Which of course, was much easier said than done.

Chapter 12

It was raining by the time Thomas returned home and handed his hat and gloves to his butler, Jones. Climbing the stairs, he headed along the dimly lit hallway and continued toward the third door on the left. Carefully, he opened it and stepped inside, immediately conscious of the easy breathing that came from the bed. He moved toward it on silent feet until he was close enough to study the sweet innocence of Jeremy's face, now veiled in shadowy darkness. Thomas felt his heart clench. With each day that passed, he looked more and more like his mother—a living reminder of unrestrained love and of his irrefutable failure.

Returning downstairs, Thomas entered the parlor where he found his mother enjoying a sherry. She was reading a book and looked up when she heard him come in. "There you are." Setting her book aside, she folded her hands in her lap and gave him her full attention. "I thought I would see you for supper."

"I decided to eat at the club." He crossed to the sideboard and proceeded to pour himself a brandy.

"A note would have been helpful. I waited over half an hour for you to arrive. You always join me in the evenings."

Glancing at her, he wondered at how youthful she looked in spite of her advancing years. She was in her fifties now with the occasional gray hair starting to show, but that did not detract from her beauty. "Forgive me. I should have informed you, but there was much on my mind. Returning home at a specific hour so as not to disappoint you wasn't one of them."

She sat back as if he'd slapped her, but then her expression hardened, her spine straightened and her chin tipped up. She glared at him much like Lady Amelia was prone to doing these days. "Sit down, Thomas." The use of that name sent a tremor scurrying through him. She rarely used it unless she was very displeased with him. Because of that, it always carried a sharpness to it, like a blade slicing away the last twenty years of his life until he was but a little boy feeling the shame of whatever wrongdoing he had committed.

So he sat and faced her, aware he'd made her the subject of his irritation once more. She didn't deserve it. Not after everything she'd had to suffer already. He opened his mouth to speak, to apologize yet again for the rotten mood he was in, only to be cut short by her staying hand.

"I do not want you to tell me how sorry you are," she said. "What I want is for you to explain what you are going through." Her expression softened. "Perhaps I can help or offer some sort of advice."

"I very much doubt that," he told her grimly, then took a sip of his drink.

She gave him a dubious look that suggested she thought him naive. "You won't know that unless you open up to me. This is what . . . the third time this week you have given me some cutting remark?" She sighed, and as she did so, her entire body seemed to deflate. "Something is going on, and I would like to be able to help." When he didn't answer, she asked, "Is it this business with Lord Liverpool?"

"He made no effort to gain support for my bill." The anger and frustration he felt hardened his words. "At least I was able to convince Hawthorne and Wilmington. They would have backed it as a personal favor, but Liverpool?" He shook his head. "His dismissal probably shouldn't surprise me when not even you were willing to give your support."

"That is unfair. I encouraged you to do what you could—for Jeremy's sake. The problem is I am no longer sure it would be in his best interest to inherit a duke's title. And before you start getting defensive and insist I am against him, I am not. I love that boy with every piece of my heart. His existence means the world to me."

Nodding, he reached out and covered her hand with his. "I know." Their eyes met, and for a moment their mutual pain hovered between them.

"It might be easier if you were to marry."

The comment made him withdraw his hand. He leaned back and downed the remainder of his drink in one quick gulp, relishing the way it burned his throat and numbed his mind just a little.

"That is not an option."

"Be reasonable, Coventry. You must think of the continuation of your title."

"Prewit can inherit," he said, in reference to his cousin. "Or one of his sons, if he happens to die before me."

"Well yes, I suppose that is true, but what about sharing your life with someone who cares for you? What about children?"

"I already have a son, in case you have forgotten."

"Forgive me. I did not mean to—"

"As for a life partner . . ." A vision of hazel eyes entered his mind. "She would have to know everything, and I am not prepared to share that much with anyone. The amount of trust required . . . It simply isn't possible."

She seemed to consider this and, to his surprise, she nodded. "You are probably right."

"What?"

Picking up her glass, she set the rim to her lips and drank. "I see no point in pursuing a hopeless topic." Returning the glass to the table, she suddenly smiled. "Let us discuss Lady Amelia instead, shall we?"

His entire body revolted against the idea. "Why?"

"Well, we are responsible for her until her brother's return."

"You must not forget about Lady Juliette," he said in the hope of avoiding a lengthy discussion on Lady Amelia alone. With the state he was in, he might not survive it.

"Of course not. But she is not our main concern.

She will have at least another year in which to prepare herself for courtship while Lady Amelia must make an attachment as soon as possible." She expelled a breath. "Lady Everly agrees that Mr. Burton and Mr. Lowell both make excellent suitors for her. What I wish to know is your opinion."

He tightened his hold on his glass and made an effort not to bare his teeth when he spoke to her next. "Mr. Burton is a bore—an amicable bore, I will grant you, but a bore nonetheless. Certainly, she may enjoy his kind gentility at first, but after a year or so she will begin to feel trapped. The man simply hasn't a passionate bone in his body. Unless he is speaking of sheep, that is."

"Well." His mother stared at him from behind a pair of wide blue eyes. "You have given that quite a bit of thought, I must say."

Wincing, he tried to dismiss her implication. "It is something that became glaringly obvious to me earlier today when I encountered him in the park. He was out walking with Lady Amelia."

"Ah." She nodded as if this were the solution to every puzzle that had ever existed.

He clenched his jaw. "What does that mean? *Ah?*"

She gave a little shrug. "Nothing. Tell me your thoughts on Mr. Lowell."

Hesitating, Thomas wondered briefly about her quick dismissal of his question. It felt as though she was trying to distract him from something, though he couldn't for the life of him figure out what. So he pushed his wariness aside and formed a response.

"He is handsomer than Burton, but his reputation

isn't nearly as clean. That being said, I do believe he will be faithful to the woman he chooses to marry and . . . given his rakish streak and his academic interests, he will definitely prove to be a more interesting companion."

"You have no concern about his club?"

"Its exclusivity, and the fact that even the king enjoys a membership there, prevents me from being critical of it. Certainly, there are no doubt those who find it scandalous, but such is life, Mama. One cannot please everyone."

"So then you would recommend Lowell? He is your preferred match for Lady Amelia?"

His entire body seemed to strain against the idea. It repelled him to think of her wrapped in another man's arms when he . . . *Damn!* He hadn't even kissed her, so what claim could he possibly think of having? None. That was what. And this whole possessive streak he was on—this itch to shout at someone or hit something—was getting out of hand.

"Yes," he managed to say while his throat closed around the word, strangling it as he pushed it past his lips.

His mother studied him. "You look like you did when your father and I denied you that rifle you wanted when you were a child."

He blinked. "What are you talking about?"

"Don't you remember?" Her eyes had taken on a faraway look. "You saw it in a shop window when we walked to church one Sunday morning. It was a splendid thing, I have to admit, but you were much too young—only ten, if I recall." She shook her head as if trying to clear her mind. "In any case, you were very displeased to be denied it, and your face . . . it bore the same petulant expression it does now."

"Don't be absurd." Averting his gaze, he focused all his attention on trying to rid himself of the panic creeping into his bones.

"Perhaps your grumpiness this past week is not only because of Lord Liverpool's lack of cooperation."

Don't say it.

He clasped the armrest while she continued. "Perhaps Lady Amelia is partly to blame, as well?"

His head snapped around to face her. "That is ludicrous, Mama. She is Huntley's sister—a woman whom I have been charged to protect no matter how bloody difficult she likes to make that task at times."

"You certainly have a strong opinion on the matter," his mother murmured. She tilted her head as if contemplating what to do with him.

"It would be impossible not to, all things considered. The task of protecting her reputation is not a simple one and you, if I may remind you, did not make it any easier when you decided to put her in that shocking gown at the Elmwood ball last week."

"I still think you overreacted about that."

"Overreacted?" His voice had reached a pitch that he had to admit was quite unacceptable and utterly uncouth. So he blew out a deep breath and leveled his tone. "Her breasts were practically spilling out of that bodice, Mama. It was . . . unnerving."

"Hmm . . ." She said nothing further, just watched him with interest until he muttered something he had to apologize for immediately after. "I thought she looked lovely," his mother continued, "but that is neither here nor there. We obviously have two very different opinions on the matter."

"Obviously."

"The important thing is she caught Burton's and Lowell's attention." The smile that followed was a little too sweet. "Whatever your thoughts about them may be, I am sure she will make a wise choice for herself. What I quite like is that they do not disapprove of her buying that house and turning it into a school. Lady Everly informed me that both gentlemen have made donations in order to help."

"As have I," he reminded her with a grumpiness he desperately wished to get rid of.

"Yes, but you were compelled by duty while they were merely being generous."

He kept quiet while counting to twenty since speaking at that exact moment would probably result in tears. When his blood had cooled a little, he stood and returned his empty glass to the sideboard. "I will wish you a pleasant evening now, as I am going back out."

"Where to?" She sounded a little alarmed, which was to be expected since he was not prone to going out late at night.

"I cannot say, but this house is too small to contain my aggravation at the moment. A bit of fresh air should do me some good."

Having shed the fine clothes he'd worn for the better part of the day and replaced them with a plain pair of brown trousers and a jacket to match, Thomas hailed a hackney carriage and directed it toward Seven Dials. From there he walked the remainder of the way to the Black Swan Inn, locating it easily enough on account of all the noise the place emitted.

Stepping inside, he pushed his way past a thick throng of people who'd gathered next to the door. The sound of violins and the stomping of dancing feet produced a boisterous atmosphere that he couldn't quite say he disliked. There was something unrestrained here—no rules to govern one's every move, except for the rule of common decency, though he knew many of the patrons did not even practice that.

Still, he could feel the weight of his responsibilities begin to lift from his shoulders as he crossed the floor to the door leading out to the courtyard beyond. Stepping through it, his blood began to sing in response to the fight that he saw taking place. It was masculine power at its best, just pure muscle and strength against one's opponent. Moving forward, he joined the crowd of onlookers and considered the men whose faces were both puffy and swollen, their bodies soaked from the onset of rain.

"Well, well, well . . ." The thick voice that spoke at his shoulder had Thomas turning around to find Carlton Guthrie grinning back at him. "Didn't think to see ye 'ere, Yer Gr—"

"Heathmore will do," Thomas said, offering up his last name to prevent the man from revealing his title. "You should know that by now."

"Aye." Guthrie glanced around. "Matthews ain't with ye?"

"No. He is abroad at the moment." Figuring Huntley would not approve of him sharing details about his life with a man he disliked, Thomas refrained from elaborating. "So I have come alone this time."

"Need a good thrashin' do ye?" Guthrie's lips curled back to reveal a row of surprisingly perfect teeth. In fact, if it weren't for his mustache, the stubble that dotted his jaw and the unkempt state of his hair, the man would actually be quite handsome. He would also look a hell of a lot younger than one imagined him to be at first glance.

"I've had a bad week," Thomas confessed. "I believe hitting something might do me good."

Nodding, Guthrie stuck out his hand. "It'll be three pounds to enter."

"When I was last here, it was free," Thomas muttered, not because he couldn't afford the sum but because he didn't want to be taken advantage of.

"I 'ad to lure ye in first." Guthrie smiled broadly, eyes flashing with devilish glee. "Now that ye're lured, it'll be three pounds."

"What about them?" Thomas asked with a nod directed at the two men who were still throwing punches. "How much did they have to pay?"

"They're me men, Heathmore. I'm trainin' them fer the next match so I'll be payin' them an' not the other way around."

"I see." Thomas pulled his coin purse from his

pocket and counted out the money, then handed it to Guthrie.

"Thank ye very much, kind sir. Ye can toss yer 'at an' jacket o'er there if ye like." He pointed toward a stack of crates that stood beneath an overhang. "These two'll be done soon so ye'd best prepare yerself 'cause I'm puttin' ye against Smith."

It wasn't until he stepped out into the middle of the courtyard a few minutes later that Thomas understood what Guthrie had meant about preparing himself. Because the man he now faced bore a crisscross of scars on his cheeks and appeared to have risen from a medieval battleground ready to murder any man in his path.

Flexing his fingers, Thomas peered through the sheet of falling rain, his hair already smeared across his forehead. He balled his hands into fists, raised his arms and planted his feet in a solid stance like Huntley had taught him. The hours of exercises his friend had forced him to endure had physically changed his body. Gone was the softness to his belly that most men of leisure possessed, replaced instead by taut rows of muscle. His shoulders had widened as well, while his arms bore evidence of finely honed strength. It would be to his advantage now, he realized when Smith stepped into his space with a punch that was neatly avoided as Thomas moved out of its path.

He turned and rose onto the balls of his feet, dodging first this way, then that, before pulling his arm back and pushing it forward, directly toward Smith's face. *Thwack!* His opponent's head was flung back. Blood flew from his nose in a spray of crimson droplets that mingled with the rain.

Christ, that felt good.

So did the blow Smith landed next, straight to Thomas's chest. It bit at his senses in an energizing way that had him punching back. Head lowered, he beat his way forward, demolishing every damn problem that clung to his brain; his sister's unnecessary death, Jeremy's questionable future, Lord Liverpool's unwillingness to help and every temptation Lady Amelia offered.

His mind lingered on that last issue while he delivered another blow to Smith's face and then yet another. Rage burned his eyes, but Thomas didn't care. He just had to expel his baser instincts—the unforgiving urge he had to capture her lips with his own, to pull her into his arms and this mad desire he had to undress her. A fist slammed into his shoulder, sending him back, but not for long. If he could only stop picturing her naked. Perhaps then he would be able to go on with his life in a reasonable way. He staggered for a moment but regained his balance just in time to avoid getting punched in the face.

Shifting sideways, he stared at Smith. Both were panting now from exertion, and he saw when he raised his fists once more that they were raw and bloody. The pain didn't bother him though, quite the contrary. He welcomed it in an almost perverse way, hoping it would bring some satisfaction—that it would erase the frustrated state he was in by replacing it with a different kind of ache.

It did no such thing, he realized later when he made his way back home. His body still responded to every thought he had of her. And there were many since they included the products of his own erotic imaginings. Even now, beaten as he was, he felt himself stir at the thought of just seeing her again, of how her mouth would curve with pleasure when he offered a compliment or how her eyes might blaze with anger if he displeased her. Both affected him equally. It no longer mattered what mood she was in or whether she was happy to see him or not. He just wanted her, plain and simple, and he didn't know what the bloody hell he was going to do about that.

As it happened, there was one thing that would serve to dampen his ardor, though he did not realize this until he returned home and found a note waiting for him on the silver salver in the foyer. Unfolding it, he read the few lines and felt his heart lurch.

Holy hell!

He raced upstairs to his room while doing his best not to wake those who slept. Pulling out dry clothes from his dresser, he exchanged them for the wet and filthy ones he wore. He then grabbed a piece of paper and penned a hasty note to his mother, which he slipped beneath her bedroom door. Nerves tight and heart pounding, he headed back out. All in all, he'd spent no more than ten minutes at most inside his house before hurrying toward St. Giles. There, surrounded by a firefighting unit and with smoke billowing out of every available opening, stood the house Lady Amelia had bought, like an eerie lantern glowing in the dark.

He hadn't seen it when he'd gone to the Black Swan earlier, nor when he'd returned. The quickest route for him had not required the use of Oxford Street. Now, he sorely wished it had done. Perhaps then he might have discovered this sooner.

"What happened?" he asked a heavyset man who was busy directing a hose from the fire engine while two other men worked the pump.

"Not sure. Perhaps someone tossed a cigar into the weeds, but it's tough to say. I believe we should have it contained soon. We managed to catch it before it got too big inside—would have had to tear down the building then."

"You don't think that will be necessary now?" Thomas asked as he watched the smoke rise to the sky. "Looks pretty bad in there."

"I suppose that depends on one's perspective," he said. "I've seen worse."

Thomas didn't doubt it, given the man's profession, but it still didn't change the fact that Lady Amelia would be devastated by this news. How the hell was he going to tell her? "I would like to help," he said, not only because saving the building would be in his own best interest, considering the money he'd already spent on it, but because he needed to know he'd done something.

"You can help man the other fire engine over there," the man said. "I believe one of those fellows could do with a break."

Thanking him, Thomas hurried over to where the other men were pumping and offered to take one of their places. It was tough work, especially after the fight, but he found a rhythm soon enough and put all his strength into pushing as much water as possible through the hose. If the house was unsalvageable, they could try to find another—he could certainly afford the expense—except Lady Amelia had been so set on this one he suspected no other place would do in her mind. So there was really nothing for it. They would simply have to muddle through as best as they could and make the most of whatever remained in the morning.

Chapter 13

Amelia was halfway through her breakfast when Pierson came to announce that the Duke of Coventry had come to call.

"That is rather early," Lady Everly said. She returned her teacup to its saucer. "We are not expecting him to arrive for another three hours."

"He is asking for a private word with Lady Amelia." Pierson's expression conveyed no hint of his opinion on such an unusual occurrence. "Shall I show him to the parlor?"

"Please do." Lady Everly pushed herself out of her chair as soon as Pierson had exited the room. She looked at Amelia. "Stay here until I return."

Nodding, Amelia watched her leave the room.

"What do you suppose all of this is about?" Juliette asked.

Amelia met her inquisitive gaze. "I've no idea."

"But you do know why Lady Everly has gone to speak with him first."

The way in which her sister said it suggested that

Amelia should have some idea, except she didn't. "Not the faintest."

Juliette rolled her eyes. "Think about, Amelia. He arrives unexpectedly and asks to meet with you in private? Lady Everly obviously went to inquire about his intentions."

"Which would be what, exactly?" A distinct tone of annoyance had slipped into her voice because she now sensed where this conversation was going. "He hasn't come to propose, if that is what you are thinking."

"He might have," Juliette said with a hopeful smile.

Pushing her plate aside, Amelia leaned back in her seat and crossed her arms with a huff. "No, he might not. And please stop insisting that he feels enough for me to ever do so."

"I think you're wrong about that."

"On what grounds?" Amelia stared across at her sister.

She shrugged, then took a sip of her tea. "It's just a feeling I have."

A feeling. What good did that do when Amelia had a long list of facts stacked against the possibility of Coventry ever making her that sort of offer? First, her background made her completely unsuitable. Second, she was too independent for his liking. Third, he found her aggravating, as evidenced by the fact that she'd been subjected to his temper three times already in little over a week. Fourth, he had no desire to marry anyone—he'd told her as much. And fifth, he was a duke for heaven's sake! She might as well set her sights on the Pope for all the difference it made to her chances of success.

"Amelia?"

Blinking, Amelia realized Lady Everly was talking to her. She must have entered without her noticing. "Yes?"

"You need to hear what Coventry has to say. As long as you leave the parlor door open, I have no issue with the two of you being alone for a moment."

Unsure about Lady Everly's somber tone, Amelia hesitated. She glanced at Juliette, who shook her head as if to say that she no longer had any idea of what to expect.

"Very well." Amelia got to her feet and made her way toward the door. For reasons she couldn't explain, it felt as though she was heading for the gallows. Which made her wonder if she might have done something else that he did not approve of—something of which she was not yet aware.

By the time she arrived in the parlor, she almost expected him to look tense and irritable. "Coventry?"

He was standing by one of the windows, looking out onto the street. At the sound of her voice, he turned around and faced her, revealing a face that bore no resemblance to the one she'd seen when last they'd met.

"Bloody 'ell!" The words were out before she could stop them, the shock of seeing his eyes outlined in shades of blue and purple so shocking, she forgot herself completely. Another bruise colored the left side of his jaw while a vertical line of dark red upon his lip suggested he'd been bleeding. "What 'appened?"

"What *happened*?"

Befuddled, she shook her head. Was he seriously correcting her English right now? Slowly, she moved toward him. "Were you attacked?" It seemed like a logical question, given his appearance.

To her surprise he grinned, though only for a second. "No. I engaged in a boxing match at the Black Swan last night."

She could only stare at him before calmly asking, "Are you mad? You're an aristocrat, Coventry. You don't belong in that place."

"Perhaps not, but I needed the sport." Before she could ask him why, he quickly changed the subject. "But I am not here for you to study my rare coloring. Rather, there is a matter of great importance I must discuss with you." When she waited for him to continue, he gestured toward a nearby armchair. "Perhaps you will be more comfortable sitting down?"

Her heart lurched as a rush of foreboding swept through her body. "What is this about?"

"I will tell you in a moment." Again, he swept his hand toward the chair. "Please."

Unsure of where this was going, Amelia moved across the floor on leaden feet and took her seat. He, on the other hand, remained standing. Something intense brewed in his eyes. She saw he was clenching and unclenching his jaw, and the action only put her all the more on edge.

"What is it," she finally asked, unable to stand

the anticipation of what he would say for one more second.

He drew a deep breath before he spoke. "There has been an incident."

His solemn tone made her insides wither. "What are you saying?"

"The house you bought caught fire last night."

Every hope she'd had of him not conveying some terrible news was gone in a heartbeat. She shook her head. "No. That cannot be."

"I saw it with my own eyes. When I arrived at the scene, the fire brigade was already doing their best to put it out, so I stopped to help pump water."

"But . . ." Breathing was suddenly difficult. "Is it . . ." Oh God, she could barely bring herself to ask the necessary questions.

"It was not burned to the ground, if that is what you wish to know. In fact, the entire structure is still standing due to how quickly the flames were brought under control. But there is some considerable damage." Moving toward her while she processed that bit of information, he paused by her side. And then, quite unexpectedly, she felt his hand settle upon her shoulder.

It was both comforting and disconcerting, the inappropriateness of the gesture quite forgotten by her as it shoved her misgivings aside, replacing them with a keen sense of solidarity—an unspoken promise that they would get through this together. It was so touching she feared she might weep. So she bowed her head, hoping to hide the emotion that no doubt showed in her eyes.

"I thought you might like to go to see it for yourself. If anything, doing so may help put your mind at ease since I do believe the house can be saved."

Gulping a breath of air, she clutched the armrest and gave a curt nod. "Yes. I believe you're quite right." Disregarding how weak she felt—as though it was she who had taken a beating instead of him— she rose to her feet on legs that did not feel capable of carrying her weight. Still, she forced her spine into a rigid line and pushed up her chin. "Allow me to ready myself and to inform Lady Everly of our outing. I'll only be a moment."

When she'd completed her tasks, she found him waiting in the foyer, ready to depart. With all of the riotous emotions that had attacked her during the last half hour, she'd hardly had time to notice how dashing he looked in a burgundy jacket and charcoal breeches. And although his face did look like a bad artist's canvas, there was no denying his handsome features—that ever-present glint of responsibility that shadowed his eyes or the terribly attractive curve of his mouth.

Catching herself, she allowed him to escort her outside to his carriage. Her palm settled comfortably against his as he helped her alight, and when he settled himself across from her, she could not help but wonder what it might be like to have him touch her with greater insistence. What a silly thing to even consider at a time such as this.

"Does it hurt?" she asked a moment after the carriage had set off down the street. "Your face, that is."

"Not too much. It looks worse than it feels."

"Did you at least win?"

He smirked. "I did indeed."

"Good." Her concrete nod made him smile. "But I still don't see why you had to go there. The neighborhood isn't safe, Coventry. Any number of terrible things could have happened to you, given your appearance."

"Oh?"

"You cannot hide your wealth, which could have made you an easy target for any number of villains."

"Not too easy of a target, I should hope." He leaned forward. "Or is your opinion of me so low that you think me incapable of surviving a few unpleasant muggers?"

"Of course not. But there are murdering scoundrels there too, men who would not hesitate to use a knife if it got them what they wanted."

"And knowing this," he said while leaning closer still, "you had no qualms about going there yourself without escort."

She saw the mistake she had made in her argument, but that didn't change the fact that the more she thought about his little adventure the previous evening, the more it worried her, because really, what if something had happened? What if he'd been cornered and killed? Such incidents were not unheard-of.

"I went during the day and I did not actually enter St. Giles."

"Even so, you are a woman, and therefore at far greater risk than I would ever be."

"Oh, for heaven's sake, Coventry. Why must you be so difficult?"

He looked at her with a thoroughness that immediately made her regret the outburst. His eyes narrowed ever so slightly, and then he quietly said, "Perhaps because your actions insist that I have to protect you from even yourself."

"And who will protect you from yourself?" She stared into his dark brown eyes. "Who will be there to stop you the next time you think of asking a stranger to ruin your handsome face?"

The edge of his mouth tilted. "You think me handsome?"

She watched his gaze change to a warmer shade, the effect of it sending a dart of heat straight to her belly. Her stays felt suddenly tight against her breasts, and her throat had grown uncomfortably dry. Awareness crackled in the space between them. Why on earth did she have to say that?

Deliberately sitting back, she looked away and responded crisply. "In an ordinary sort of way." She dared not glance at him while she sat there staring at nothing in particular, for she could feel him watching her with a closeness that threatened to reveal everything she felt for him. Which was something she simply could not allow.

Eventually, he shrugged. She wasn't sure how she knew that he did so, but there was something about the way in which the air shifted and the carefree tone of his voice as he said, "Then I must confess that I find your face enchanting. In an equally ordinary sort of way."

Without thinking, her eyes shot toward his, only to find that his face was even closer now than it had been before. "You are impossible," she said, since staying silent would do her no good at all.

"No more than you, I imagine."

His hand came up, the astonishing touch of his fingers against her cheek jarring her senses and sending her reeling. Her breath caught in her throat. A series of shivers caressed her skin. If only she could keep her stomach from rolling over so she could enjoy the intimacy of the moment a little. Instead, she remained completely stiff and unsure. What was he doing and what did he expect her to do? She really wasn't the least bit sure, but the studious look in his eyes had vanished, replaced by a dangerous gleam that excited her while at the same time filled her with no small amount of trepidation.

"Whatever shall we do?" He asked the question as if to himself—the contemplative tone hinting at deep thought and consideration.

"I . . . I . . ." *I cannot speak. You've addled me with your nearness.*

"Hmm . . ." His gaze dropped to her mouth, the color of his eyes now concealed behind lowered lashes. The air grew thick around them, and once again, Amelia struggled to breathe as she began to detect his intention. He would kiss her. Right here in the carriage. She didn't even care about the reason behind such abandon or the consequences that were sure to follow. All she could do was wait, her entire body perched on the edge of her seat while her heart threatened to burst from her chest and—

The carriage drew to a shuddering halt and Coventry quickly leaned back. "We are here." Hard lines masked any hint of longing on his part, the look in his eyes now one of practical determination and resolve. It was as if the moment had never happened—as if all it had been was a figment of her own imagination.

And yet . . . And yet, she could not deny the lingering feel of his fingers against her cheek or the craving that had consumed her seconds ago. It had not been of her own making, but of his. *He* had instigated it. His eyes had reached inside her to confirm it, and when she stepped down from the carriage, assisted by the steady touch of his hand, she realized he'd shown her something she'd never thought to inspire in him until now: unrestrained desire.

The revelation was so acute it forced her to suck in a breath. For a second, she went completely still, her hand still clasping his while she pondered this new idea. Was it really possible? Glancing up, she considered his expression. It showed no hint of such emotion, yet she'd felt it, she was absolutely certain of it.

"My lady." His tone was gentle but curt, reminding her of time and place, and the fact that she ought to release his hand.

She did so swiftly, all thought of a mutual attraction evaporating the instant she turned to look at her house. Her hands came up to cover her mouth and drown out the cry that escaped as she took in the scene. Black patches marred the wall above two of the window frames. The front door was charred, and the lock appeared to have been broken, no doubt so the firemen could get in and put out the flames.

Disheartened, Amelia climbed the steps and went inside, her heart plummeting even further at the sight she beheld. The stairs had collapsed in a pile of debris that now sat in a pool of water. Lifting the hem of her gown, she walked on through to the parlor, the library, the ballroom and finally the dining room. With each step she took, she felt her heart drop a little bit more. There was water everywhere, and most of the window frames had been burned away, the glass gone to leave nothing but gaping holes in the walls.

An ache began to fill her as she thought of the extra expenses. At least one wall would have to be torn down completely, and parts of the floors and ceilings that had looked fine before now bore evidence of irreparable damage. By the time she came to a halt before the glassless dining-room windows and looked out into what had once been an overgrown garden, she felt raw inside. Not a hint of color remained. Everything was encased in black.

"We can fix this." Coventry's voice summoned her attention but failed to lift her spirits. He came to stand beside her.

She continued to look out at the hopeless display of destruction. "I suspect it would cost a small fortune to do so. Certainly more money than I have at my disposal." Her voice took on an absent tone as she fought the pain that threatened to swamp her.

"Listen to me." When she failed to respond to his demand, he turned her with the force of his hands so he could look at her directly. His features were set in firm lines, portraying a keen determination that she completely lacked at that moment. "We can fix this. The house is not beyond repair, and I will happily supply the necessary funds until you are able to pay me back through your fund-raising."

She stared at him in surprise. "Why would you do that?"

"Does it matter?"

Exhausted from having to recognize that she had failed before she'd really begun and now faced with a good solution, she did not feel like arguing with him. So she shook her head. "No. I suppose not. But you are assuming that my fund-raising events will be successful enough to cover the expense. Your plan is not without risk."

"No." He gave her a fleeting smile. "I don't suppose it is. But I believe this is more important to you than any amount of money will ever be to me."

Her composure finally crumbled in response to his undeniable generosity, and when the first tears rolled down her cheeks, he pulled her into his arms. With her face snug against the soft wool of his jacket, she inhaled and found herself cocooned in a rich fragrance of musk and sandalwood. One hand settled against her waist, holding her to him while the other soothed along her spine. It was lovely, this intimate closeness. She could feel the strength in his shoulders and chest as she leaned a bit closer, pressing more firmly into the warm embrace he offered.

"I don't know how to thank you." Her words

were muffled against his jacket, but he heard her nonetheless.

"No need. I am simply happy to ease your concerns."

A few more seconds ticked by before she reluctantly pulled away. "Forgive me," she felt compelled to say, "I was overwrought by the shock of it all."

Reaching up, he tucked a loose curl behind her ear and looked at her with such overwhelming kindness she almost started crying once more. "There is absolutely nothing to forgive since you have done nothing wrong. If anything, I overstepped, though I do believe circumstance will forgive me for doing so."

"Without a doubt," she agreed. There was no hint of the heated longing with which he'd regarded her in the carriage, only a friendly countenance. It made her wonder if she'd been wrong to suppose he might ever have thought to kiss her. She'd been so certain before, but if she'd been right, now would have granted him apt opportunity. Yet there was nothing to suggest he even considered such a thing.

Unsure of what to make of that, she chose to set her mind elsewhere. "Can you please inform the laborers today that we are ready to take them on? I would like them to start work as soon as possible."

"Of course." They walked out to the foyer where they exited the house and returned to the carriage. "Does Monday still suit you in terms of visiting the lumber mill, glazier and stone mason?"

"Yes. I have no other plans for that day."

He nodded. "I would recommend you take some time either today or tomorrow to consider your first fund-raising event. Lady Everly can advise you, but I think it would be good to start engaging people in your project."

"I will attend to it as soon as I get home. Thank you, Coventry. Your kindness today has been such a comfort while your friendship . . . I cannot tell you how much it means to me." Even though it would never be nearly enough. With Coventry, she would always long for more.

Chapter 14

~~~~~~~~~~⟞⟝⟞⟝~~~~~~~~~~

An entire week had passed since Amelia had gone to see the results of the fire. A crew of laborers had been hired, and they were now busily removing all of the damaged wood from the structure. In the meantime, she and Coventry had placed an order for cherrywood flooring, crown glass windows and enough marble tiles to replace the ones that were cracked in the ballroom. The rest would simply be polished as well as possible since replacing the entire floor would be an unnecessary extravagance.

This had occupied three of her days so fully that she had allowed no time to meet with Mr. Lowell or Mr. Burton, who'd both come to call on her twice while she'd been out. Juliette and Lady Everly had met with them instead, but their disappointment in having to forgo Amelia's company had apparently been made very clear, which was why Lady Everly had insisted she let them escort her to Gunther's for an ice by the time Friday morning rolled around.

The excursion had been pleasant enough, and their interest in the progress she was making with the school had helped a great deal in keeping her focused on their conversation. Now, standing with her sister in the Falconrich ballroom, Amelia saw them make their approach together with another gentleman whom she easily recognized as Doctor Florian.

"Good evening, ladies," Mr. Lowell said once he and the other men came within speaking range. Mr. Burton was wearing a grand smile as usual, while charm oozed from Mr. Lowell's smooth countenance. He would no doubt have had the ability to weaken Amelia's knees a little if it wasn't for Coventry. The duke had made her completely immune to any other man's attention. "We have been looking everywhere for you."

"It is such a crush though," Burton said. He glanced around at the many people who filled the large room. "You must forgive us for not finding you sooner."

"Of course we do," Juliette said while Amelia offered the men a reassuring smile.

Doctor Florian addressed Juliette. "It is good to see you looking well again, my lady."

"When I told my brother that I expected to find you here this evening, he insisted on seeing you for himself," Mr. Lowell said with a grin.

Amelia's gaze shifted to Florian. *Brother?* She hadn't realized the connection and never would have without Lowell mentioning it. The two men looked nothing alike. Lowell's hair was dark, while Florian's was a rich shade of copper. Lowell's face was more angular than Florian's and yet in spite of that, it was Florian who looked most severe. "But . . ." She could not contain her dismay. "You are brothers?"

Florian finally allowed the faintest hint of amusement to show as the edge of his mouth twitched ever so slightly. "I chose to be addressed as Florian when I became a doctor in order to distinguish myself from Lowell. It is my middle name."

"And a fine one at that," Lowell said with a wide smile. Sobering slightly, he added, "He is very thorough when it comes to his patients. Takes quite an interest in them even after they are fully recovered, which is why he was so eager to see you again, Lady Juliette."

"I have always felt that tending to the sickly and helping them fight their ailments creates a bond of sorts." Florian's expression grew increasingly serious as he spoke. No hint of a smile played about his lips anymore, and his eyes held nothing but deep contemplation now. "I often see people at their worst—I help when no one else knows what to do—and they place their faith in me with the hope that I will do whatever is in my power to find a cure. It is a great responsibility, but it is also the most rewarding work I have ever done."

"You make it sound like a vocation," Juliette said with interest.

He gave a curt nod. "Indeed, that is how I consider it."

"Which is admirable," Mr. Lowell said. "I do not think many of us manage to find such purpose in our lives, though it does appear as though you have done so too, Lady Amelia. Your efforts to make a school for the poor are absolutely remarkable."

She couldn't help but blush a little when all three gentlemen nodded their agreement. "You have said so several times already."

"One cannot say it enough," he insisted.

"He is right," Mr. Burton said. "We have discussed the matter at length and have concluded that no other young lady would have thought to dive into such an endeavor. A dowager might, though she would undoubtedly have been dissuaded by the fire. That you intend to persevere speaks highly of your vision and your insistence on seeing this through."

"I could not agree more," Doctor Florian said. "You are the sort of person who stands to change the world. I expect you will achieve great things and that this school is only the beginning."

"Which makes one envy the gentleman who will one day accompany her on this journey," Mr. Lowell said with a wink that made Amelia chuckle. "It is unfortunate she cannot marry all three of us."

"What a scandalous thought," Juliette said with a grin.

Doctor Florian nudged his brother. "Have a care, Lowell. Can you not see you have shocked them?"

"Then allow me to redeem myself on the dance floor," Mr. Lowell said. "I trust we can find a minuet or a reel to engage in?"

"Of course." Amelia handed him her dance card while Juliette gave hers to Doctor Florian.

"Not a minuet or a reel, I see," Mr. Burton said

when it was his turn to pick a dance. He glanced at Mr. Lowell, whose eyes now twinkled with mischievous delight. "You scoundrel." He wrote his name and then returned the cards to Amelia and Juliette.

Amelia lowered her gaze to study hers and then quickly looked up again. "You have chosen the waltz?" She stared at Mr. Lowell, who offered a boyish shrug by way of explanation.

"Nobody else has done so yet, so why not?"

Why not indeed? When she'd arrived at the ball an hour earlier and met Coventry, he'd quickly excused himself without claiming a dance. She hadn't seen him since, though she supposed his absence did give her the opportunity to try the waltz with someone else. And since she would probably end up marrying either Mr. Lowell or Mr. Burton instead, it might be wise of her to allow them the honor instead of giving it to Coventry.

Pushing the duke from her mind, she consequently resolved to enjoy the evening with her sister and the three gentlemen who were more than happy to give them their full attention. In fact, they were very polite and attentive, bringing refreshments, inquiring about their interests and escorting them out to the terrace whenever the heat in the ballroom became too insufferable.

"My lady," Mr. Lowell finally announced. "It is time for our dance."

Already exhausted from her reel with Doctor Florian, the minuet with Mr. Burton and a cotillion she'd danced with a baron, Amelia did her best to look as enthusiastic about the prospect of torturing her feet some more.

"You are delightful," he said when he finally held her in his arms and guided her across the floor. His steps were precise, though not nearly as smooth as Coventry's.

"Thank you. You are very kind to say so."

A sparkle turned his eyes a dazzling shade of aquamarine. He gripped her hand a little bit tighter while adding more pressure to the spot where his palm met her back. "I only speak the truth, Lady Amelia, and the truth is that you are the most remarkable woman I have ever had the pleasure of knowing."

"Are you always this charming?"

He flashed her a grin. "Not at all. I'm making a particular effort for you."

A little discomforted by his flattery and the direction in which she suspected it might be leading, she chose to direct the conversation elsewhere. "Have you ever traveled abroad?"

A frown puckered his brow to confirm his surprise with the unexpected question, but he quickly recovered and he spun her about, leading her expertly between two other couples.

"Yes. I did a tour of the Continent a few years ago right after the war ended. Rome was particularly impressive—more so than Paris."

"I would love a chance to see those places for myself," Amelia confessed. "And other, much further destinations, as well, like Egypt and China. The cultures are so vastly different, I hear. They are sure to make an impression."

"So there is an adventurous streak inside you just waiting to break free," Mr. Lowell murmured. "I was not aware, though I have to confess that I find this new insight extremely intriguing."

She wasn't sure why it would be. In her mind, the urge to explore what lay beyond England, to see the wonders of the world for herself, was such a natural thing she couldn't imagine not wanting to do so. "And why is that?" she asked.

"Because if there is one thing I do not enjoy, it is monotony, so I welcome adventure with open arms and applaud it."

Unable to argue with that since she rather agreed, she allowed herself to simply enjoy what was left of the dance while imagining what a life might be like with a man like Mr. Lowell by her side. He would, it appeared, support her ambitions while accompanying her to various parts of the world. Granted, a spark did not exist, but that didn't mean they couldn't enjoy each other's company or that they wouldn't feel some affection for each other eventually. He certainly wasn't displeasing to look at, and he did show a keen interest in what she had to say, which was definitely something she liked.

"Please join me for a moment," he said after the dance had ended. "There is something I would like to say, and it must be done in private."

Unsure of where this was going, Amelia looked around in the hope of finding a familiar face. "I should probably consult with Lady Everly or the

Dowager Duchess of Coventry before allowing you to lead me away like this." But they were already exiting the ballroom and heading through to a hallway beyond.

"You may rest assured that I have no intention of compromising you if that is your concern."

"I . . . ah . . . well . . . Would being alone together not lead to ruination anyway?" She'd always been told to keep a chaperone with her.

"Not as long as we keep the door open," he said, ushering her into a comfortable parlor and carefully closing the door most of the way. "There. See? It remains respectably ajar."

"I would be more comfortable if we opened it more."

He ignored the comment and pulled her toward an armchair instead. "Please. Have a seat, my lady. Your feet must be tired from all of the dancing."

Unable to deny that, she sank down onto the chair with a thankful sigh. He, however, did the most extraordinary thing, dropping to one knee beside her and reaching for her hand. His eyes met hers, and she realized then with alarm that something awful was about to happen—something she now knew with startling clarity that she did not want.

And yet, she felt powerless to stop it as he gazed into her eyes and said, "I have spent an eternity looking for the right woman—a passionate, life-loving lady with whom to share my days and nights." The "nights" part made her cringe for he followed the word with a slow calculation of her body, his eyes lingering a moment too long on her breasts. "Considering Mr. Burton's keen interest in you, I feel compelled to act quickly before he chooses to make you an offer." His hand tightened around her fingers. "My dearest Lady Amelia. It would be the greatest honor if you would agree to be my wife. We will travel the world together just as you wish, I will build you a library with books of your choosing and . . ." He looked away briefly as if overcome by emotion, then turned a blazing pair of eyes on her. "I will fill your life with exquisite passion—of that you have my word."

She stared at him in absolute shock. This was anything but a simple proposal. This was a declaration of need and desire, which wasn't at all what she had expected. Apparently the man had been holding back his yearning for her, though there could be no denying it now. He drank her in, his entire body taut with the expectation of her answer.

Which reminded her that it was her turn to speak. What on earth would she say? What *could* she say? Until she'd realized his intentions, she'd been quite set on marrying either him or Mr. Burton since Coventry wasn't a realistic possibility. But then every part of her body, every fiber of her being, had rebelled against the hopeful gleam in Mr. Lowell's eyes. She'd wanted him to stop— had prayed for him to do so in order to let her flee. It had apparently taken a rather impassioned proposal for her to realize that she would not settle. Not where the rest of her life was concerned.

"I am . . . incredibly flattered that you would consider me in such a way," she managed to say. "But I must decline."

He stared at her as though her words made no sense, then gathered himself and asked, "Is there something else you require? Something else I can do to convince you?"

"No. I'm sorry. I just . . . I wish to marry for love, and as wonderful as you are and as kind as you have been, I must admit that I do not feel more than friendship for you."

He averted his gaze. "And Burton? Do you love him then?"

"No. I do not, and if it is any consolation at all, I can assure you that I will not be marrying him either." She pushed out a deep and agonizing breath. "You see, the trouble is my affections lie with a man who I cannot have."

His eyes found hers once more, and she saw that he was giving her comment some serious thought. She shouldn't have said anything, but the hopelessness that now swamped her had made her want to confide.

"Is it Coventry?"

When she nodded, he gave her a sympathetic smile and rose to his feet. She stood as well, her hand still clasped by his, and for a long moment, they simply looked at each other without either uttering a word. Eventually, he took a step back and bowed over her hand, kissing her knuckles at the exact same moment the door to the parlor opened and Coventry walked in.

His eyes found Amelia before shifting to Mr.

Lowell who presently straightened himself and released her hand. All pleasantness vanished from Coventry's features in a second. He marched forward with a glower.

"What the hell is going on here?" he asked in that same angry tone Amelia had now grown accustomed to having directed at her.

"Nothing for you to concern yourself with," Mr. Lowell said. He stepped around the duke and headed for the door. Pausing there, he looked back at Amelia. "Thank you, my lady. I hope you enjoy the rest of your evening."

The door clicked shut as he exited the room, leaving her alone with a man whose temper had once again risen to an uncontrollable level.

Thomas wasn't sure what to think. Indeed, he found he *could* not think as long as combustive heat drummed through his brain in a blazing inferno of violent emotions. Body tense in an effort to hold himself in check lest he send a vase flying against the nearest wall, he stared at the woman who continued to send him into fits of fury. She looked absolutely lovely this evening with her curls loosely piled at the back of her head. A dress sewn from golden silk gauze afforded her skin with a warm hue that made her appear as though she was bathed in sunshine.

He'd welcomed her when she'd arrived but his reaction to her—the quickening of his pulse and the way in which his chest had tightened with longing the moment he'd met her gaze—had prompted him to retreat to the gaming room. Remaining there had seemed like an excellent solution until his mother had sought him out and insisted he make more of an effort. When she'd mentioned Lady Amelia's waltz with Mr. Lowell, something primal had taken root and he'd not wasted another second in seeking her out. Fortunately, he'd managed to catch a glimpse of her retreating form from the opposite side of the ballroom, so he'd had some idea of where to find her. What had not worked in his favor was the massive throng of guests who'd kept on blocking his path while he'd tried to reach his destination.

And then, once he did reach it, he'd been handed an image that had made his blood boil in his veins. Clarity had fled his mind, replaced by an intrinsic need to toss Mr. Lowell aside so he could take his place. It was an urge that defied all logic—one that warred with his common sense. He could not be more than friends with Lady Amelia, but he would be damned if he was going to allow Mr. Lowell to lay a hand on her instead.

Selfish bastard.

"Have you no care for your reputation?" he asked. Perhaps speaking would drown out his conscience.

"Of course I do."

He waited for her to elaborate, but she did not, which forced him to ask, "Then what were you thinking to let yourself be alone with Mr. Lowell like that?" When she only glared at him, he took a step toward her. "Answer me, Lady Amelia."

"Or what?"

Clenching his jaw, he moved closer still. "I could tell Lady Everly," he threatened. "Maybe that will teach you to take better care since you do not seem to worry about my regard for your safety."

Amelia's eyes widened with just the right amount of trepidation. "Please don't."

"No?" He came to a halt directly before her. "Then perhaps you will answer my question and tell me what you were thinking to let yourself be alone with Mr. Lowell."

"I wasn't. Thinking, that is."

She crossed her arms, and his eyes instinctively dropped to the perfect swell of her breasts. Flexing his fingers, he fought the itch that compelled him to touch her right there—to explore the soft shapes with his hands. His gut tightened at the thought of taking such liberty with her, his mind creating all sorts of arguments in his favor. Except she'd been here with Mr. Lowell, and she had not looked the least bit displeased by the man's attentions. That thought grated.

"What did he want?" Thomas asked, though he supposed the man had wanted exactly the same as what he did. Again, he clenched his fists and fought for some measure of calm.

"He wished to make me an offer of marriage." She spoke so matter-of-factly she might as well have been speaking of current events or the weather. "I declined."

Relief swept through him on a wave of unequivocal joy. It banished most of the anger, returning him to a state of comfortable relaxation though he still had to understand her reasoning. "Why?"

"Because I do not love him." Her answer was simple and to the point. "I know your mother and Lady Everly were quite set on him, and frankly, so was I until a few minutes ago when I realized that marriage ought to accomplish more than satisfying everyone else's dreams."

"I see."

"Do you really?" Her tone was not the least bit pleasant but rather accusatory.

"You wish to make a love match, and since you have not found the right man with whom to do so, you will continue to wait for him to come along."

"And will you chase him off, as well?" she asked without the slightest hint of surrendering the subject anytime soon.

Thomas braced himself. "Of course not. What a ridiculous thing to ask when you know I want you to make a happy match for yourself."

She stared at him, her breaths coming in the same uneasy way his had the moment he'd burst into the room. "You are unbelievable!"

"I—"

"You have done nothing but stand in the way of such a possibility, frightening Mr. Burton with your dukely authority and then telling me he isn't good enough when he most certainly is. And now, with Mr. Lowell, you act as though he has committed some terrible wrong when all he did was extend the most wonderful proposal a woman such as myself could possibly hope to receive."

"He was charming, was he?" Thomas felt the edge of his anger begin to return.

She pinned him with a glare. "Incredibly so."

"Then perhaps you should reconsider and accept him after all." Incensed by her high regard for the man, Thomas leaned in, crowding her with his presence.

"Perhaps I should!"

Her head was tilted back so she could look up into his face, her breaths hitched with the undeniable irritation that poured off her in waves. She looked like a valkyrie about to decide his fate—a stunning image of strength and self-preservation.

Perhaps it was his reaction from earlier, that sting of fear that had shot through his limbs when he'd thought he might lose her to Lowell. Or perhaps it was simply the fiery beauty that spilled from her soul. Whatever it was, he found himself dipping his head and closing the distance.

He'd made a valiant effort to keep a respectable space between them, but all of that crumbled the moment his mouth met hers. It happened so swiftly she had no chance to escape. For a second, he contemplated retreat, but then her lips moved and her body curved toward his. Her arms found their way around his neck while little sighs rose from her throat in a sensual plea for more. It made him wonder why the hell he hadn't kissed her sooner.

Spreading his hands across her back, he felt her gown ripple beneath his touch. She clutched at his head as if needing that extra bit of closeness. Adjusting his position, he obliged, deepening the kiss in an intimate exploration that sent hot blood thundering through his veins. She tasted divine; the fruity flavor of expensive champagne still lingering on her tongue. But what drove his fervor higher was perhaps her eagerness, for it proved she was just as hungry as he.

His hands slid lower, discovering the body that hid beneath her gown; a slim waist, the flaring of hips, and the soft flesh of her bottom curving against his hands. He dug his fingers into it, forcing her hips toward his in a powerful insinuation of what he wanted. Her gasp mingled with his breath as he kissed her harder, his mind wandering to a wide variety of possibilities—to a conjured image of fewer clothes between them, of her spread out against his sheets while he . . .

A clock chimed, announcing the hour, and Thomas's thoughts came to a jarring halt. What the hell was he doing? This was Huntley's sister he was kissing, not some widow with whom he could share a night of pleasure. Demands would be made if this went any further, and that was without considering the very real possibility of Huntley killing him. And then there was his life to think of. It was complicated and messy. The last thing he needed was to add a wife to it. Which was exactly what he would have to do if they got caught in such a fervent embrace.

He released her so fast she almost stumbled. "Forgive me." It was all he could think to say. "I don't know what came over me."

"Don't you?" The passionate look in her eyes faded until they began to shimmer with a horrible hint of tears.

He felt like an ass. "Amelia," he said. "My job is to keep you safe, not to compromise you. But we have been spending a lot more time together lately and I . . . I would not be a man if I had not considered kissing you at least once. And if I can so easily succumb to temptation, then others will too, which is why I have been so intent on protecting you from situations such as this."

She looked increasingly horrified. He was reeling in his effort to explain. All of his words were coming out wrong, but to think he'd just started down the path that had led to his own sister's death—the concept that he wasn't any better than the man who'd compromised Melanie—made him want to run from Amelia as fast as he possibly could.

How could he have succumbed to his baser urges with her when he of all people ought to have known better? Disgusted by his behavior, he told her frankly, "This cannot happen again. You must know that." He had to tell her the truth. "I am not . . ."

The man you think me to be.

He ran his hands through his hair, knowing what had to be said but fearing the effect it would have on her opinion of him. But since it was the right thing to do, he determined to try anyway. "My life is complicated and—"

"I understand." The wretchedness with which she spoke was devastating.

"I don't think you do." He held out his hand,

uncertain of how to offer comfort without making matters worse. "Amelia . . ."

She turned away from him and walked to the door. Without uttering another word, she opened it and slipped out into the hallway beyond, leaving Thomas behind with a wretched feeling of loss and regret.

Chapter 15

Without planning to ever rise from her bed again, Amelia rolled onto her side and covered her head with her pillow when she woke the next morning. Coventry had kissed her, and it had been the most spectacular thing in the world.

Until it hadn't been.

She groaned as she recalled what had happened and the manner in which he'd apologized for his regrettable behavior. *I don't know what came over me.* He might as well have been speaking of some hideous hat he'd bought on a whim.

Pulling her duvet higher, Amelia snuggled into its warmth. She had no desire to do anything today or to see anyone or go anywhere. She simply wished to remain here alone until she forgot about that wonderful kiss and the awful way in which it had ended.

A knock sounded at the door.

"Go away. I'm still sleeping."

Footsteps padded across the floor.

Amelia groaned. "Juliette, I am warning you. I wish to—"

"It is not Juliette." Lady Everly's voice was warm and kind. "I thought I would come and check on you since it is rare for you to sleep so long."

"We had a late night," Amelia explained.

"And it is now two o'clock in the afternoon. The duke is waiting for you downstairs."

That got Amelia to sit up straight, her hair falling about her face in wild disarray. "Why?" She honestly hadn't thought he would come today of all days, inconsiderate man.

"He claims the two of you agreed to go and check on the building site."

Amelia stared at Lady Everly's expectant gaze. "I never . . ." She shook her head and let the words die. Accusing him of lying would not be very helpful to anyone since such a statement would likely lead to a series of other deductions that would invariably reveal what had happened in the Falconrich parlor the previous evening. So she gritted her teeth and resolved to get through the day as best as she could. "Sorry. I should have asked my maid to wake me earlier."

"I will ring for her now so she may help you dress." Lady Everly moved to the bellpull and then to the door. "Do try to hurry. I believe His Grace is quite eager to be on his way."

Amelia grimaced as Lady Everly departed the room. It was just her luck to have to endure the company of a man she loved when he did not love her in return, and his lack of love for her was making her hate him enough to go mad. Thankfully, the maid brought tea and sandwiches with her when she arrived so Amelia was able to eat while having her hair combed and set. She gave herself one quick look in the mirror once she was ready, deciding the rich lavender color of her simple day dress was quite acceptable—especially since she was *not* trying to impress anyone. Far from it.

"Good afternoon, Lady Amelia," Coventry said, greeting her when she strolled into the parlor.

She forced a smile that felt tight around the edges. "Your Grace," she said, deliberately using the honorific.

He frowned for a second, then seemed to recover. He produced a pleasant smile. "Are you ready to depart?"

"Certainly." She turned and strode toward the foyer with him on her heels. Even now, as irritated as she was, she could not deny the awareness she had of him. His masculinity was so overwhelming that escaping it would be impossible. Which only served to annoy her even further.

Tempted to scream, she clamped her mouth shut and allowed him to hand her up into the carriage. Climbing in after her, he took a seat on the opposite bench, his every move alerting her to his presence though she refused to look in his direction. Her eyes were stubbornly trained on a tree she was able to see out in the street.

"May I say that you look radiant today?"

No, you may not.

She forced back the tart remark and muttered a thank-you, instead.

The carriage jerked into motion and the tree

vanished from sight. An awkward silence flooded the carriage, interspersed only by the faint rattle of wheels and clanking of hooves.

"Amelia."

Coventry's voice beseeched her to listen, though she still refused to look his way.

"Yes?"

"I am sorry about what happened yesterday."

Her hand clutched at the edge of her seat while her fingertips dug into the upholstery. "Stop saying that!" She couldn't bear to hear him apologize again.

"Considering your mood, I feel that I must."

That did it.

She snapped her head around to meet his gaze, ignoring the way his brow furrowed with concern. "My mood?" He just stared at her, no doubt taken aback by her cutting tone. "Is it not to your liking? Would you perhaps prefer it if I pretended that nothing has changed between us?"

He seemed to consider that and then finally said the last thing she'd expected him to say. "Yes. I believe I would."

Anger clutched at her brain, threatening to dismantle it with its overpowering strength. "You . . . ass!"

"I should not have kissed you, Amelia. It was a mistake to do so and I am—"

"Tell me you're sorry one more time, and I will never speak to you again."

He closed his mouth and stared at her with contriteness. Eventually, he blew out a breath and ran one hand through his hair, scattering the neatly combed locks. "How do I fix this?"

"I don't know. Ordinarily you should probably ask for my hand."

His eyes widened with dismay. "You know I cannot marry you. My life is—"

"Complicated. So you have said, but you are also a man of honor and duty—the sort of man who does the right thing. Ordinarily."

A look of terror entered his eyes. She would have pitied him if she hadn't been so unbelievably angry and hurt. Swallowing, he seemed to prepare himself, then slowly leaned forward and reached for her hand. She allowed the gesture though she did not care for the pleasure it wrought. At the moment, she'd no desire to be overwhelmed by the profound effect he had on her. She didn't want to revel in the gentle touch of his fingers or be infused with longing and want. She did not want to care, but she did so anyway. Desperately.

"Amelia." He spoke hesitantly. "You ought to know that I have a son."

Amelia sat as if frozen. She stared up at Thomas's familiar face and saw caginess there. Her reaction to what he'd revealed mattered, and yet she wasn't sure whether to hug him for being so honest or throttle him for keeping his son a secret for so long. Eventually, she just sank back against the squabs with a defeated sigh.

"Why would you keep that from us?" Not just from her but from Raphe, as well. Granted, they'd known each other for only a couple of months, but with all the events that had taken place since, Amelia knew Raphe considered Thomas a brother. He would never have kept something this important a secret.

There was also the way she felt about the matter. Their recent differences aside, it hurt her to imagine that he hadn't trusted her with the fact that he was a father. *But he's doing so now, Amelia.* Gazing into his dark brown eyes, she waited for him to answer.

"I have made a habit of never mentioning Jeremy to anyone," he told her frankly. His palm rested against his thigh, producing a stiff posture of resolved control. "As a duke and an active member of parliament, I do not have the luxury of avoiding public scrutiny. With Jeremy's illegitimacy in mind, I have always sought to protect him from that."

She understood him immediately. Exposing a child to possible insults and unfavorable whispers before he was ready to either ignore them or respond in kind, would be cruel. But Thomas's comment raised a whole new question.

"Who's the mother?" Other questions followed until a stack of them formed in her mind: *Do you love her? Why haven't you married her? How could you be so reckless with your lovemaking?*

"I cannot tell you that," he said.

"But—"

"There are people in my life that I seek to protect at all cost." Shifting, his foot scraped against the floor of the carriage. "All you need to know is that Jeremy's mother died in childbirth and that I have

pledged myself to raising Jeremy with the same op-
portunities available to legitimate children. It has
taken up a great deal of my time these past five
years, but I am determined." His voice shook with
emotion, and if she wasn't mistaken, his eyes shone
with a sheen of moisture.

Reaching out, Amelia clasped his hand in her
own. "I respect and admire your decision."

His jaw tightened. "Thank you." A moment passed
before he continued. "This is why I have decided not
to pursue any woman in earnest." He gave her a serious look. "Courtship and marriage take vast amounts
of time and energy."

"You're a busy man." She knew she stated the
obvious but could think of nothing else.

He squeezed her hand. "The fact that I am accompanying you on outings and to balls at your
brother's request should tell you something about
my high regard for you and your family. That
being said, and especially in light of what transpired between us last night, I would urge you to
refrain from hoping for a deeper connection with
me. Because honestly, I do not have room for that
right now."

Doing her best to maintain a calm demeanor
and hide her inward scream of frustration, Amelia
slipped her hand from his and offered a pleasant
smile that would never convey how she truly felt.
"It was just a kiss. If you think it caused me to have
expectations, then you are mistaken."

"You've seemed to fluctuate between hurt and
anger since it happened. You also suggested that I

should ask for your hand, so I naturally assumed the kiss meant something to you and that my . . . withdrawal . . . caused you pain."

"Then allow me to alleviate your concerns." Deliberately, she thought of all the housework she'd had to do when she'd lived in St. Giles. It helped push aside her emotions. "I am neither hurt nor angry, simply worried that my lapse in judgment last night would give you cause to think less of me."

A frown appeared upon his brow. "Amelia—"

"What happened between us was a mistake. I think we can both agree upon that." And since they had now arrived at the house, she was saved from having to endure another second of this conversation. Exiting the carriage with his assistance, she proceeded up the steps and through the front door.

A group of hardworking men were reconstructing the stairs, the banging of hammers and loud chatter a thankful distraction from Amelia's tumultuous emotions. "How are you progressing?" she asked as she went to take a closer look.

"Quite well, I'd say," one man told her. "T'will be faster once the floors 'ave dried—that's takin' a right long time, that is. But once it's done, we'll be able to plane 'em an' sand 'em before puttin' in the fresh planks."

"And the walls?" Amelia asked.

"We'll get to those once the floors are good an' sturdy."

Thanking him for the update, Amelia continued through to other parts of the house while Coventry remained in the foyer. He probably had no desire to be alone with her again since that would require them to either talk or feel as though they ought to be talking. She was grateful she didn't have to do either and silently thanked him for the consideration.

By the time he returned her to Huntley House, they'd said no more than a handful of words to each other, which was regrettable since it only increased her foul mood. What she truly wanted was to forget—to erase yesterday from her mind in order for her and Coventry to go on as friends. She missed their amicable repartees, but neither could she summon the courage required to get past the gaping hole in her chest. So when they arrived at her door, she bid him a good day and went inside, not offering him another glance.

When Thomas arrived home, he slammed the door so soundly behind him the entire house shook. Jones came running while his mother emerged from the parlor. "Is everything all right?" she asked.

He gritted his teeth. The last thing he wanted to do right now was explain himself. "I need a drink," he muttered after handing his hat and gloves to Jones.

Striding past both of them, he entered the parlor and went straight to the sideboard. Pouring a large measure of brandy, he downed it in one swift gulp and then poured himself another.

"What happened?" His mother's voice was gentle.

He turned to face her, aware that he probably wore a dark scowl. "I would rather not speak of it."

"You went to see Lady Amelia though—to escort her to the house?"

Her probing question made him grimace. "Yes." He drew in a breath and stared into his glass.

When he said nothing further, she asked, "Was the progress on the house not to your satisfaction?"

"It is not the damn house, Mama." Wincing, he immediately apologized for the expletive, then pinched the bridge of his nose in an effort to ward off an encroaching headache.

"Oh. I see." She crossed the floor and lowered herself to the sofa while he watched her every movement.

Finally, when she said nothing further, he asked, "What do you mean by that?"

Tilting her head, she eyed him with no small amount of pity. "Only that Lady Amelia must be the cause of your annoyance. Yet again."

"We had a disagreement," he confessed. His mother just watched him, waiting for him to continue, so he did. "She believes I insulted her, which I may have done although doing so was not my intention." On the contrary, his intention had leaned in a far more lascivious direction. "Naturally, I apologized, which she did not take kindly to at all. If anything, it only made matters worse, and now she refuses to speak with me at all." He approached the sofa and dropped down into the chair closest to it. "Frankly, I am somewhat confounded by the whole thing—by her reaction and my response to it. I feel . . . uncharacteristically contentious."

"Hmm . . ." Studying him for a long moment, she said, "The fact that you would insult her to begin with is very unlike you. I don't suppose you would care to elaborate on your poor misjudgment?"

"Not especially."

"I did not think so." She met his gaze for a long moment during which he remained completely still. He feared she might uncover the truth in the depths of his eyes. "What I would advise," she eventually continued, "is for you to take a good long think about what Lady Amelia means to you."

He instinctively flinched. "She is a friend or, more precisely, the sister of a friend."

"Is that all?"

"Of course it is." She could be nothing more. It wouldn't work if she were, which was why he wouldn't allow it.

"Then there is really no hope for you, is there?"

He sat back, a little unnerved by that comment. "What do you mean?"

"As far as I am aware, it is uncommon to get all unhinged on account of a person that one does not care strongly for. Unless of course one is mad, which you must surely be since you deny any deep attachment to Lady Amelia. So, there is no hope for you. You clearly belong in Bedlam."

He stared back at the petite woman who'd raised him—the woman who always spoke demurely— and he wondered how exactly he'd managed to make her go off on such a confounding tangent.

"Mama," he said as he emptied the last of his brandy, "your logic is distressing."

"That you would think so only proves my point even more."

"And what exactly is your point, besides me being mad and belonging in an institution for the mentally insane?"

She smiled then—the sort of smile that a mother might give a child who was trying to learn how to walk. "You are obviously developing a tendre for her."

He felt his entire body go numb. "I am *not!*"

"Very well then." She stood and walked to the door. Pausing there, she looked back at him with warmth and more understanding than he possessed at that moment. "You will recognize the truth soon enough, Coventry, and when you do, I suggest you embrace it."

He waited until she was gone, then muttered a series of curses.

She was wrong, damn it. He was *not* losing his head over Amelia. He *would* not lose his head over her. Except, if he were to be completely honest with himself, he had to recognize that he already had. His mother was right. Why else would he get so wound up over their falling-out?

The answer was simple. He missed how easy their relationship had been before he'd ruined it with a kiss. There was nothing easy about it now. She'd gotten beneath his skin and taken up residence in his heart. The hurt in her eyes when he'd disengaged from her had been palpable. It had twisted his gut and prompted him to voice his regret even though he regretted no part of what had transpired between them. On the contrary, he'd savored every exquisite moment. But she could not know that—not without promises being made.

With a heavy sigh, he stood and went to get changed. A good fight at the Black Swan was awfully tempting at the moment. Perhaps he could have his feelings for her punched out of him. At least then he would no longer suffer the wretched pain of caring about how thoroughly he'd managed to wound her.

Chapter 16

"**T**his just came for you, my lady." Pierson held the salver toward Amelia so she could retrieve the letter.

Opening it, she read. "It's from the dowager duchess," she said, looking at Lady Everly, who'd been in the middle of instructing Amelia and Juliette in how to hold a fan correctly before the butler had entered. "She is inviting me to join her this afternoon for tea."

"Then you must go," Lady Everly said without blinking.

"But . . ." Amelia read the letter again while trying to detect if this might have been Coventry's doing. "Is it not odd that she would invite only me?"

Lady Everly shrugged. "I shouldn't think so. You are the elder sister and the one we are most eager to find a suitor for. I am sure she just wishes to offer some private guidance."

More puzzled than ever by that remark, Amelia refolded the piece of paper and continued with her lesson. She would not worry about the visit, she told herself, even though her heart began to pound at the idea of having to face the duke again. It was his house after all, so she might run into him, which was something she wasn't prepared to do quite yet. Not after the argument they'd had the day before. Which was why she immediately asked his butler if he was at home upon being admitted to Coventry House at precisely three o'clock that afternoon.

He shook his head and relief swept through her. "No, my lady, but Her Grace awaits you in the parlor. If you will please follow me."

Showing her into the spacious room, Amelia greeted the dowager duchess with a short curtsey that hopefully didn't look nearly as awkward as it felt. The dowager duchess smiled. "Thank you for joining me, Lady Amelia. I was not sure if your schedule would allow it."

"I am grateful for the invitation, though I must confess I find it a little surprising."

The older woman laughed and gestured for Amelia to take a seat on one of the sofas. "My son did mention your forwardness."

Amelia bit her lip. "I'm sorry. It does appear as though I have a tendency to speak without thinking sometimes."

"Oh, you need not apologize to me, dear. I find you quite delightful and refreshing. I can see why Coventry enjoys your company."

The comment, accompanied by a welcoming

smile, gave Amelia pause. She suddenly wondered what exactly Thomas had told his mother about her, or rather, how much.

Steeling herself, she watched as the duchess poured tea. Her curiosity continued to climb. Eventually, she had to ask, "Why didn't you invite my sister?"

Nudging a teacup in Amelia's direction, the dowager duchess said, "Because as charming as I find her, she is not the subject of my interest. You are." When Amelia stared at her in amazement, the dowager duchess's smile broadened. "You see, I can be forward too."

Silenced by that comment, Amelia picked up her teacup and took a sip.

The dowager duchess looked at Amelia with assessing eyes. "The thing is that I find myself intrigued."

"By me?"

Surely not.

The dowager duchess gave a slow and very deliberate nod. "Coventry has taken notice of you, and as his mother, I therefore feel it is my duty to evaluate you myself."

Momentarily startled, Amelia wasn't sure whether to laugh or cry in response to such an outrageous opinion. Training her features to the best of her abilities, she spoke softly in an effort to come across calmer than she actually was. "If you imagine that he might be thinking of courting me, then you are mistaken. Your son and I are friends, Your Grace. Nothing more."

The dowager duchess sipped her tea while eyeing Amelia over the brim of her cup. Returning the fine piece of Wedgwood porcelain to the table, she simply said, "We will see about that."

Oddly perturbed by the comment and the thought of the poor woman hoping for something that would not be, Amelia allowed her to turn to other subjects of conversation. When the lady asked about her past, she held nothing back as she spoke of the difficult life she'd led in St. Giles and how Mayfair posed an entirely different challenge.

"The minuet is proving to be particularly difficult," she said when they started discussing ballroom etiquette. "My feet always feel as though they're moving in the wrong direction when I dance it."

"I have seen you dance it several times now, and in my opinion you do not do it too badly."

Amelia laughed. "That doesn't sound very reassuring."

"As long as you continue to practice daily, you will master it eventually."

Appreciating the confidence with which she spoke, Amelia reached for a biscuit. She was just about to bite into it when a slight movement off to one side caught the corner of her eye. She glanced toward it, pausing at the sight of a small face peeking out at them from behind the doorjamb. His eyes were beautiful—a rich chocolate color, wide with interest.

Forgetting that she was sitting in a formal parlor with a dowager duchess, Amelia set her biscuit aside and placed her hands over her eyes. Carefully, she parted them just enough to meet the boy's gaze before covering her eyes again. She repeated the gesture, noting that more of his face had come into view—a handsome mouth that failed to smile even as he joined in her game.

For the next several minutes, Amelia covered and uncovered her eyes while the boy stepped further into the room. When he was well inside the doorway, she dropped her hands to her lap and smiled. He averted his gaze and shifted from foot to foot, his body twisting as though he was thinking of fleeing. So rather than drawing too much attention to him, she focused on the paper that stuck out of his pocket.

"What do you have there?" she asked, pointing to the rolled-up sheet.

His gaze slid sideways, and Amelia became suddenly aware of the dowager duchess again. The lady hadn't spoken a word since the boy's arrival, and Amelia chose to ignore her now, in favor of encouraging him to speak. Instead, he silently took the paper she'd pointed to out of his pocket and stepped closer still. He handed it to her without a word, and she unrolled it to find a stunning display of color. It didn't look like anything in particular, but that didn't make it less beautiful.

"You're a true artist," she murmured, studying the way that splashes of yellow and orange mixed with blues and greens. "To capture a feeling is no easy task, but this . . . this makes me think of warmth and happiness, of the sun rising above the world. It's beautiful, and you should be very proud."

The boy, all serious and terribly quiet, glanced at the dowager duchess once more, and so did Amelia this time. She looked at the woman who'd easily smiled and laughed just moments before. Her eyes now gleamed with a watery sheen and her lips had begun to tremble.

"My grandson," she managed to say with a hoarse whisper. "His name is Jeremy."

"I'm very pleased to meet you, Jeremy," Amelia said, returning her attention to the child. His eyes were dark like his father's, but his hair . . . She felt her chest constrict as she gazed at the trait that he must have gotten from his mother.

Forcing aside the ugly feelings of jealousy that threatened, Amelia patted the seat beside her and asked, "Will you join me?"

Jeremy seemed to consider. Eventually, he drew closer and claimed the spot. Still, he did not smile or show any other hint of emotion. Instead, he crossed his arms and began swinging his legs back and forth. Amelia considered him more closely, aware that there was something peculiar about his behavior that reminded her of Bethany.

She picked up the tray with biscuits and offered it to him. "Would you like one?"

When he shook his head, she set the tray down. She glanced at the dowager duchess who looked increasingly distraught for some odd reason. "Are you all right?" Amelia quietly asked her.

The dowager duchess responded with a nod. Swiftly, she stood, paused, looked at Amelia and Jeremy, then turned away while muttering a hasty, "If you will please excuse me for a moment."

Amelia stared after her. Everything about this

visit seemed strange. Deciding that nothing she'd learned so far would help her through it, she chose to let her instinct guide her and addressed Jeremy once again. "Do you like animals?"

He stilled beside her. A moment passed, and then he nodded.

"Dogs?"

He nodded again.

"Do you own one by any chance?"

A shake of his head and she had her answer.

The painting he'd made caught her eye once more. Jeremy might be a quiet introvert, but his art provided an insight to great imagination. She pondered that for a second—the do's and don'ts of the idea taking shape in her head. She was in a duke's home, after all—a guest invited to tea. And yet . . . Jeremy clearly needed some sort of amusement. She longed to make him smile and considered the way in which Raphe had sometimes succeeded in getting Bethany to do that.

So she asked him plainly, "Would you like to play a game?"

For a long while, he said nothing, and then he finally spoke his first word to her.

"Yes."

When Thomas arrived home from parliament, he instantly knew that something was amiss. For one thing, his butler wasn't there to greet him at the door. This had never happened before. Not during the day. Thomas took off his hat and removed his gloves, placing both on the foyer table. And then he became aware of laughter—a child's laughter. He shook his head. It wasn't possible.

As he headed down the hallway that led toward the parlor, he saw his mother and his butler standing outside the door looking into the room like a pair of secretive spectators. "What—"

"Shh!" His mother turned to him with a finger pressed to her lips. She looked overly emotional—possibly as if she'd been crying.

What the devil?

Respecting her wish for silence, he eased his pace and stepped forward with a soft tread. Another bit of laughter and what sounded like . . . neighing? Thomas frowned. None of it made any sense until the butler moved aside so he had room to observe the scene for himself.

His mouth dropped open, not so much because of the overturned tray of biscuits that littered a very expensive carpet, but because of Lady Amelia. She was crawling about on her hands and knees, heedless of what that might do to her gown, and with Jeremy riding upon her back as if she were a pony. Whinnying, she plodded about. A sudden shake of her body made Jeremy laugh, and whenever she ducked down or rose up a little, he howled with amusement. And in that moment, Thomas felt his heart swell as warmth cascaded through him. He'd never seen Jeremy this animated before. It was little wonder that his mother appeared to be overcome.

Amelia reared to one side and then turned about while Jeremy clung to the back of her gown. A laugh broke from her lips, as well. Her delight was undeniable until she spun toward the door, her eyes settling on the feet that stood there. Freezing, she looked up at her onlookers from behind a few locks of unpinned hair. She blew at the locks with charming abandonment. Her cheeks were bright from exertion, her eyes conveying every piece of kindness that filled her heart to overflowing.

"Jeremy," she said. "I think it's time for us to stop for a moment."

The boy's face fell. His mouth twisted and he crossed his arms, but he didn't move or speak. Thomas stepped toward him. "Jeremy," he told him gently, "you must climb down from Lady Amelia's back so she can get up." The boy's eyes did not make contact. As usual, it was as if he wasn't hearing what was being said. "Jeremy," Thomas tried again, "if you do not climb down, I will have to pick you up."

Jeremy jerked his head just enough to convey his displeasure. He began twisting from side to side, eyes fixed on the carpet. "No," he muttered. "No, no, no."

"I mean it," Thomas told him sternly. Jeremy didn't answer. Instead, he unfolded his arms and swung his fists hard. Thomas rushed forward, but before he could reach Jeremy, the child had managed to hit Amelia in the back of the head.

"Ow!"

"Oh no!" he heard his mother exclaim as he wrapped his arms around Jeremy's body and lifted him up and away from Amelia.

"No, no, no!" Jeremy chanted, legs kicking,

while Thomas walked from the room and climbed the stairs to the nursery. There, he lowered himself to the floor and held on tight while Jeremy cried in his arms.

"**D**oes this happen often?" Amelia asked the dowager duchess as she followed her through the house to the garden. The day was warm and pleasant, the fragrant scent of jasmine and roses so enticing Amelia could not resist taking a closer look at the flowers. Some birds twittered from a nearby tree, adding to the charm of the overall experience.

"Only when Jeremy gets overly excited. He . . . is not spoiled, you know. The reaction he had in there was not simply on account of him being deprived the fun he was having." The dowager duchess sighed. "It is not so simple, and perhaps I was wrong to invite you here and to show you. Coventry is bound to have a few choice words with me later."

"Because he wouldn't want me to know that he has a son who is . . . slightly different from other children?" When the dowager duchess's eyes filled with pain, Amelia placed her hand on her arm in comfort.

"He believes it is his responsibility to protect Jeremy before all else."

"And rightfully so," Amelia said as they began a slow walk. "The world can be incredibly cruel." She knew that firsthand. Considering how hurt she had been as an adult by a few unkind words, she couldn't imagine what it might do to a little boy.

"It is not that Coventry does not trust you, but you have to understand that this is his closest kept secret. It is in his nature to protect it as well as he can."

"Then he may indeed consider my coming here a betrayal."

"A necessary one, I should think," the dowager duchess said with a sad little smile. She glanced at Amelia as they followed a path leading back to the terrace.

Her tone caught Amelia's attention. "How do you mean?"

"Only that I want him to be happy and that I hope my actions today will accomplish that in the end."

Her cryptic remark gave Amelia pause, but she had no time to analyze it in detail since Coventry returned at that same moment, eating up the distance between them with a solid stride. He reached them in under five seconds.

"Mama." His eyes were full of seriousness. "Might I speak with Lady Amelia in private?"

"Of course. I need to remove a few dry petals from some of those flowers over there anyway."

Amelia watched her walk away and instantly wished she could stay by her side. Instead, she now had to face the tall presence of the man who stood before her. He wasn't smiling, but he didn't look angry or high-handed either, which was of some relief since she was quite tired of being annoyed with him, as well. Because although it still hurt to have him push her away, she understood his reason for doing so better now, even though she would have to make him understand how unnecessary it had been.

"Your mother was right to bring me here," she said. One dark eyebrow rose into a pointed arch. "And you were mistaken when you decided to treat Jeremy as if there is something wrong with him."

"He is not like other boys, Amelia."

"Perhaps not, but that doesn't mean that he should be hidden away in this house. What will that teach him?"

Sighing, he shoved his hands in his pockets. "I do not know. You saw the way he reacted in there. Imagine what would happen if he had such an episode out in public. He would be ridiculed— laughed at."

"By some, I'll grant you that. But I would never be that cruel. Nor would Huntley or Gabriella or Juliette. Surely you know that." He nodded a little but did not look entirely convinced, so she decided to be as candid as possible. "The truth is, I am not completely unfamiliar with his kind of behavior."

His eyes sharpened with interest. "What do you mean?"

"My sister, Bethany, had trouble relating to other people's emotions. She often seemed anxious, would remove herself to a corner and simply stand there swaying back and forth until someone hugged her. It wasn't easy, taking care of her and always worrying about the next episode, so I completely understand what you're going through, Coventry, as do my siblings."

"I . . . I had no idea."

"There was no reason for me to mention it until now."

Dropping his gaze, he shifted his feet, then looked at her again with a stricken expression that tore at her heart. "Did . . . I mean . . . I know Bethany died, and I cannot help but wonder if perhaps . . . if perhaps . . ." He shook his head and then covered his eyes with his hands, concealing his dread from her view.

Amelia's heart went out to him. "She caught pneumonia one winter and never recovered. Her death, as awful as it was, had nothing to do with her state of mind."

The sigh of relief that escaped him was shaky. "I see." He swallowed and looked about before addressing her once again. "You are right. My mother did well to invite you here today. Not only to meet Jeremy, but because it forces us to address the tension between us. I have been trying to think of what to say to you next and have found nothing fitting."

"Is that why your face looks a little bit bluer than yesterday?"

His mouth tilted with the hint of a mischievous smile. "Perhaps."

"So you have ignored my advice and gone back to St. Giles?"

"Of course not."

She couldn't help but grin. "You're a terrible liar."

"Hmm . . . perhaps I should practice more?"

"No. Don't you dare. I appreciate your honesty." She started toward the terrace, and he fell into step beside her. On the opposite side of the lawn his mother appeared to be giving a shrub a great deal of attention. "Now it is my turn." This wasn't going to be easy, but she felt she owed him an explanation for her churlish behavior. "The fact of the matter is that I *wanted* you to kiss me, Coventry, and when you did, it was the most wonderful thing I'd ever experienced in my life. But then you had to go and ruin it with apologies. You took something special and turned it into this terrible, regrettable mistake."

"I acted on instinct," he explained, "and I am sorry for it. Not for the kiss, but for the carelessness with which I treated you after the kiss. You deserve better from me, Amelia." Reaching the terrace, he turned to face her. His hand found hers, his thumb gently stroking her palm while he leaned a bit closer. A shiver tickled her insides. Her breath caught in her throat. "Perhaps I ought to tell you how much you affect me?"

Was it possible for a pair of stays to tighten on their own accord? Amelia didn't know. In fact, she could barely think as his thumb stroked a path to her wrist. It settled there, pressing against her pulse. "I, er . . . ah . . . I affect you?" She spoke with a squeak, her nerves completely frayed by the prospect of him provoking her so intensely while his mother remained but a short distance away.

"More than you can possibly imagine." There was a decadent depth to his voice that made her skin tremble. His thumbnail scraped against her palm, stirring a slow delicious ache somewhere deep down inside. "Keeping my distance from you—not acting rashly—has taken tremendous restraint. But . . ." He drew his hand away and stepped back. "Restraint is what is required if we are to avoid a scandal and preserve your reputation."

Dazed by his need for control in her presence, Amelia barely managed a nod. "Of course."

"Not to mention that your brother will not be pleased to find you compromised by the man who swore to protect you. I cannot let him down. To do so would make me no better than . . ." He clamped his mouth shut with a brusqueness that hinted at anger. "We must keep a respectable distance. This cannot happen again."

She tried not to let the finality of his words vex her. Instead, she focused on his unspoken words. "No better than whom?"

His jaw clenched and his eyes hardened. Gone was the man who'd seductively told her of his desire seconds earlier. "It does not matter."

"I disagree."

"Amelia." His voice held a note of warning. "It is a private matter, and I will ask you to respect that."

Taken aback by his violent tone, she retreated a step just as Coventry's butler came out on the terrace. "Lady Amelia," he said, walking toward her with a salver. "This has arrived for you. It seems it was forwarded from your house."

Concerned about the urgency, Amelia thanked him and snatched up the letter. She quickly tore it open. "It is from the chief laborer at the house. There has been an accident." Her hand began to tremble so she offered the letter to Thomas. "Part of the roof collapsed on one of the workers. It does not mention his condition."

"Then let us go and assess the situation for ourselves. The sooner we do so, the sooner our minds can be put at ease."

Agreeing with him, she went to say goodbye to his mother, all the while wondering if she ought to abandon her project and sell the building before anything else could go wrong with it.

Chapter 17

~~~OO~~~

The sight that awaited them was horrific. Beams of wood, roofing tiles and other debris covered a man whose voice pleaded weakly for help.

"Stay back," Coventry warned Amelia as he shrugged out of his jacket and handed it to her. They were in one of the second-floor bedrooms with three other men who were all trying to lift away the larger pieces of wood. Coventry quickly went to offer his assistance while Amelia watched from the doorway.

Looking up, she glimpsed the sky through the gaping hole in the ceiling. The man who'd gotten hurt must have been on the roof and fallen straight through. They would have to investigate further—especially to make sure this did not happen again.

"I think we may need a doctor," Coventry said. Crouching to move away pieces of plaster, he glanced toward Amelia. "Perhaps you can ask my coachman to fetch one. Florian will do, if he is available."

Eager to help, Amelia hurried back downstairs to deliver the message. She then asked the laborers still working in the foyer if they had any water for her to give their injured friend. One of them went to fetch a jug and a cup.

Returning upstairs with it, Amelia arrived just in time to see the injured man being pulled from underneath a large beam. He was coughing and wheezing, his lungs no doubt filled with the thick white dust that covered the floor. She poured some water into the cup and handed it to him. He accepted it with eager hands, setting it to his mouth and gulping it down.

"I think his arm may be broken," Coventry said. "And there is a large bump on the back of his head. He is in a great deal of pain."

"What is your name?" Amelia asked the man as she crouched beside him.

"Rob," he said with a grimace.

"I'm sorry you got hurt, Rob." She refilled his cup and he drank some more water. "Can you tell us what happened?"

Rob stared straight back at her, then nodded. "I was tryin' to clear the spots that needed fixin'. You know, removin' broken tiles an' markin' the places where rain 'ad gotten in since those will likely be pretty damaged. I stepped forward onto an area that looked solid enough an' me foot went straight through. Lost me balance an' fell, hittin' me chin on a bit of chipped tile in the process." He pointed to the cut he'd received.

"I have sent for a doctor," Amelia told him. "He will hopefully be able to set your arm if it is indeed broken."

"Hurts like the devil, that's fer sure. If ye'll pardon me language, me lady."

Patting him gently on the shoulder, Amelia stood and faced Coventry. "I want to take a closer look at the damage."

"I just did so while you were helping Rob." His expression was grim. "You are not going to like this."

Bracing herself for what would no doubt result in another large expense, Amelia followed Coventry to where the ceiling had given way. She stared up at the visible parts of the roof's structure and frowned as she studied the broken off ends of four beams. "I would have expected a more uneven break." She pointed to one of the beams. "That almost looks as though it was cut, it's so perfectly straight."

"That is probably because it was."

She lowered her gaze and met Coventry's. "Are you saying this was sabotage?"

"That is what I believe. Yes."

"But . . ." She shook her head, trying to make sense of such a possibility. "Who on earth would want to do such a thing? I have no enemies, as far as I know and . . ." A thought struck her. "Oh God. Do you suppose the fire might not have been an accident either? That perhaps someone is trying to chase us away?"

He appeared to ponder that for a moment, his face a mask of serious contemplation. "I suppose it is a possibility, though we cannot know for certain."

"No. But if we suppose that this is the case, a

meeting with Mr. Gorrell might be in order. He did say there was another interested party."

Coventry nodded. "You're right. At the time I believed it was something he had fabricated in order to make you pay more than the house was worth. But if that was not the case and there really was another buyer, then that individual must have wanted this house very badly to offer such huge sums for it."

"In which case they might have been very angry when they discovered that Mr. Gorrell had sold it to me." She cast another glance at the damaged ceiling before addressing Coventry once more. "I think we should head over to Mr. Gorrell's office as soon as Doctor Florian has finished tending to Rob. The sooner we solve this mystery, the better."

It was another half hour before Doctor Florian arrived, but it took him only a couple of minutes to confirm that Rob's arm was indeed broken. Since setting it would require more supplies than he'd brought with him, the doctor suggested taking Rob back to St. Agatha's Hospital with him. The two departed by hired hackney while Amelia and Thomas took the ducal carriage to Mr. Gorrell's office only to find it closed.

"That is odd." Thomas stared at the locked door. "His clerk ought to be here if not the man himself. After all, it has only just gone four on a Friday."

"Perhaps he has some business out of town?" Amelia suggested.

Thomas frowned. He glanced toward the windows, which were off to one side. "Hold on." Clasping the corner of the building with one hand, he braced himself and leaned to the right as far as he could manage.

"Oh, do be careful." It wasn't too far up, but if he fell he might still get seriously hurt, and in Amelia's opinion, one wounded man was enough for one day.

Grunting his response, he strained his neck in order to peer through the nearest window. Amelia looked around. If someone happened to see, there was no telling what they might think of the Duke of Coventry invading someone's privacy like this. So she was relieved when he quickly returned to the ground unnoticed. "It has been vacated," he said, "and quickly, I might add. There were things tossed about—papers and such. I would say he left in a hurry."

Amelia felt a shudder go through her. "Do you think he ran from the same person who tampered with the roof?"

"It is becoming increasingly likely. The only problem is that with Mr. Gorrell gone, we might not be able to discover who it is."

She thought about that for a moment, then had an idea. "There might be a way." Bracing herself for his disagreement, she said, "It is common knowledge that Carlton Guthrie runs St. Giles, and with the house being right there on the edge of it, he might be able to help."

"That's not a bad idea."

Amelia blinked. What? No argument? No telling her that Guthrie was not to be trusted? No reminder of the fact that her brother had barely escaped the man's clutches and that he'd be furious if he found out they'd sought his help?

"I was expecting you to say no. Instead, you seem surprisingly at ease with the suggestion. Why is that?"

He gave a nonchalant shrug and started back toward the carriage. "I am well acquainted with Guthrie and have no issue with requesting his assistance in this matter."

"I beg your pardon?"

Stopping next to the carriage, he turned and offered her his hand. She didn't budge, which resulted in a sigh. "Allow me to hand you up and I will explain."

"Promise?"

"You have my word." Pleased by that assurance, she allowed him to do his gentlemanly duty. She took her seat, as did he, and the carriage set off. His contemplative gaze found hers, there was a pause and then, "Your brother introduced me to Guthrie several weeks ago. Huntley was teaching me how to box and thought it would do me good to experience a less polite setting than Gentleman Jackson's. If you ask me, he also missed the rougher fighting St. Giles had to offer. Guthrie was there. We had a few beers together."

Amelia stared at him in stupefaction. "So the two of you—a pair of dukes—decided to not only take an excursion into the slums for a bit of sport, but to also keep the company of one of London's most notorious criminals?" She was going to have some choice words with Raphe when he returned, considering all the lectures he'd given her and Juliette about adhering to propriety and protecting their reputations. Hypocrite!

"Huntley may not like Guthrie much, but he has known him a long time. He spent most of his life in St. Giles and—"

"So did I, if I may remind you. We lived there together, don't forget. But that did not prevent you from flying into a fit when I merely skirted the edge of it."

"That is entirely different."

"Oh really? Is that because you are impervious to danger while I am but a frail woman who must be protected by rules and governed by men whose wisdom surpasses my own in ways that I cannot ever hope to comprehend?"

Expelling a breath, he pinched the bridge of his nose and closed his eyes. "Can we please stick to the subject at hand? We have already argued over this once already, and I am reluctant to do so again."

Feeling peevish, she sat back and crossed her arms. "Very well."

"Thank you." He opened his eyes and regarded her steadily. "The point is that Guthrie knows me."

"Did he facilitate your most recent fight? Is he the reason why your face still looks all blotchy?"

"Yes, but we digress. *Once. Again.*" He pinned her with a look that said he would not be bullied by her. "As long as I offer him an acceptable sum, he will answer whatever questions I give him."

"Whatever questions *we* give him, you mean."

"No." His expression changed from serious to forcefully decisive. "*You* are going home while *I* am going to meet with Guthrie. I will stop by your house later to let you know what I have discovered."

"You domineering, aristocratic, high-handed fop!" To her surprise, he grinned, which only annoyed her more. "What?"

"There is something utterly charming about you when you are angry." A spark lit in his eyes. "It makes me want to be reckless, even though I know that I mustn't."

Her anger evaporated in an instant as his words settled over her. He was speaking of kissing, and she suddenly longed to feel his embrace once more—to simply surrender no matter the consequence.

"Oh."

It was all she could say while she sat there hoping he might decide to ignore his better judgment.

"And now you look adorably befuddled."

"I do?"

He nodded before averting his gaze and looking out of the window. "Ah. We are here."

Amelia felt his pronouncement like a jolt. He'd teased the very depths of her sensuality with his heated perusal and she was now expected to forget it? To descend from the carriage and return to the company of Lady Everly and her sister as though nothing had happened?

Well, nothing *had* happened, technically. He'd just spoken a few words, but those words had made her clamor for him with a desperation that would likely leave her feeling restless for several days after. It also had a distinct influence on her mood, which was once again prickly. But since the only person with the power to change that had no intention of making the effort, she allowed him to help her down and escort her up to the door, which Pierson held open.

"I will return later to inform you of the progress," Coventry said. "It should not take too long." And with that he departed while she remained there, trembling with a need that would not be sated.

Swearing beneath his breath, Thomas walked from the street where he'd asked his driver to wait and headed toward the Black Swan. He'd been mad to confess the effect she had on him, for it had only made her look more alluring. Aware of his want, she'd allowed a glimpse of her own, her lips parting and eyelids lowering while her breaths had grown labored. She'd been just as aroused as he by that one proclamation, and it had taken every bit of restraint he possessed not to leap across the carriage and take what he wanted. But he would not behave like a scoundrel even if he had begun to think like one. She was worth more, the only problem being that he wasn't sure he was the man to supply it.

But what then?

He'd effectively chased away both of her suitors, so unless someone else showed an interest, she'd likely fail to achieve what Huntley had hoped for. Except, Thomas would probably take a dislike to that man as well and sabotage his efforts to marry her. In which case she might end up a spinster and . . . perhaps then he could ask her to be his mistress. *Would she agree to such an arrangement?* he wondered.

A sigh escaped him as he turned a corner and strode forward, ignoring the stench of refuse and the curious stares of the bedraggled people he encountered along his way. Even if she did, he knew it wouldn't be fair to her. She deserved to marry and have a respectable family—children that she could dote on. But marriage? Would he actually be capable of entering into such a binding union with her?

For the past five years, Jeremy had occupied his every thought and concern. Every action had been carried out with him in mind. He'd worked so bloody hard to ensure the boy's future only to find himself struggling more now than ever before.

Perhaps his mother was right and he needn't do so alone. Perhaps Amelia would offer some much-needed support with regard to Jeremy's upbringing. She certainly seemed to understand him, had experienced a similar issue with her sister, and showed a degree of patience with the boy that would likely work wonders.

Granted, he was basing his deductions on one brief encounter, so maybe he ought to invite her back. Jeremy would no doubt be thrilled. He'd enjoyed her company immensely until Thomas had put an end to it. But would Amelia be able to accept the complete truth about Jeremy's birth? Would she be willing to keep it a secret, even from her siblings?

Yes.

He knew it instinctively. She would hold the truth close to her heart, if not for his sake, then for Jeremy's, and she would do so whether she agreed to marry him or not.

That turn of thought gave him pause. Was he really going to propose to her?

He considered the benefits their marriage would bring. She would be his to seduce at leisure, her body would warm his bed, and the craving he had would finally be sated. But there was more to it than that, wasn't there? For one thing, he genuinely cared for her and enjoyed spending time in her company. For another, she would make an excellent mother for Jeremy.

As for the downside . . . he couldn't really think of one at the moment.

Arriving at the Black Swan, he saw that the place appeared more dilapidated during the light of day. The paint peeled on the entire facade and the railing out front looked more crooked than he remembered. Inside, the dim interior lacked the life that filled it in the evenings, lending a depressing air of abandonment to it.

Passing the only occupied table, Thomas crossed to where a woman was sweeping the floor. "Is Guthrie around?" he asked, holding a coin in her direction.

She snatched it up and pointed toward a corridor. "Last room at the end. Knock before you enter."

As if he'd consider doing otherwise.

He headed toward the room in question.

"May I have a moment of your time?" he asked

Guthrie after being admitted by a Scotsman who went by the name of McNeil.

Guthrie's face transformed into one of welcoming politeness. He waved Thomas closer. "My, my, what an unexpected honor." He gestured toward an empty chair that stood on the opposite side of the table at which he sat. Thomas stepped forward and claimed the seat. "Would ye care fer a pint?" Guthrie indicated a jug. "I can ask McNeil to fetch another mug."

"Thank you, but that will not be necessary." Leaning forward, Thomas placed his elbows on the table and met Guthrie's calculating eyes. "I am here to discuss a house with you."

"A house?" Guthrie's surprise was undeniable.

Thomas nodded. "The one on the corner of Bainbridge and High Street."

"That run-down stack of bricks?"

"It was recently purchased by Huntley's sister, Lady Amelia."

Guthrie's eyes widened. "I was not aware of that."

It was Thomas's turn to be surprised. "I was under the impression that you knew everything that went on in St. Giles. At least that is what Lady Amelia and Huntley have told me."

"And they would have been correct a few weeks ago before my best informant went missing. I'm guessing he was either turned by Bartholomew or murdered," he grumbled, mentioning the only crime lord whose infamy could surpass his own, if only because Bartholomew's well-polished appearance and wealth allowed him to mingle with a higher class of people than Guthrie would ever manage to do. "If I ever find him, he'll wish it was the latter."

"Then you are probably not in a position to help since the information I need pertains to more recent events."

"Such as?" A keen interest gleamed in Guthrie's eyes.

"The solicitor who arranged the sale of the house mentioned another buyer—some individual willing to outbid Lady Amelia until I stepped in and threatened the solicitor with ruining his career. He must have seen me as a more immediate threat because he immediately gave in and Lady Amelia managed to complete her purchase. Since then, however, there has been a fire and today an act of sabotage causing one of the workers to get seriously hurt. The solicitor has also quit town—his office has been vacated. I came here with the hope that you might be able to give me some idea as to who might be behind all of this."

Guthrie leaned back in his chair, reached for his beer and took a slow sip. When he set the mug down, he wiped his mouth with the back of his hand before saying, "I can still give ye my opinion."

"I would be happy to hear it."

"That house was once very grand. Its location is of particular interest since it sits between the good part o' town and the not so good part."

"How do you figure?"

"Well . . . let's say that ye want to take advantage

of both sides. Let's say ye're in the business of prostitution and ye'd like to start caterin' to a richer clientele. A house like the one Lady Amelia purchased would make a prime location."

"I suppose that is true," Thomas muttered. He wasn't quite sure where Guthrie was going with this.

"Now, let's also suppose that ye'd like to gain a foothold in St. Giles."

"Disregarding the various assumptions you are making, I don't suppose a name comes to mind?"

Guthrie beamed. "Now that ye mention it, I do believe one does." Crossing his arms, his eyes narrowed above a smirk. "If I'm to theorize, I'd say Bartholomew's yer man. He 'as the means to do it. He's also been after me territory fer years. Tried to win it earlier this summer when 'e had 'is man, The Bull, fight Huntley, but failed. I wouldn't put it past 'im to try an' acquire a house like the one Lady Amelia bought an' turn it into a brothel or opium den."

"Are those his primary sources of income?"

"Aye, but in the worst way possible."

"How so?"

Guthrie started to look uncomfortable, which was disconcerting. "Aside from the expected romp, he's known to offer the sort of experiences that those with particular tastes will pay good blunt to enjoy. With that house in his possession, I believe 'e'll be lookin' to offer the wealthy somethin' only the lowliest bawdy 'ouses provide at the moment."

"You imagine a twisted, drug-infused El Dorado

for the rich and perverse?" Thomas asked and Guthrie nodded, his mouth now set in a flat line. "You could be wrong."

"I bloody well hope I am, but if I'm not and 'e somehow manages to take control of that house, a lot of me people will suffer. Which is why you can count on me to do me part. I'll try to look into the matter, now that ye've made me aware of it."

"Thank you. I appreciate the help since Lady Amelia and I have no plan on quitting our own plans for that house. We intend to turn it into a school for the children of St. Giles, and not even Bartholomew is going to stop us from doing that."

"I'll certainly wish ye luck," Guthrie said. "A school would be welcomed. But don't underestimate a man like Bartholomew. He's a ruthless villain if ever there was one, and with fewer scruples than me."

Taking his warning to heart, Thomas left the Black Swan after offering Guthrie ten pounds for his trouble. He then collected his carriage and made his way back to Huntley House so he could brief Lady Amelia just as he'd promised.

Chapter 18

Sitting on a chair in Coventry's study two days later, Amelia eyed the man whom her brother had only ever mentioned when referencing someone worse than Carlton Guthrie. *Bartholomew.* She did not know his full name, nor did she care to. When Coventry had mentioned his possible involvement in the recent events pertaining to her house, her concern had left her with a deep chill in her bones.

She looked to where Lady Everly and the dowager duchess sat and was grateful for their presence. Perhaps it would prompt Bartholomew to act with some decorum even if she and Coventry failed to do so.

"I cannot imagine why you would wish to see *me*, Your Grace," Bartholomew drawled. He was an older man and shockingly well-dressed, considering his profession. Apparently crime had served him well, and the time he'd spent in Newgate years ago had not affected his fondness for proper tailoring. Rumor had it he'd been imprisoned for only a few days because of his good connections and a few well-placed bribes.

"Really?" Coventry asked with a note of sarcasm. He leaned back and studied Bartholomew with a keen eye that Amelia found rather reassuring. The villain was not about to get the better of him, of that she was quite sure.

"I'm afraid so," Bartholomew said. Smirking, he looked up at his associate—a heavyset man who probably served as Bartholomew's protector when out about town.

Coventry drummed his fingers against his desk for a moment, then said, "A house was recently sold on the corner of Bainbridge and High Street. Two parties bid on it, Lady Amelia being one and the other being yourself."

Bartholomew snorted. "You're wrong about that, Your Grace. I never tried to buy such a building."

"Is that so?"

"Of course it is." Bartholomew suddenly grinned. "One house would never be enough for me. Not when it comes to St. Giles. I'm rather looking to take the entire neighborhood, you see."

"So Guthrie says."

"Oh? You spoke to my favorite rival, did you?" Shaking his head, Bartholomew stretched out his legs and sighed. "I suppose he's the one who brought you sniffing around my feet, hoping to catch a scent of something nefarious. Well . . ." His eyes hardened, and Amelia suddenly saw the man so many people feared. "Perhaps you ought to take a closer look at Guthrie himself. That gin business he's in may need a new location."

"The house caught fire last week," Thomas said, ignoring Bartholomew's comment, "and two days ago one of the workers fell through the roof. Turns out the beams had been cut to allow for the accident."

"And I suppose you're going to blame me for that too?"

"I probably wouldn't have, but Mr. Gorrell's sudden disappearance does seem to raise some suspicion."

"Forgive me," Bartholomew murmured, "but who is Mr. Gorrell?"

"The solicitor in charge of the sale." Coventry narrowed his gaze. "He mentioned another buyer—someone wealthy enough to make the sort of offer that was meant to dissuade others—an exorbitant amount, considering the state the house is in and its location."

"Yet *you* paid. There is no doubt a long line of other individuals willing to acquire the place for whatever strange reason they might have. *I*, however, am not one of them."

Amelia pondered that statement and the convincing manner in which Bartholomew delivered it. Perhaps they were wrong about him? All they had was an idea cultivated by Guthrie.

"I rather suspect you might be," Coventry said.

Bartholomew sighed. "Very well, let us suppose that I am. You still have no evidence to prove it, do you?" When Coventry failed to answer, Bartholomew shook his head. "Honestly, I cannot imagine what you hoped to achieve by asking me to come here. If a confession was your aim, you ought to know that I never confess to anything." He stood and turned toward the door. "Come along, Mr. Smith. The duke has wasted enough of our time today."

"I will be launching an investigation," Coventry added.

His words made Bartholomew pause with his hand on the door handle. He looked back at Coventry. "Feel free to do as you please. I certainly have no plan to stop you."

"That man is a snake," the dowager duchess proclaimed as soon as Bartholomew and his compatriot had quit the room. "Those light green eyes made my skin crawl."

"He is right though," Coventry murmured. "We cannot prove that he is involved, and he certainly will not be making a confession."

"But perhaps confronting him like this will warn him off," Lady Everly suggested.

"It is a possibility." Coventry looked across at Amelia and met her gaze. He gave her a regrettable smile. "I am sorry I could not achieve more."

"Don't be. Now that we know we're being targeted, we'll hire some watchmen to keep an eye on the building both day and night. If someone tries to cause harm again, they will hopefully be caught."

"Perhaps you ought to refrain from visiting the house in the meantime," Coventry said. "I do not like the idea of subjecting you to possible danger."

"Don't be ridiculous." She could feel her entire

person revolting against the idea. "I need to stay apprised of what is going on."

"Coventry can easily do so," Lady Everly said. "I think he is right to insist on keeping you away from there until all threats have been eliminated."

"But this is my project, and the threats are not as big as all that when all I am doing is assessing the progress for a few minutes here and there." She could hardly believe what was happening now.

"Even so," the dowager duchess chimed in, "caution is advised. Especially *because* this is your project, Lady Amelia. If anything were to happen to you, it would probably be the end of it."

Disliking that ominous thought, Amelia reluctantly agreed. "Very well," she said, "but if a week passes without incident, I am going back for a quick visit."

With a sigh, Coventry looked to his mother, then to Lady Everly before eventually meeting Amelia's gaze. "Fine." His curt affirmative spoke of deep apprehension on his part.

The dowager duchess rose, signaling an end to the conversation. "It has been a trying hour. Perhaps you would like to have a refreshing cup of tea?"

"Oh indeed, that would be welcomed," Lady Everly said. She preceded the dowager duchess out of the room.

"I was actually wondering if I might be able to see Jeremy again," Amelia said.

Turning in the doorway, the dowager duchess raised an eyebrow and then looked toward her son.

"Perhaps you can engage Lady Everly in a bit of conversation, Coventry, while I show Lady Amelia up to the nursery?"

"I would be delighted to," Coventry said. He circumvented his desk and came to a halt before Amelia. "Thank you for taking an interest in him." The appreciation with which he spoke was profound.

"Having made his acquaintance, I cannot imagine not doing so," she said. "He is a bright child."

"Yes, he is."

There was something about the way Coventry spoke that almost appeared insightful. She found that a bit strange since he was Jeremy's father and would obviously know just how wonderful Jeremy was.

"After you," Coventry said, his words scattering her thoughts.

She glanced at him, producing a smile in response to the warmth that shone in his eyes, and then followed his mother from the room.

Entering the nursery, Amelia searched the room for Jeremy until she spotted him by one of the windows. A cushioned bench there allowed him to sit and look out at the street below, his arms crossed against his chest while his small frame rocked gently back and forth.

"We'll be all right," Amelia told the dowager duchess. "If you would like to return downstairs, I will join you in a few minutes after I give him the gift I've brought with me."

"You brought him a gift?" The dowager duchess's voice was but a whisper of incredulity.

"It's nothing much, but I saw it in a shop window earlier today and thought he might enjoy it."

"Well then. I will leave you to it."

Thanking her, Amelia walked toward the window announcing her presence by speaking Jeremy's name so as not to startle him. "May I join you?" she then asked. He didn't respond nor did he look at her. She paused for a second, then lowered herself to the vacant spot beside him on the bench and turned her gaze outward. "I thought there would be more people out walking at this time of day." Still no response. She considered a couple of ladies approaching from the northern end of the street. A gentleman coming from the south tipped his hat at them as he passed.

"Thirty-seven."

Amelia glanced across at Jeremy. "Thirty-seven. . . . people?" She could only guess.

"Thirty-seven ladies since noon and forty-three gentlemen. Five children and eleven dogs."

"I see. You live on a busy street."

He looked at her with a blank expression. "That is ten fewer people than yesterday, but the same number of dogs." He turned away from her again.

They sat in silence for several minutes. Amelia watched a bird land on the roof of the opposite building, then opened her reticule and pulled out a wooden cube. "I brought this for you," she said, holding the item toward him.

"What is it?" His eyes remained fixed on something outside.

"A puzzle. You have to take it apart and then put it back together again. I thought you might enjoy it."

Abandoning whatever it was that had held his interest, he dropped his gaze to her outstretched hand. A long moment passed during which Amelia wondered if the boy would accept her offering or not. In the end, she placed it on the bench between them and stood.

"I must return downstairs now, but I do hope to see you again soon."

"Will you give me another ride then?"

She nodded, even though he wouldn't see, his attention now fixed on the cube. "If you like."

When he said nothing further, she backed away before turning around and leaving the room. It was hard, trying to engage with a person who showed no hint of what they were thinking or feeling, and it was so much worse when it was a child whom one expected to laugh and play. It made her wish there was more she could do to help, except she was not really in a position to do so. She was merely a friend, and that was probably all she ever would be.

"What is your impression?" Lady Everly asked on their way home in the carriage. "Of the duke's son?"

Startled, though she'd known the question would come, Amelia considered her answer carefully, then said, "He is extraordinarily bright for his age. I enjoyed his company very well indeed."

Lady Everly stared straight back at her. Amelia forced herself to hold her gaze. "They are opening up to you. More so than to anyone else. Her Grace's attentiveness to you is also quite noticeable. I cannot help but wonder why that might be."

"I do not know. Perhaps you were right when you suggested that her invitation to tea had something to do with my need to marry more quickly than Juliette. She might simply be studying me in order to find my most appealing qualities."

"Hmm . . . I do not think it is quite that simple."

"You do not?"

"No." Lady Everly's expression turned pensive. "I think she is laying the foundation for something else, like pairing you off with her son."

Amelia's mouth dropped open. "What?"

Lady Everly nodded. "Yes. That has to be it. She has obviously taken a liking to you, and with the death of her daughter in mind, she may be hoping to keep you around. Which she would be able to do if you were to marry the duke."

"I think that is quite a conclusion to make on the basis of one private visit and my introduction to Master Jeremy."

Lady Everly smiled. "Not when nobody else I can think of has ever laid eyes on the boy. He is fiercely protected, and yet you managed to ingratiate yourself enough to obtain a private meeting with him."

Unwilling to explain that she'd only been allowed it because she understood Jeremy's behavior and would never judge him for it, Amelia averted her gaze and looked out the window. "You are mistaken about the dowager duchess's intentions, my lady. She knows as well as I that I would not make a suitable duchess. To presume otherwise would be a mistake."

"If that is what you truly believe, then there is something wrong with your self-esteem. Because it is my opinion that you deserve to marry the man of your choosing, even if that man does happen to be a duke."

Chapter 19

It wasn't particularly warm, Amelia decided the following day when she entered the tent that had been erected in her garden. The fund-raising event Lady Everly was helping her host was proving to be a remarkable success, however. Most of the people who'd been invited had arrived, many of them providing gift baskets that had been raffled off a few minutes earlier. She would have to count the revenue later, but with several items going for one hundred pounds, she knew she would be pleased with the result.

Shivering in response to a chilly breeze, she drew her shawl tighter around her shoulders. At least the sun was shining, but there was still a brusqueness to the air that made her wish she would have worn a spencer.

She reached for a jug of lemonade.

"Allow me," a deep voice said at her shoulder.

Turning, she saw it was Mr. Lowell who'd approached. Amelia moved so he could have the honor of pouring. "How have you been?" he asked, handing her a full glass.

She took a sip, then told him about the fire and the accident, which she felt he had a right to know about as an investor.

His face became a mask of concern. "Thankfully you are all right though. It could have been worse."

"Yes, I suppose that is true."

An amicable pause followed until he asked, "What about you and Coventry? Are there any developments there?"

She looked away and began regarding the finely dressed people who mixed and mingled on the lawn. Coventry was conversing with his mother. She'd greeted them both upon her arrival, but had quickly excused herself to come here—an easy escape from the man, but not from her feelings.

"No. Not really."

Lowell stuck one hand in his pocket and looked out over the crowd. "That is a pity." When she didn't respond, he said, "I am not the sort of man who would wish you ill because you turned me down. On the contrary, I like both of you well enough to hope that everything works out to your advantage. And Coventry is a good man. He deserves to find happiness."

She frowned and glanced back at where he stood. Lord and Lady Wilmington had joined him and his mother. He was laughing now in response to something that was being said. "He has never struck me as being particularly *un*happy."

"That is because you have nothing with which to compare. He used to be far more"—he seemed to struggle with finding the right word, eventually settling on—"light-hearted."

Amelia shrugged. "Most people change with age."

"I agree. But Coventry changed overnight. He went from being a carefree friend whose company was always easily available to a man who suddenly chose to avoid Society as much as possible."

"He lost his sister." And the mother of his child had died soon after, if Amelia's calculations were correct. His heartache must have been unbearable.

Lowell expelled a deep breath. "Yes, he did." Finishing off his drink, he set the glass aside and excused himself, leaving Amelia alone to ponder their exchange.

Allowing her gaze to wander to where her sister stood, she decided to go and join her, since recent events had prevented her from spending much time in her company.

But just as she prepared to do so, she heard a woman say, "He has to be the handsomest man I have ever seen."

Amelia paused. She glanced around but saw no one, then realized the voice must have come from the other side of the tent canvas. A different voice responded with a girlish giggle. "Can you imagine the coup if either of us were to win him?"

Curious, Amelia sipped her lemonade and stayed where she was, ignoring the rule that said eavesdropping was rude.

"Mama would be thrilled," the first voice said. "To win a duke . . ." She sighed as though speaking of a great romance.

Amelia's ears perked up. They obviously weren't speaking of her brother, since he was already married, which had to mean that they were referring to Coventry. Who else could it be unless there remained a young and eligible duke whose acquaintance she hadn't yet made?

"It is unfortunate that looks aren't everything," the second voice spoke. "I am not sure I am ready to raise another woman's child."

There was a pause. "It certainly is a great responsibility."

"I rather think it an uncertain bargain since no one I know has ever set eyes on the boy. Coventry keeps him hidden away for some reason."

Aha! So they *were* talking about Coventry. Amelia's pulse leaped.

"He is a protective father." Another pause, and then, "Anyway, it is pointless for either of us to even consider him in earnest since it is highly unlikely that he will ever want to marry. From what I hear, his mistress was a stunning beauty of great intellect. He loved her dearly and was heartbroken when she died. The boy is all he has left of her."

Amelia's heart stilled.

"I know. It's so unbearably tragic." There was what sounded like the ruffling of skirts. "Perhaps we should set our sights on someone else then. What do you think of Viscount Tibs?" The women, two young ladies to whom Amelia had been briefly introduced earlier, stepped forward and began heading toward the house while continuing their discussion. Neither looked in Amelia's direction. They remained oblivious to her presence.

She stood as if frozen, her fingers tightly curled around the glass she still held. Coventry had loved and lost. His sister *and* his mistress. To think of the choice he'd made to raise his son alone—the awesome responsibility such a task embodied—was incredible. Until that moment, it hadn't occurred to her that he might have been emotionally attached to Jeremy's mother or that her death could have broken his heart. It should have done, but it hadn't, and the thought of it now made her lips tremble with pain. She suddenly felt her eyes prick. Her chest tightened around her heart.

"Amelia?"

She blinked, startled to see that Coventry now stood before her. How could she not have noticed his approach? Attempting a smile, she tried to push her maudlin ponderings aside and don the mask of the efficient no-nonsense person she'd taught herself to be.

"I was just about to join my sister. Would you like to come with me?" Her voice sounded far too chirpy.

Coventry frowned. He was looking at her with an expression so serious it felt excruciatingly uncomfortable. "Are you all right?" His frown deepened, and she instinctively averted her gaze. "You look as though you may be about to start crying."

"Don't be silly," she said with a forced bit of laughter.

"Did someone say something disagreeable to you?" He clearly wasn't believing her. "I saw Lowell keeping you company earlier." Severity clung to his words. "If he—"

"You needn't worry. He did not make another proposal or say anything untoward. On the contrary, he was perfectly courteous." She felt a sudden need to pick up her skirts and run. Instead, she squared her shoulders and focused on taking deep breaths. What on earth was happening to her? She sensed she was losing control.

"Then what is it?"

She met his gaze. "I don't know," she told him plainly, "I feel quite unwell all of a sudden and . . . I think I would like to retire to my room."

He stared at her for a long drawn out moment as if considering whether or not to press her further. Eventually he gave a curt nod and said, "Very well. Allow me to escort you inside."

"But what about all the guests? This is my event. I am the hostess. I cannot simply leave."

"Of course you can," he assured her, already leading her toward the terrace. "Lady Everly and I can easily step in so you can go rest."

Entering Huntley House, he guided her into the hallway and toward the stairs.

"I don't know what came over me." Something had to be said. Anything to fill the unbearable silence that had settled between them as they walked.

"Are you sure it wasn't something Lowell said?"

She gave a decisive nod. "Yes."

"Then what was it?"

They'd come to a halt at the foot of the grand staircase, and she became aware of the expectant look in his eyes as he studied her face. How could she possibly tell him her heart was breaking because of what she now knew? How could she ever explain the pain that came from knowing he was bound to a ghost—a woman against whom she stood no chance of winning?

Unable to find the right words and unwilling to try, she shook her head. "A lot has happened recently. I fear it has exhausted me."

He drew in a breath and slowly nodded. "Very well then."

She thanked him for his attentiveness before climbing the stairs on wooden feet while wondering why it felt as though she had lost him when he had never been hers to begin with.

Surrounded by darkness, Amelia stood by her bedroom window that evening, gazing up at the wide expanse of night sky dotted by sparkling flecks of silver. She had left her home in St. Giles almost three months ago. So much had happened since then. Her brother had fallen in love with an earl's daughter and married her. Amelia and Juliette had been introduced to the queen—an incident that had almost ended in disaster when she'd walked too close to a vase. Thankfully, Gabriella had caught the precious item and stopped it from falling, but not without Amelia being reminded of how little she belonged in this world of wealth and power where even the smallest misstep could lead to disaster.

It had gotten better over time. Her lessons had helped her improve upon her speech and her comportment. These past three weeks while Raphe had been away, she'd taken on the task of building a school, had changed her life in a more meaningful way. She finally felt as though she had a purpose—as though her existence could be about more than just looking pretty, saying the right things and making a good match. It had rebuilt the confidence she'd lost upon overhearing the cruel remarks being made about her and her siblings several weeks earlier. What those young ladies had said did not matter. What mattered was her ability to make a lasting difference in the world and how well her efforts to do so had been received by others.

She would be lying if she denied how well it pleased her to know that Coventry had been impressed by her efforts. The chance she'd been given to spend more time in his company had given her something else as well—an awareness of the sort of attraction that could exist between a man and a woman. He'd made her feel beautiful and desirable. He'd taught her that standing up for what she believed in would earn the sort of respect that would not be easily forgotten. So although he might never be able to love her as she loved him, she would always cherish the kiss they had shared and the words he had spoken when he'd told her how much she tempted him.

A movement outside drew her attention. She looked down, squinting through the darkness. For long seconds after, she saw nothing and was about to turn away and return to her bed when a figure stepped out from the shadows on the opposite side of the street. It was a man, his silhouette suggesting a sturdy build. Pausing, he looked toward Huntley House, then raised his hand to his hat and tipped it in her direction before walking away.

A chill went through Amelia. He couldn't have seen her, could he? She was shrouded in darkness and mostly hidden behind the thick curtains. And yet, she felt as though he'd been looking straight at her. Worse than that, that he'd wanted to make her aware of his perusal.

Drawing back, she wondered if he might be one of Bartholomew's men. If so, his presence could only be perceived as a threat. Which meant that actions would have to be taken. For starters, she would have to let Coventry know as soon as possible, a decision that led her straight back to Coventry House the following day, with her maid accompanying her on the fifteen-minute walk she'd decided to take in order to get some exercise. She'd spent far too much time sitting down recently, either on chairs or on sofas or in carriages.

But as they made their way toward Wimpole Street, the hair at the back of her neck began to rise. She looked over her shoulder just in time to catch a flash of movement. Her breath caught and she quickened her pace.

"I feel as though we are being followed."

Heather gave her a look of concern. "Perhaps we ought to hire a hackney for the remaining distance, my lady."

They turned a corner. "I do not see an available one at the moment, but I think you are right. We shall flag down the very first one that comes into view."

As it turned out, every hackney that rolled by was already fully occupied, and since they were taking the shortest route, the streets were not busy enough to allow for the sort of traffic that one might find on Oxford Street or Piccadilly. Amelia looked back once more and spotted a man, his head bowed low as he walked some distance behind them. She wondered if it might be the same man she'd seen last night. Perhaps she ought to stop and confront him?

No. That would be a terrible idea—the sort of idea that neither Raphe nor Coventry nor anyone else of sound mind would ever approve of. If he did work for Bartholomew, as she suspected he might, he'd be dangerous too. It would be foolish to risk a confrontation with him. Especially when she had Heather to think of, too.

So she kept her pace brisk and breathed a sigh of relief the moment she stepped inside the foyer at Coventry House. The butler took her bonnet and then showed them through to the parlor. "Please wait here while I inform His Grace of your arrival," he said before exiting the room once more.

"My lady," Coventry said when he came to greet her seconds later. "What has happened? My butler said you looked distressed when you arrived, and

I have to say that even now your complexion appears a bit pale."

"I apologize for coming here like this without invitation. I know how busy you are and—"

"Amelia," he told her gently, disregarding propriety in spite of Heather's presence.

Feeling a flush of heat creep into her cheeks, Amelia glanced toward her maid and was grateful to see she was keeping herself busy with a tiny book that she must have brought along in her reticule.

Coventry's hand pressed gently against Amelia's elbow, causing her to jump. She returned her attention to him as he nudged her toward the other side of the room so they could speak more privately. "You are always welcome here. There is no need for you to concern yourself about that. So please tell me what it is that has upset you."

Inhaling deeply, she allowed the tension she'd felt on her way over to ebb a little. "There was a man in the street last night. It looked as though he was watching Huntley House, and when he eventually left, he tipped his hat toward the window where I was standing."

"That is no small matter," Coventry said. His brow knit with concern.

"And then today when I walked over here, I had the distinct feeling that I was being followed."

"After seeing that man last night, you should have taken a carriage."

"You're right." His eyebrows rose with surprise. "I just didn't want to acknowledge the possible danger, and with the weather as pleasant as it is and being in Mayfair, I did not think that there would be any threat."

He studied her a moment. "Did you see someone today who looked suspicious?"

"There was a man with a downcast face who kept walking some distance behind us. He disappeared right before we got here."

Muttering something that sounded like a curse, Coventry raked his fingers through his hair and considered her. When he spoke again, he sounded more serious than ever before. "No more walks. If you need to go somewhere, you take the Huntley carriage or my carriage with drivers who can be trusted."

"What about the park? Surely I will be all right going for walks there as long as someone comes with me."

"Not unless that someone is me." He must have seen her look of dismay because he quickly added, "Your safety is paramount. We must not risk it for any reason. Not as long as there may be a threat and certainly not when that threat may very well come from Bartholomew."

"Do you suppose he might be trying to rattle me?"

"It is possible. And if that is the case, then I fear this is only the beginning. In which case, you must remain vigilant." His fingers found hers in an intimate caress that pushed most of her worries aside, replacing them with helpless longing instead. "If anything were to happen to you . . ." Stepping back, he shook his head. "Nothing will, as long as we take some precautions."

"Can I still go to Vauxhall on Saturday?" Lady Everly and the dowager duchess had suggested the outing since Amelia and Juliette had never visited the pleasure garden before. "I am rather looking forward to it."

"I think that will be fine since you will be part of a larger group. I hear that Burton and Lowell will be there, as well." He winced just enough to convey his displeasure.

"Lady Everly thought it prudent to invite them."

"I take it she does not know of Lowell's proposal or the fact that you turned him down." When she shook her head, he said, "It surprises me that he would agree to keep your company after that."

"Perhaps he has set his sights on Juliette instead? Such a thing is possible."

"I suppose it is." His eyes turned a deep shade of chocolate, and then a smile touched his lips, affording him that dashing look that invariably weakened her knees. "Thank you for your kindness toward Jeremy yesterday. The gift you gave him was very thoughtful. He has made great use of it since."

"Did he manage to solve it?"

"Yes. It didn't take him long. And the pleasure he found in doing so was unmistakable. I . . ." He paused, and Amelia spied a look in his eyes that she'd never seen before. It spoke of deep comprehension and resolve. He darted a look in Heather's direction before returning it to her. "There are things I must say to you, Amelia—things that will hopefully help you understand why I have been so reluctant to pursue a deeper attachment with you. It is not that I do not care for you, but that I—"

"Please." She couldn't imagine what might have prompted him to tell her this now, but she had to stop him before he broke her heart all over again. She could not bear the thought of having to listen while he spoke of the love he'd felt for his mistress and how he would never feel that kind of love again. She'd come to terms with it—accepted it—but she had no desire to be tortured by it.

"There is no need for you to explain."

"Of course there is."

She shook her head. "I would rather you didn't."

A frown appeared upon his forehead. "Amelia—"

"Oh! I thought I heard voices," the dowager duchess said as she entered the room.

Stepping away from Coventry, Amelia went to greet her. "I came to inform your son of an incident." She then relayed a brief version of what she'd told Coventry earlier about the man she'd seen in the street.

"How unnerving," the dowager duchess said with a look of distinct alarm. She addressed her son. "You must escort Lady Amelia and her maid home from here. I absolutely insist upon it."

"My thought exactly," he murmured.

"But first," the dowager duchess said, "I do hope you will stay for luncheon. We are having mushroom pie and mackerel."

Thanking her for the kind offer, Amelia walked with her to the dining room while Coventry followed behind. She'd escaped his explanations, thank God, but she was still very much aware of his presence and of the thoughtful way in which he watched her later during the ride home. It was almost as if he was plotting and planning something, though she couldn't for the life of her figure out what it might be.

Chapter 20

❦

As reluctant as Amelia was to hear what he had to say, Thomas knew he had to have a serious word with her. Considering the developing relationship between them and his recent thoughts of marrying her, he was going to have to make her hear him out and then see where the truth would take them.

Arriving at the pleasure garden with his mother that Saturday, they approached the supper box where Amelia, Juliette and Lady Everly were keeping company with Mr. Lowell, Mr. Burton, Viscount Tibs *and* the Earl of Yates. Worst of all, Viscount Tibs's head was dipped toward Amelia's while he spoke, and she was looking very amused by whatever the hell the man was saying.

"Calm yourself," his mother murmured before they drew within earshot of the group. "You look as though you're prepared to go to war."

"If there is one to be fought, Mama, then I am ready for it."

His mother chuckled, and then they were suddenly greeting the others and finding places to sit.

Lady Everly, who'd risen when they'd arrived, waved them into the spot she'd vacated, denying Thomas the chance to sit beside Amelia. *Annoying woman.*

"You look lovely tonight, ladies," Thomas said, glancing at each of the women in turn. He allowed his eyes to linger a second longer on Amelia, but she failed to meet his gaze when she thanked him for the compliment.

"We are fortunate to be in their dazzling company," Mr. Lowell said, his eyes on Amelia as he spoke. She blushed in response to the compliment, which made Thomas feel like punching the man.

Christ!

The woman had turned his head.

His chest tightened against a deep inhalation of breath. He did his best to calm himself. She was exceptional, her beauty and character more enticing than any other. And he . . . God . . . the way he felt about her. He'd be damned if he could put it into words, but he knew he ached to be close to her, to hold her in his arms and to bask in her vitality.

Sweetmeats arrived, but he wasn't hungry. At least not for food. Amelia leaned across Tibs to say something to her sister, and Thomas almost leaped from his seat when he saw the man's eyes fill with pleasure. Only his mother's staying hand kept him from acting irrationally.

"I have been taking a look at the bill you proposed," Yates remarked. He popped a piece of sweetmeat into his mouth.

Thomas shifted his gaze to meet the earl's. "Thank you, but it does not appear as though it will be accepted. So perhaps we ought to discuss something else since such a topic is unlikely to interest the ladies." A discreet reminder that politics was not to be discussed in polite society.

"On the contrary, I find myself intrigued," Lady Juliette said.

"It is a tiresome matter," Thomas stated.

"Are you saying we lack the patience or skill to comprehend it?" Amelia asked.

His mother tried to hide a snort, and he knew right away he'd lost the fight. "No. Of course not." What else could he say when all eyes were now trained on him? He glanced at Amelia, who'd finally decided to give him her full attention. Well then . . . "I was trying to change the law of inheritance."

Tibs barked with laughter, then grew immediately still when he saw that nobody else was laughing. "You are serious?"

"There are no assurances for illegitimate children. Many end up discarded by their fathers, and that is wrong. Men need to be held accountable. They have to know that they cannot simply go around begetting children without consequence."

"You sound rather passionate about it," Mr. Burton commented.

"He has a bastard of his own," Yates murmured.

The comment, as matter-of-factly as it was spoken and without the slightest hint of malice, still felt like a sharp stab to Thomas's chest. He clenched his jaw and stared back at Yates. "I would be much obliged if you did not speak of him like that."

"My apologies, if I offended you," Yates said.

"I actually consider your bill rather progressive, if you must know."

"What about the part concerning the titles?" Thomas asked, curious now to hear his opinion.

"Well, as long as it is up to the individual, I—"

"Wait," Tibs interrupted. "What are you proposing with the titles?"

"That a peer may choose to let his illegitimate son inherit it," Thomas replied.

A stunned silence settled over the group for a second, and then Amelia said, "I think that—"

"Ludicrous?" Tibs suggested.

"It certainly sounds like an uphill battle," Mr. Lowell remarked.

"I was going to say that I find it an admirable endeavor." Amelia lowered her lashes and snatched up a piece of sweetmeat before adding softly, "I wish you the best of luck with it, Your Grace. There are no better causes than those that favor children."

"And on that note," Lady Everly said, effectively ending the conversation, "I would like to recommend a walk so we may enjoy the Cascade when it begins."

The group left the supper box and Thomas immediately went to Amelia, offering her his arm before anyone else had a chance to do so. She accepted, but not without him noting her hesitation.

"We need to talk," he told her plainly. They took the lead and began heading along the walk that would take them to one of Vauxhall's main attractions. He'd seen the Cascade several times before and was sure Amelia would find it intriguing.

"About what?"

He drew her a little bit closer. "Us."

Gasping, she turned to him with a start. "I don't—"

"Are the lights not magnificent?" Yates asked as he and Juliette drew up alongside them. "How many do you suppose there might be?"

"Thousands, I should think," Mr. Lowell said from directly behind Amelia. He and Tibs were escorting Lady Everly together with Mr. Burton.

"It certainly is a magical display," Juliette whispered. "I never thought to see anything like it."

"It reminds me of the *Arabian Nights*," Yates said. "Have you read it?"

"No, I have not had the pleasure."

Slowing his pace, Thomas allowed Yates and Juliette to move ahead so they could continue their conversation in private. "I do believe your sister has found an admirer."

"Perhaps." She let him draw her to the side so they didn't hold the others back. "But I sense that her interest lies elsewhere."

"Oh?"

"I won't say with whom yet, for I am not completely sure."

"Come," Lady Everly said, passing them with Tibs and Burton, "I can see the crowd gathering. If we do not hurry, you will not be able to see a thing, and that would be a pity since this is bound to be unlike anything you have ever witnessed before."

Approaching the Cascade, Thomas deliberately slowed his pace even further and glanced around. They had reached the periphery of the crowd, but when Amelia moved to follow Lady Everly through it, he held her back.

"No," he told her plainly.

Her eyes rose toward his, and he saw then the tragic despair she was trying to hide. "Let me go, Thomas." His given name, spoken like a plea almost brought him to his knees.

"Amelia—"

"Stop." She tugged on her arm, but he wouldn't release her. "Please," she begged.

He shook his head and drew her back, away from the crowd and toward a copse of trees shrouded in darkness. "You *will* listen to what I have to say, damn it, and you will do so now."

"**W**hat do you think you're doing?" She was heart-broken, embarrassed and furious all at the same time, and the bloody man who'd stirred all these feelings in her would not allow a reprieve.

"Giving you the knowledge you need in order to make an informed decision," he retorted, steering her between the trees until they found themselves at a safe distance from all sound.

Confused, she stared at his dark silhouette and quietly asked, "What does that mean?"

He drew a deep breath. "We need to address the attraction between us, and I need to tell you the absolute truth about Jeremy."

"Please don't." She had no desire to listen to one more word. Not when it would involve the greatest love of his life.

"Amelia—"

"Damn it, Thomas!" She hadn't meant to become overwrought, but he was pushing her fragile emotions to the limit. "I know you had a mistress whom you loved beyond all reason. I know it broke your heart when she died giving birth to Jeremy, and I know I will never be as important to you as she was, so then what is the point here? What do you want from me?"

Silence fell and for a long moment, there was nothing but their breathing—hollow and deep like they'd both run a mile.

When he finally spoke, his voice was low and ragged. "Do you have any idea what such words do to me?"

His change of tone unbalanced her. There was something about it that heated her skin and made her think of decadent pleasure and warm caresses. But it was fantasy of course. This was the Duke of Coventry, a man who'd made his lack of interest in heading down that particular road explicitly clear. And yet he took a step closer, and his hand was suddenly on her arm, his fingers trailing a long delicious path up over her shoulder, across the sweep of her collarbones and toward the opposite side of her neck.

"Please don't do this." She would die if she let him continue. Her heart would simply shatter. Because this could never be and the pain of that . . . oh God . . . "Please stop."

His hand stilled against her cheek. "What if I told

you there is no mistress, no ghost for you to measure up to, no long lost love—no memories shared with another woman more important than you?"

Her heart stopped beating. Or that was how it felt. And in that moment, Amelia would have given everything in the world in order to see his face and to know if what he said was true.

"Explain yourself."

His hand fell away, and a brief pause followed. She fought the urge to beat the answer out of him, holding herself completely still and under remarkable control.

"Jeremy isn't my son, Amelia. He is my sister's boy."

Her lips parted, and she spoke on a breath of air. "What?"

"Melanie was seduced. When she died in childbirth, I swore to protect Jeremy as if he were my own."

"The illegitimate son of a duke is less scandalous than the son of an unmarried lady and a . . ." She blinked. "Who is Jeremy's father?"

The air seemed to shift around them, and when Thomas spoke again, his voice was tight. "An undeserving cad who denounced them both."

"A gentleman?"

"A young man with a title, but hardly a gentleman." A breeze disturbed the leaves around them, and Amelia instinctively shivered when Thomas said, "It was Fielding's younger brother."

The memory of words spoken by Raphe flew

to the front of Amelia's mind. She drew a sharp breath. "And Fielding did nothing, did he? That is why you dislike him so much."

"He discovered the affair, which took place at one of my estates during a house party. Desperate to cover it up and avoid the scandal of a hasty wedding, Fielding helped his brother quit the country before I found out about it."

"And once his brother returned?"

"He remains in exile, though I might still seek retribution if I choose to do so. But since the matter is best forgotten, I have decided against such a course of action."

And with that knowledge, and the rest of what he'd just told her, came the greatest amount of respect she'd ever had for another person. Thomas had risked scandal, sacrificing his own future and denying himself the revenge he no doubt longed to execute, all to protect his sister and nephew.

"The point is," he added, and she felt his hand on her wrist this time, "I have spent the past five years telling myself I cannot marry, that I do not have room for a wife and that I must face my responsibilities alone. But perhaps I am wrong." His fingers moved to her waist, and he was suddenly pulling her to him. "Perhaps Jeremy needs a mother."

Her breath caught. "What are you saying?"

His other hand reached up to cup her chin, his thumb gently stroking along her jaw and producing a spark of tender warmth that slid all the way to her toes. "I have seen you with him, Amelia, and he has never looked so happy before, not to mention your genuine concern for children in general and your positive outlook on life. There is no doubt in my mind that Jeremy would benefit greatly from your continued presence and . . ." He fell silent, muttered an oath and finally said, "I am not proposing—at least not until we are both completely certain that marriage would work—but I *am* telling you what my intentions are."

"And what exactly would they be?" she asked. Holding her breath, she waited for him to respond.

He blew out a breath. "I would like you to give me a chance to court you."

Thrilled by the prospect, she would not ruin the moment by asking him how he felt about her. The fact that he trusted her with Jeremy's care and upbringing was proof enough of his high regard. And perhaps . . . at least now there was more hope than there had been before that he might one day feel as deeply for her as she felt for him. The answer was simple. "When would you like to begin?"

"Right now." His hand swept to the back of her head, and he was suddenly pulling her to him. His mouth met hers in a simple caress that almost brought tears to her eyes as a lifetime of yearning welled up inside her—the longing to be held and cared for so acute she could scarcely bear it.

Her arms went around his neck, and she pressed herself to him, arching against his chest for closer contact while his hand at her waist moved toward her back, flattening over her spine. "Amelia." Her name whispering across her cheek as he kissed his way toward her neck left sizzling embers in its wake.

"Yes." Her fingers tunneled through his hair. She would take advantage of this chance to touch him without apology. This was what she'd dreamed of, this casting aside of rules and strictures. His mouth pressed against the edge of her jaw, teeth scraping the tender skin in a predatory way that sent pleasure bursting through her. "Thomas . . ."

His mouth found hers once more, silencing her in an open offering, ridding her mind of all thought. She could only feel, his firm body pressing into her softness, his hands sliding over her in exquisite exploration, and his kiss . . . Deep. Hot. Demanding. It was unlike anything she'd ever experienced before—more primal than their previous one—an elemental claiming of sorts. And it threatened to drive her mad with unexpected need.

So she clung to his shoulders, fearing her legs might suddenly fail to carry her weight. It seemed entirely possible given the weakened state she was presently in, drugged by the taste and scent of the man she loved, unable to fathom how keenly he was ravishing her; as though she were some rich elixir he would never get enough of. It felt so wonderfully right, so utterly thrilling and perfect—a melding of souls so divine it threatened to make her weep.

And it was over much too soon for her liking, his voice sighing her name as he eased her back. She felt his breath against her face, heavy and rapid.

"Dear God," he murmured, his lips caressing her cheek. "If you only knew what you do to me, Amelia."

"I wager it can't be much different than what you do to me," she whispered, her voice casting a web across the darkness.

He held her still, and she felt his lips trail a path toward her neck and the rough vibrations of a growl in response to her words. Pulling her to him once more, he buried his face in the curve of her shoulder and carefully bit her flesh. She gasped in response, both surprised and allured by his primitive method of branding. And as heat rushed through her, straight from the point of contact and all the way down to her toes, she wished they were somewhere else—somewhere private.

If only . . .

As if sensing her concern, he drew back once more, this time with greater deliberation. "It is time for us to get back to the others before they become aware of our absence."

All he'd offered was a courtship with the possibility of marriage. No guarantees until he was certain. To be found like this—to have his hand forced . . . She was suddenly eager for them to return to the others and ensure that all was well and that their absence had gone unnoticed.

So she followed him out from between the trees to the dimly lit walkway where the crowd still watched the Cascade. They'd made it back in time. She breathed a sigh of relief, which was swiftly snatched away at the sight of Lady Everly. She was bearing down on them with a disapproving glower that could have chilled an iceberg. The rest of their group followed in her wake, all with wide-eyed incredulity.

"What on earth were you two doing between those trees just now?" the dowager countess hissed, coming to a halt before them. Everyone else remained a respectable distance behind, except for Thomas's mother, who wore a look of distinct disappointment.

"We—"

"Never mind," Lady Everly snapped, silencing Thomas's reply. "I do not want to know, but I expect you to call on me first thing in the morning, Your Grace." She took a step toward him, her voice lowering even more. "And when you do, I suggest you have an offer in mind."

"You need not worry," Thomas told her crisply. He gave Amelia's hand a quick squeeze before releasing it. "I have every intention of doing the honorable thing."

Amelia's heart crumpled. There was no warmth in his voice, no talk of his affection for her. In the blink of an eye she'd become an obligation rather than a choice. Pressing her lips together, she squared her shoulders and raised her chin. "I would like to leave now." Away from all the censorious stares. Away from him.

They parted without pleasantries or smiles, and as Amelia sat silently in the carriage that would take her back to Huntley House, she felt sorrow's heavy embrace, reminding her that she was doomed.

"**W**hat were you thinking?" Thomas's mother asked when they entered their parlor later, breaking the silence that had accompanied them all the way home.

He ran his fingers through his hair. "I made a mistake, Mama."

"That goes without saying."

He dropped onto the sofa, and after a moment she went to sit beside him. "Did you see Lady Amelia's face? She looked like a trapped animal."

Guilt filled his lungs, making it hard to breathe. "It is my fault. She heard the rumor about me having a mistress, and I wanted to dispel it. I wanted to let her know that I wasn't pining away for some long-lost love, but that I—" He passed the palm of his hand across his face and sighed. "It no longer matters. I have backed both of us into a corner, tainting our future with doubt. She will always wonder if the only reason I married her was because I had no other choice but to do so."

"Isn't it?"

He met his mother's knowing gaze. "Of course not. I would have married her eventually for countless other reasons. You know that."

"Then I suggest you tell her as much." She rose and went to the door. "I am going to retire now, but just so you know, I believe this will all work out well for both of you in the end. Especially if you take a moment to consider how you truly feel about her."

How *did* he feel?

The question lingered long after his mother had left the room. He definitely liked her. A lot. Which he decided was a good start. And he really enjoyed kissing her. The chemistry between them was extraordinary. No need to worry about that. He was also deeply touched by her ready acceptance of Jeremy and of the complicated nature of his birthright. She would make an excellent parent, and she would keep Jeremy's secret safe. He felt it in his bones. But was there anything else? A stronger attachment that surpassed all else? He simply wasn't sure.

You think of her when you're not with her.
You worry for her safety.
Her opinion matters to you.

But did that mean he loved her? Shaking his head, he headed up to bed, hoping the morning would bring enlightenment with it.

It did not. If anything, it brought only more questions and feelings of uncertainty. Not that he ever questioned doing the right thing. What he did question, however, was the impact a hasty marriage would have on his relationship with Amelia. And this was without considering how Huntley might react once he returned. Bloody hell, what a mess he'd made.

"I trust you have given this matter some serious thought," Lady Everly said when she met him in the Huntley House drawing room later.

"Of course." He gave her a steady look. "I have every intention of doing my duty."

"How romantic of you," she murmured. When he didn't respond, she puffed out a breath. "I fear you may find Amelia quite stubborn, however. When we parted last night, she did not seem amicable to the idea of marriage."

"She feels trapped." But that wasn't all. "And she feels as though she has trapped me."

"Is that how you feel?"

"No. Not at all." He thought of everything that had happened within the last twelve hours. "It was not supposed to go this way. All I meant last night was to talk to her."

"Alone? In the dark?" She shook her head. "Do not pretend you were not aware of the risk." She gave him a frank stare. "Or that all you did was talk."

He turned away from her, chastised by her gaze. "You are correct, of course. I know that. And now it is time for me to make things right. If you will permit, I would like to take her out for an hour or so."

"I doubt she will agree to it."

"Just tell her I intend to visit her property so we can have a look at the progress." That ought to convince her to share his company.

"Very well," Lady Everly agreed. "But only if you take a chaperone with you. After all that has happened recently, I fear I cannot trust you to be alone with her."

Accepting the reprimand that was his due, Thomas dipped his head in acquiescence and then waited while Lady Everly went to speak with Amelia.

Chapter 21

Exiting the carriage on High Street, Amelia thanked Thomas for his assistance before continuing up the front steps of the house. She did not wish to keep his company today. Indeed, she had no desire to be in the same city as him or even the same country. But she did want to see what progress had been made by the workers since her last visit to her property, which left her with very little choice. She would simply have to accept his escort even though the events of the previous evening filled her with discomfort.

"Amelia."

His voice reached her in a whisper and with a great deal of urgency. She chose to pretend she hadn't heard him since she'd no desire to engage in a lengthy discussion about scandal and duty, and what they must do now in order to preserve their reputations. It would probably involve a proposal, which was something she did not wish to endure when his heart wasn't in it.

So she stepped forward and glanced around. "Oh

look. The staircase is almost finished. A bit of sanding and varnish will probably do it. What do you think, Coventry? Should we have a runner put down or shall we leave it as is?"

"It will probably be easier to keep clean without the runner, and since this is to be a school and not a house, I do not believe there is a need for one either. But that is not what I wish to discuss at the moment." She hurried on through to the ballroom, leaving him to follow in her wake if he wished. Or not to, as she hoped. He chose to follow. "Amelia. Can we please—"

"The windows are being nicely prepared." Crossing to where a couple of laborers were repairing the window ledge with a fresh layer of brick, she addressed them with a smile. "I see you have removed all the wood casing that was here before."

"It was either burned or rotted, me lady," one of the men said as he smoothed out a blob of cement. "No need to worry though—this'll be good an' ready by the time the new windows arrive."

Thanking him, she hurried onward before Coventry had a chance to stop her. "Watch your step," she said. "There are some gaps in the floor here." It looked as though all of the damaged planks had been removed in the dining room. Fresh ones sat in one corner, ready to be put into place.

"Can you please stop?" Coventry's voice hinted at severe exasperation. "We need to talk about last night, Amelia."

"I do not wish to."

"That much is obvious," he grumbled.

She reached the dining-room door, hoping to escape on through to the hallway beyond and continue from there to some other part of the house. But he'd apparently had enough of the chase and reached out to grab her wrist. A gasp escaped her as he pulled her back straight into him, his other arm circling her waist and holding her close while his breath warmed the side of her neck.

"Release me." They were in a house full of other people for heaven's sake. Anyone could walk in on them at any moment and minimize her chance of avoiding marriage. "This isn't proper."

"Neither was last night," he murmured, his voice a low vibration that skittered through her and tickled her senses. "You did not seem to mind my closeness then."

"That was different." Heavens, she sounded so breathless, and she felt . . . she felt as though she might melt right here in his arms.

"How?"

Closing her eyes, she did her best to gather her thoughts. He'd made no promise of marriage until they'd been caught. He had not spoken of love or even of affection. Desire was what drove him, but that would not be enough to last her a lifetime.

You can have what you've wanted for so very long.

Don't throw it away.

She forced a good deal of steel into her bones and, pulling away, she turned to face him. "The cover of darkness prompted me to be reckless, but it was a mistake. The kisses we have shared, both last night and before, were mistakes."

He frowned at that. "Are you certain?"

"Absolutely."

"And there is nothing I can say to dissuade you?"

"No." She crossed her arms for good measure.

His eyes held hers. "That is a pity." Without elaborating further, he strode around her and exited the room.

It was her turn to follow. "What do you mean by that?"

He shrugged. "I thought you would make an excellent mother for Jeremy. He likes you a great deal."

That he would sink so low as to use an innocent child as a bargaining tool . . . Still . . . "I like him a lot too, but I cannot allow myself to consider marriage on that basis alone." They'd reached the foyer where Heather stood waiting.

"Then explain it to me. Tell me what you need me to do, and I will see to it immediately." His expression had turned rather desperate. "Christ, woman." He looked about ready to give her a good shake. "Do you not see that your entire family's reputation hinges on us doing the right thing now?"

She stared at him, the last hope of a happy resolution to this problem crumbling. "And therein lies the problem." She turned away from him and headed for the door before he could see the emotion that stung her eyes. "Come along, Heather."

"You have to accept the consequences of our

actions," he called after her, prompting her to swing back around and glare at him.

"No, I do not. As long as I quit Town for a while, I have no doubt that everything will be fine. My siblings and I have survived worse than the gossip a private conversation with you at Vauxhall Garden might cause."

"It was more than a conversation, Amelia."

"Nobody knows that yet. But if we marry, they most certainly will." She was trembling now with the anger and hurt he was causing. "The matter is closed. I will not discuss it any further, and right now, all I want to do is to return home. Will you please escort me?"

He hesitated a moment while she held her breath. Eventually, he inclined his head. "Of course." He extended his arm, gesturing toward the door and she happily hastened toward it, desperate once more to be free of his company.

How was it possible to love someone so deeply and yet dread their nearness? She didn't quite know, but that was how it was now. Four weeks had changed everything. Her heart was no longer her own. It belonged to him. But with no assurance that he would ever feel for her what she felt for him, risking a lifetime in his company was not an option. How could it be when five minutes alone felt like endless torture?

She had no answer, but as she started down the front steps, she could hear him say, "We will revisit this issue when your brother returns. I am confident that he will agree with me."

She feared he might be right. But the fact that Coventry was willing to threaten her with such inevitability only confirmed her worst fears. His proposal had nothing to do with how he felt about her. Had she been any other woman, he would have done precisely the same thing. Because that was what was proper and because protecting one's reputation trumped everything else. Scandal had to be avoided at all cost. Such was the aristocratic dogma.

Reaching the pavement without acknowledging his comment, Amelia saw that Heather was already waiting for them inside the carriage. A couple of pedestrians were approaching from the left and another three from the right. One was a laborer who turned toward the house. She heard him greet Coventry.

"You must be new," Coventry said. "I do not recognize you."

An exchange of words followed. Amelia waited for the other pedestrians to pass, but when one of the approaching men came up alongside her, she was shocked to find his arm winding tight around her waist and pushing into her back while another man stepped close, hindering her movements.

"Ye're to leave this buildin' alone, do ye hear?" The gravelly warning raked over her. "This is so ye take us seriously."

She felt something sharp prick her side, then the sting and the pain of it sliding in deep. A scream tore its way past her throat, mingling with the cruel laughter of those who had hurt her. They pushed her aside, causing her to stumble. A shout followed, then the rapid clattering of shoes hitting the ground at a run.

Clutching herself, she felt sticky wetness seep through between her fingers. A quick inhale filled her lungs with breath, and then a hand caught her elbow.

"My lady." The coachman's steady voice was followed by Heather's more anxious tone.

"Coventry." She needed him now, her eyes frantically searching for him as she swung back toward the house. Her legs grew more and more wobbly by the second.

A hunched-over figure caught her attention. There. He was clutching his head and attempting to rise. Relief filled her. He was all right. Not as bad off as she. Which was good. If one of them had to suffer, she wanted him spared.

Raising his gaze, he looked at her then. "Dear God!" She managed to see him stagger up onto his feet, eyes wide with dread and anguish. A strange feebleness covered her brain. The pain began to recede, and she felt herself melting away into blackness.

"We need to get her home this instant," Thomas yelled, hurrying over to where his coachman was standing with Amelia in his arms while Heather looked on with a stricken expression. There was so much blood. *Too* much blood. Thomas felt his heart crumple into a painful lump of despair. "If

I climb into the carriage, can you hand her up to me?" he asked.

"Of course, Your Grace." The coachman adjusted his hold on Amelia. "You'll need a doctor, Your Grace."

"Florian's the man. I'll not consider anyone else."

They proceeded as discussed while Thomas ignored the violent pain that ricocheted through his brain. He'd been caught completely off guard—struck by a heavy object that the so-called laborer had been carrying. Stars had spun before his eyes as he'd fallen to his knees, only vaguely aware of a scream ripping the air. He now knew it had been Amelia. The bloody bastards had stabbed her and, if they didn't get help quickly enough . . . He didn't dare think of what might happen then. All he could do was clutch her to him and pray while pressing his hand to her wound.

"Will she be all right?" Heather asked from the opposite side of the carriage. Her voice was weak with concern.

"She'd better be," he told her grimly, "or I'll hunt down the villains who did this and kill them myself." He'd recognized one of them as the man who'd accompanied Bartholomew to his home. *Mr. Smith.*

Presently, he wanted to see him and his accomplices suffer for causing Amelia pain and for putting her life at risk, but he kept his creative ideas on torture to himself since such a topic would likely offend Heather's sensibilities. Instead, he gritted his teeth while the carriage rocked back and forth in response to his coachman's swift driving. Amelia groaned, her head rolling against his shoulder. Thomas pulled her closer, his arm locked tight around her while one hand did what it could to hold back the blood.

Abruptly, the carriage drew to a halt and Heather glanced out. "This isn't Huntley House. In fact, I don't know where this is."

"What the devil?" The door flew open, and his coachman looked in. Thomas wasted no time in turning his fury on him. "Where in hell and tarnation are we? I told you to—"

"We're at Doctor Florian's house. I thought it more efficient to pick him up on the way or at least leave a message for him in case he's out rather than—"

"Fine. See to it then and be quick about it." The door closed, and Thomas sank back against the squabs. Blood roared in his ears, and his eyes burned with tears that refused to fall. For five years he'd avoided this kind of tormented anguish. It twisted his insides and tore at his soul.

When his sister lay dying, he'd felt a similar pain, so acutely he'd thought he might die right there along with her. And he felt it now in every fiber of his being—a chilling promise that his life would be over if Amelia ceased drawing breath.

The carriage door opened and a bag was tossed in. It was followed by Doctor Florian's prominent figure. "Allow me to take a look," he said, crouching on the floor in front of Amelia. The carriage took off with a jolt, but the movement did not disturb the doctor. It was as if he was well accustomed to traveling in such a fashion, for which Thomas was now immensely grateful. He drew his hand aside to reveal the wound. The doctor's expression remained inscrutable. "When did this occur?" he asked. A practical question.

"Perhaps fifteen minutes ago?" Thomas wasn't sure. He hadn't stopped to check his pocket watch.

Florian nodded. "The tear in her gown suggests a thin blade, but I'll have to get her out of her clothes to examine her properly. In any case, it does look like it's in a spot that should pose no risk to any major organs. You've done well to keep pressure on the wound. Keep doing that, and she ought to recover soon enough."

He gave no indication of what "soon enough" meant, though Thomas expected it to be at least a few days, given the gravity of the injury. Still, he was thankful for some reassurance since he'd been imagining the worst possible scenarios up until that point. Florian had eased his mind a little even though he still felt responsible for what had transpired. As with his sister, he ought to have been more vigilant. He ought to have seen this coming, and he ought to have stopped it. But just as it had been with Melanie, he'd been distracted and now Amelia had gotten hurt, as well.

To say he was just as furious with himself as he was with the men who had caused this would be an understatement. He wanted to head back to the

Black Swan so he could seek out the punishment he deserved. Instead, he dipped his head close to Amelia's and whispered in her ear.

"It will be all right, sweetheart. You will get through this."

Whether or not she heard him, he did not know. He followed the endearment with a kiss to her temple though, hoping that she would at least feel cared for.

They reached the house and exited the carriage in short order, with Heather bringing up the rear. Thomas marched up the steps with Amelia in his arms and straight through the door, which was swung open wide by Pierson, who must have heard them arrive. Without stopping, Thomas continued toward the stairs with Florian right on his heels.

"What is going on?" Pierson asked.

The question was echoed by Lady Everly who arrived in the foyer together with Lady Juliette. One glance in Thomas's direction made both pairs of eyes open wide. "Is that blood?" Lady Everly asked with sudden despair.

With nothing more than a curt nod, Thomas hurried onward. "I'll explain everything later," he said over his shoulder. "Right now, time is of the essence." He reached the landing. "Which room is hers?"

"Second door on the right," Lady Juliette called.

Florian, good man that he was, pushed his way past him and opened the door. He then rushed to pull back the bedspread so Thomas could lay Amelia down.

"Help me undress her," Florian said, pulling Amelia onto her good side.

Thomas didn't hesitate, his fingers working nimbly on the buttons at the back of her gown. He tugged at the sleeves and unlaced her stays—not because they had to be removed, but because he wanted her to be able to breathe more easily.

Her gown was tugged down and her shift was pulled up in order to reveal the angry gash of crimson that had caused her to lose consciousness. Thomas stood, studying her pale features for a moment. He was aware of Lady Everly's presence somewhere behind him and was grateful for her lack of interference in a situation that would no doubt have caused others to chase him from the room in an effort to preserve Amelia's modesty.

"I will be requiring a pot of hot water," Florian said. He drew a few items out of his bag. They included squares of white linen, pincers, needle and thread, and a glass bottle containing a clear liquid. He set all the items next to each other on the bedside table.

"What is that?" Thomas asked when Florian opened the bottle and poured a bit of the liquid onto one of the linen cloths.

"Rum. I find it's stronger than brandy, and since I'm not fond of the drink myself, I've no regrets about using it like this." He held the cloth to the wound, and Amelia's eyes flew open while air hissed between her teeth.

"You're fine," Thomas told her in the most reassuring tone he could muster while gently pushing her back against the mattress so Florian could do what he had to without too much resistance. He eyed the doctor. "Perhaps some laudanum for the pain?"

"We can do better than that." Florian reached inside his bag and produced another glass bottle. This also contained a clear liquid. He handed it to Thomas. "I recommend half the dosage of laudanum. This is much stronger."

Thomas read the label. "Morphine?" He gave Florian a dubious look. "I'm not familiar with it."

"The discovery of it is recent, so it has not been commercially produced yet. However, I have used it on a few other patients and seen the results of the studies, so I have every confidence that it would be most effective in this instance. However, the decision of whether or not to administer it is entirely up to you."

With this taken into consideration, Thomas opened the bottle and poured a small measure into a nearby glass. He'd specifically asked for Florian, not because there were no other capable physicians nearby, but because he appreciated Florian's innovativeness. The man was renowned for using methods that had proven to be reliable, no matter where those methods came from or who might have discovered them. He'd traveled far and wide in search of medicinal knowledge, believing other cultures might hold the key to certain discoveries of which the English still remained ignorant. Many thought the man eccentric and anti-science. In Thomas's opinion, he was more enlightened than most. So he held the glass to Amelia's lips and gently urged her to drink.

She did so with a groan. The hot water arrived. Florian disinfected his tools and by the time he was ready, a silly grin had appeared on Amelia's lips. "Is that normal?" Thomas asked when she actually giggled.

"The results of the morphine vary, but yes, a strong sensation of euphoria is known to occur." He set his pincers to the wound and pulled out a small piece of fabric that must have gotten pushed inside by the blade.

"You're very handsome," Amelia said, looking up at Thomas. Her comment was followed by a smile. She turned her head in Florian's direction. "So are you." A sigh escaped her. "Gorgeous hair."

Without comment, Florian added more rum to the wound, then threaded the needle and started to sew. By the time he was done, Amelia had managed to doze off with a beatific expression of pure bliss upon her face.

"How long will she sleep?" Thomas asked.

"I can't be sure, but at least a few hours, perhaps even until morning." Florian cleaned his tools and returned them to his bag. "Do you know who might be behind the attack?"

"I cannot be completely certain," Thomas told him, "but I suspect Bartholomew. He has more motive than anyone else I can think of."

Florian stared at him for a long moment, then asked, "Do you intend to have him apprehended?"

Blowing out a breath, Thomas could feel the

fangs of failure drawing near once more. "I have no proof to merit an arrest besides spotting one of his men at the scene."

"Then I suggest you have someone look into his taxes. From what I understand, he owes a great deal to the Crown."

Thomas frowned. "How on earth would you know that?"

"I cannot say, but you can count on it being true. You've my word on that."

Thanking him, Thomas paid him for his help and saw him to the door.

Before donning his hat and heading back out, Thomas told Lady Everly that he would return later in the day to check on Amelia. It seemed he now had a criminal to apprehend, and he knew precisely who to turn to for help.

Chapter 22

"Tax evasion, you say?" King George punctuated the question by popping a piece of sweetmeat into his mouth. His regal eyes were bright with interest. "Are you certain Bartholomew is guilty of such a crime?"

"That is what I have been told," Thomas assured him. "And I am inclined to believe my source." One of the benefits of being a duke was having the king's ear. And since Thomas never abused this privilege, he was always taken seriously whenever he came to call.

"Why?"

"Because he is highly respected. Indeed, I would trust him with my life."

The king's expression grew pensive. "What is your interest in this, Coventry? I do not suppose you are simply looking out for the Crown's coffers?"

It was time to be honest. "The truth is Bartholomew has threatened the Duke of Huntley's sister, Lady Amelia. This afternoon, she was brutally stabbed by one of his men."

"Good God!" The king's posture grew rigid. His hands appeared to tighten against the armrests of his gilded chair. "Would it not be simpler to arrest Bartholomew for attempted murder then?"

"You know as well as I that he will escape such a charge. The blame will merely fall on the man who wielded the blade."

"So you hope to find Bartholomew guilty on a different charge entirely." The king gave a thoughtful nod. "A smart move, on your part. The only problem I see is that a thorough investigation would have to be carried out. We will have to involve the accountants, and that is going to take time. However . . ."

"Yes?"

"Keeping the attack on Lady Amelia in mind, I propose we send the guard out immediately and arrest Bartholomew on the assumption that he is guilty. It will then be up to his lawyer to prove him innocent, allowing us the necessary time we need in order to find some proof. These things can be dragged out with a bit of bureaucracy. There is also a good chance that more incriminating facts will rise to the surface if we offer his people rewards in exchange for reliable information."

"As long as Bartholomew pays for his crimes, then I am happy."

"You may rest assured then, Coventry, for I am certain justice will be served in this instance. I thank you for bringing the matter to my attention."

"Thank you, Your Majesty." Thomas stood and

executed a bow. "I will leave Bartholomew's address with your secretary on my way out."

Drifting back to consciousness was decidedly unpleasant, Amelia thought. She was becoming increasingly aware of a horrible ache in her side. And the headache! Good Lord, she could not remember experiencing so much pain before she'd drifted off in a delirious state of bliss. Now it felt as though her skull was being sliced into little pieces.

"My dear."

She recognized Lady Everly's voice and tried to open her eyes. Thankfully, the curtains had been pulled tightly shut, shrouding the room in muted tones that were wonderfully soothing.

Lady Everly drew close and reached for her hand. "How are you feeling?" she asked.

Amelia blinked, tried to adjust her position and instantly groaned in response to a sharp twinge. "Not my best." She sank back against the plump pillow with a sigh. "What happened?"

"A vile miscreant stabbed you." Lady Everly's voice trembled with emotion. She squeezed Amelia's hand. "The duke brought you here with Doctor Florian who tended to your wound. He said it wasn't too serious—that a good rest should lead to a speedy recovery."

Amelia nodded, acknowledging her understanding of the situation. "Where are they now?"

"Both departed three hours ago. Coventry did

say he would come back later in the day to check on you."

Amelia's heart expanded with that thought, then deflated again when she recalled the last words they'd spoken to each other before the attack. She regretted the tone she'd taken with him. He hadn't deserved it, no matter how frustrated she'd been by his insistence that there was no choice for them but to marry. It still annoyed her, but she now had other things to think about, like the possibility of her brother returning home to find her like this. The mere idea of having to explain it all to him was exhausting.

"Is he all right?" she asked Lady Everly. "I do not recall if he was injured in any way."

"If he was, he made no mention of it to me. His entire focus was on you, Amelia." Withdrawing her hand, Lady Everly poured a glass of water and helped Amelia drink. "I understand your hesitation regarding marriage, but I do believe you ought to reconsider."

Amelia groaned. "Must we discuss this now?"

"No, but I would like you to hear my opinion on the matter since it likely differs from most." She set the glass aside and perched herself on the edge of the bed. "I was prevented from marrying the man I loved, and so I married for duty instead. It wasn't the worst union in the world, but it wasn't a very happy one either." She drew a deep breath and exhaled it. "Nobody can force you to marry Coventry, and if you are truly opposed, then I believe your brother to be the sort of man who will help you set up a life for yourself somewhere else, away from Society's censure. Just look at what he did for Gabriella's sister after all. But . . . I think that would be a mistake on your part. I know how deeply you care for Coventry, and instinct tells me that he cares just as much for you."

"No. He would have said so if he did."

Lady Everly chuckled. "Men can be such fools when it comes to confessing their feelings. Just mention 'love' to them and they begin to perspire. But his reaction when he brought you here earlier—his desperate stride and anguished tone—spoke volumes about the inner workings of his heart."

Closing her eyes, Amelia tamped down the giddy sensation of joy that threatened to spiral up through her. She would not allow herself to be influenced by a few words and to let hope in, only to be disappointed.

"Even if what you say is true, he and I are an impossibility. Coventry needs to marry a woman who can make him proud. He needs a wife who can fit the duchess role to perfection."

A tentative smile emerged on Lady Everly's lips. "My dear, it is time for you to realize that you can be that woman, but to do that, you must stop wearing your past like a millstone around your neck. Remember, the way people perceive you has a lot to do with your state of mind. If you think yourself unworthy, everyone else will too."

A knock on the door made them aware of Pierson's presence. "The duke is here," he said. "Shall I send him up?"

Lady Everly glanced at Amelia who hesitantly nodded. "Please do," the dowager countess told him. She waited until he was gone before saying, "I think you and Coventry have much to discuss, so I will give you the privacy you need."

She began to move away, but Amelia caught her by the hand, staying her progress. "You cannot mean to leave us alone in my bedchamber." A sudden blast of nervousness made her want to keep Lady Everly as close as possible. "It would not be proper."

"I do not think there is too much harm in it. After all, you are affianced, the door will remain wide open and you, my dear, are hardly in any position to do much of anything besides talk." She gave her hand a gentle tug, and Amelia reluctantly released it. "I will be in the sitting room if you need me," she added, referring to the small intimate space at the top of the landing. It wasn't far, but it still didn't feel close enough under the circumstances. Not when she had to contend with a very determined duke.

Another knock at the door brought said duke into the room. He greeted Lady Everly as she slid past him, making her exit and leaving Amelia quite alone with Thomas, whose dark gaze did little to put her at ease. It seemed to bore straight into her, devouring her until she felt weak with longing. Oh, if she could only develop some defense against the effect he always had on her. But every time she was sure she had built a wall around her heart, he would break it down with his mere presence, and she would respond like a moth drawn to a flame.

"I am glad to see you awake," he said, striding toward the bed where she lay. "How are you feeling?"

"As though I've been stabbed." When he paused and winced, she said, "It hurts, but it is not fatal. Let us take that as a blessing."

Pressing his lips together in a tight line, he reached her side and extended his hand. Amelia drew a sharp breath and held it in anticipation of his touch. It came a second later—the careful stroke of fingertips upon her cheek.

"Forgive me," he murmured. "This is my fault. It should not have happened. I—"

"Shh . . ." His distress made her forget her own. "You are not to blame for any of this."

He withdrew his hand, leaving coolness in its place. "I should have anticipated the attack, Amelia. I should have prevented it."

"How? None of us expected this to happen."

"There were warnings—the fire and the accident, Mr. Gorrell's disappearance. I should have stopped you from going back there after those things happened but—"

"You would have failed, Thomas." The use of his given name seemed to snap him out of the self-inflicted turmoil he was in. "I am not the sort of woman who is easily controlled by anyone."

With a heavy sigh, he suddenly lowered himself to the edge of the bed as though pushed there by an intolerably heavy burden. She felt the mattress dip beneath his weight. "No, you are not." He angled himself sideways in order to better face her. "But I still feel as though I failed you, just as I failed—"

"Stop." The word cut through his, forcing him into silence. "You have to understand and accept that people have their own willpowers. You are not their keeper, nor do you determine cause and effect. What happened with your sister was tragic, but she believed herself to be in love and as such, I doubt you would have been able to stop her from meeting Fielding's brother in secret. Especially since you were unaware of her planning to do so until it was too late." When he looked unconvinced, she placed her hand over his. "As for me, there was little you could do to keep me from that building short of having me locked in my bedchamber, and even then I am sure I would have found a way to defy your wishes."

He muttered something—a curse, no doubt— then locked his eyes with hers. "Why do women have to be so infernally stubborn?"

She shrugged as best as she could, given her position, then regretted making the movement since it pulled at her wound and sent pain darting through her. Twisting her face in response, she groaned. "Perhaps because we have become weary of being directed by men."

Turning his hand, he grasped hold of hers. "You must not overtax yourself, Amelia. The wound you sustained is still serious."

An aching smile caught her lips. "I am aware of it."

"Of course you are. I did not mean to imply

otherwise. It is just that I . . . I cannot help but worry. It is in my nature to do so."

She hadn't really thought of it like that before. It was something with which she could easily relate, having spent her life worrying about Juliette and Raphe—Bethany too, when she'd been alive. It had been the burden of having nobody but each other. Still . . . "And it will eat you up unless you relinquish control."

He snorted. "I fear that is easier said than done."

"Not when you never had control to begin with." She squeezed his hand. "The sooner you accept that, the easier life will be for you."

Frowning, he turned his attention toward their laced fingers. His thumb brushed over her skin, prompting all of her senses to fully awaken. "It is difficult to do so. Especially when there are things that I wish I could put into boxes and hold on tight to." His gaze met hers once more with an endless amount of emotion. "Marry me, Amelia."

She felt herself draw back. "No." Lady Everly had clearly been wrong.

"When will you see reason?"

His face transformed into a portrait of undeniable torment. It was as if deep feelings existed within him, and yet when he spoke . . . "You mean your version of reason? The sort of reason that involves retraining me, keeping me close and forcing me into a sheltered existence? I will have none of that, Thomas. Not from any man."

"Then what will you have? Tell me and I will provide it."

Closing her eyes, she forced back the tears that threatened. "It does not matter as long as you are unprepared to give it." She was suddenly quite tired—exhausted, really. "You should go. I need to rest."

A pause followed. "We are not done with this subject, Amelia. You and I *will* marry. Of that you may be certain."

She had no energy to respond, though the opening and closing of the front door below did catch her attention. Muffled voices rose toward them, then the sound of footsteps heavy upon the stairs. They paused at the top of the landing. Lady Everly was saying something now. Her voice was followed by a far more familiar one. Raphe's. Amelia's eyes flew toward the door just in time to see her brother enter the room. His solid pace ate up the carpet as he crossed it with a stern expression, not halting until he stood before Thomas, who'd risen to greet him.

"Coventry." Raphe's tone had never sounded so menacing before.

It filled Amelia with sudden concern. "Raphe," she tried, but he ignored her. Both men did, to her utter frustration.

"You were supposed to protect her," Raphe said in a clipped tone. "Instead, I return home to find her stabbed and compromised. Is that correct or have I been misinformed?"

"You are correct," Thomas told him in an equally blunt tone.

"Then you will have no qualms with what I must do."

"None at all. Indeed, I would expect nothing less."

Amelia stared at one, then at the other. What on earth were they talking about? She knew the answer to that question two seconds later when Raphe's fist made direct contact with Thomas's face.

Chapter 23

Thomas felt the burning ache vibrate through him. The punch had been well deserved—expected—and yet it still hurt like blazes. Far worse than any other hit he had ever received, no doubt because this one had been delivered with passion. It was personal, carrying the weight of Huntley's disappointment in him.

"Raphe!" In spite of her weakened voice, Amelia still managed to sound horrified. "There is no need for such brutality."

"Let me be clear, Amelia. The only reason I am not punching you right now is because you're a woman and also injured." He crossed his arms and glared down at where she lay. "What the hell were you thinking?"

"I can explain," she said on what sounded like a weary sigh.

"I should bloody well hope so," Huntley thundered.

Disliking the tone he was using on her, Thomas

placed himself between Huntley and Amelia. "She has endured enough for one day. The last thing she needs is for you to come home and berate her."

Huntley narrowed his gaze, and for one terrifying moment it looked as though he might unleash a flood of fury, but then he swung away without warning and paced across the floor. "You and I have much to discuss, Coventry. I'll await you in my study."

Thomas waited until he could hear his footsteps upon the stairs before turning to face Amelia once more. "I am sorry he had to arrive and find you like this."

"Yet another man who feels responsible for all that is wrong with the world." She expelled a tortured breath. "Remember that, when the two of you speak. You are so very alike."

He considered her words for a second, then bowed over her and brushed her lips with his. It was quick and gentle, yet it still managed to stir an unquenchable thirst in him—a thirst for things he now wanted with every fiber of his being. If she would only surrender to his desire and agree to accept his offer. To his way of thinking, there could be no other solution, and he was willing to bet his fortune that Huntley would agree with him once he told him all that there was to tell.

"Have a seat," Huntley said as soon as Thomas appeared in the study. He'd met Gabriella in the hallway on his way there and had given her a quick account of Amelia's situation. The duchess had immediately hurried off to see her.

Thomas sat in the chair that he always used in this room. It was comfortable—a little less rigid than the other available seat, no doubt on account of overusage. He considered Huntley, who now appeared slightly more subdued than earlier. The walk down the stairs and the few minutes that had passed had apparently eased his temper.

"Allow me to start at the very beginning," Thomas said. He then proceeded to related the events that had taken place since Huntley's departure: Amelia's pursuit of the property, her prompt purchase of it and all the trouble that had followed.

"I knew she had plans of this nature," Huntley said, reaching for the bottle of brandy that stood on a nearby tray. Turning over two glasses, he poured a measure into each of them and slid one across the desk to Thomas. "What I did not know was the location or the state the building was in. I imagined an investment opportunity in Mayfair. I also asked her to seek your assistance with it. You must forgive me for not informing you of this, but it wasn't even brought to my attention until the day before my departure. Sending word must have slipped my mind."

Thomas took a sip of the brandy, relishing the soothing effect it had on him. After being knocked unconscious and later punched, he could do with a bit of fortification. "I found out anyway though. You ought to know I tried to dissuade her."

"How did that go?"

Thomas thought back on the many arguments he and Amelia had had during the course of the last four weeks. "Your sister can be very insistent when she sets her mind to something."

Huntley grinned. It was the first sign of understanding he'd shown since his arrival. "I see that you have gotten to know her quite well during my absence." The comment instantly sobered him. Leaning back in his chair, his face took on a grave expression. "Have you really compromised her, or did Lady Everly exaggerate?"

Knowing that this would be the most difficult part to explain, Thomas braced himself for Huntley's reaction. "She and I were seen stepping out of the foliage at Vauxhall Garden by numerous witnesses."

"That hardly answers my question."

"I have kissed her," Thomas confessed.

"Is that all?"

"*Is that all?*" Thomas gaped at his friend. "Nothing else is required, Huntley. Especially not when considering our positions. She is a lady and I am a gentleman. A kiss is enough to dictate the necessary course of things."

"Did anyone see you kiss her?"

"No. Of course not. But assumptions will be made." Thomas took another sip of his drink. "One cannot take a woman into a dark and secluded spot without people thinking the worst. Her reputation will be destroyed unless I marry her."

Huntley nodded, and Thomas finally thought

he'd managed to make him see reason, until he asked, "Does she wish to marry you?"

"I hardly think that is—"

"Relevant?"

Huntley gave Thomas the sort of chastising look that made him feel like the ass that he knew he was turning into. He'd allowed lust to guide him through all of this without paying attention to Amelia's best interests. She'd tempted him, and by God he should have known better than to allow it.

As if reading his mind, Huntley said, "Ignoring her thoughts on the matter would be a mistake."

"Then what do you propose we do?"

"I'm not really sure, but I will not force her into an undesirable marriage." When Thomas opened his mouth to protest, Huntley held up his hand, silencing him. "My parents had one of those, and it affected not only them but their children, as well."

"But the scandal will be enormous." He could feel himself floundering without the support he'd expected to receive from Amelia's brother. "Your entire family will be affected. Think of Lady Juliette!"

Tilting his head, Huntley seemed to consider that for a moment. Thomas held his breath. "We will get through it if we must," Huntley said, smashing all hope Thomas had of a quick resolution. "What matters most to me is my family's happiness, not accommodating other people's notions of what must be done. And since we have recently gotten ourselves through an equally large scandal, I am confident that we can face another without too much harm being done. Lady Juliette can easily wait another year before seeking a husband in earnest. By then this whole thing will have been forgotten. Especially since the very same people who are likely to criticize us will be equally pleased to have my good favor."

"But—"

"Unless of course there is something besides duty that prompts you to ask for Amelia's hand." Huntley raised a daring brow. "Is there, Coventry?"

Thomas stared back at the man who'd become a close friend in recent months. His insides rebelled at the very idea of letting Amelia go, of not holding her in his arms again and feeling her lips move softly over his. Rising, he crossed to the window and looked out into the street.

"She has captivated my interest." He spoke to the glass pane while envisioning her joyful smile and the temper that sometimes happened to overtake it—especially when *he* managed to vex her. Shaking his head, he allowed a grimace. "I can think of little else when we are apart. My every thought these past few weeks have been of her, of seeing her again, of helping her with the school, of . . . of . . ."

"Yes?"

Struck by a sudden spark of clarity, Thomas turned to face Huntley, who was looking annoyingly smug and amused. "Are you enjoying yourself at my expense?"

"Absolutely, but that does not answer my question." Huntley's smile broadened. He waved his hand. "Do go on. I believe you are about to have an epiphany."

Of kissing her and touching her . . . of sating both their desires.

Thomas wisely kept those thoughts to himself. But the imaginings he'd had! They'd left him in a painful state of discomfort most nights. And yet he knew it was more than lust and his duty to protect her that kept her on his mind. It was the bond that had formed between them and the fondness it had provoked. He cared for her. Deeply. More deeply than he had ever cared for any other woman.

Marriage had always seemed so impossible to him, until she had stepped into his life and convinced him that with the right woman, it would not only be possible but also wonderful. Ever since that realization, he'd not simply wanted her as a permanent part of his life, he'd *needed* her, just as keenly as air was required in order to breathe. And when she'd been hurt . . . it had felt as though he'd been mortally wounded. Which could only mean one thing. Couldn't it?

"I love her," he said, acknowledging the truth for the very first time. The words felt good. They brought with them a new kind of reality—one in which winning her might be possible after all since he now had the chance to stop acting the fool and woo her with every bit of affection she truly deserved. "I love her so much I can scarcely believe it."

"In that case, you have my blessing, provided that she agrees."

Thanking him, Thomas said goodbye to Huntley

with the assurance that he would return in a few days when Amelia was feeling better. He could only hope that he hadn't ruined his chances with her for good.

Sitting in the sunroom with Gabriella and Juliette, Amelia enjoyed her cup of tea and the freedom of leaving her bedchamber behind. She'd spent three long days in that room and was seriously considering not ever going back to it. Sleeping down here on one of the sofas would be a welcome change, though she doubted Pierson would approve.

"Now that we know all about Amelia's love interests, let us hear about yours, Juliette," Gabriella teased. She'd been relentless with her questioning ever since learning that Amelia had been pursued by no fewer than three gentlemen, two of whom had proposed. And since flowers had been pouring into the house over the last couple of days, it had been a difficult subject to ignore.

"I cannot relay anything nearly as interesting as Amelia," Juliette said.

"But there is someone?" Gabriella prodded.

Juliette shrugged. "Not exactly. Lord Yates has shown some interest, I think, though I am reluctant to consider making a match with him."

"He is both titled and amicable," Amelia said.

"Qualities that I appreciate, but hardly enough to stir my heart."

Gabriella smiled. "I see we have another romantic in our midst."

"Is it wrong to want love?" Juliette asked with a pitch to her tone that made her sound rather defensive.

"Not at all," Gabriella told her. "Have you perhaps met a man who might encourage such deep affection?"

Juliette paused and then shook her head. "I don't think so."

Amelia wondered if that was entirely true, considering the blush that appeared on her cheeks. Choosing to give her privacy, she decided not to pursue the subject further, which was made easier by Pierson's arrival. "The Duke of Coventry to see Lady Amelia."

"Finally," Gabriella murmured before saying, "Do show him in."

Amelia looked to Gabriella. "Finally?"

Gabriella smiled. "The man is obviously struck by Cupid. I'm surprised he managed to stay away this long."

Amelia frowned. She would not argue the point no matter how false she knew it to be. The only thing Coventry was doing was giving her what he thought might convince her—an overwhelming and very expensive display of roses. While she appreciated the effort, she wished he would have avoided it since it only made denying him all the more difficult.

But then he arrived, and she realized it would be hard enough to continue doing so even without the flowers. The man was simply stunning, clad in a beige jacket with a taupe velvet collar and breeches to match, his brown boots complemented the earthy tones of his ensemble. Hair slightly tussled, he approached with an armful of pretty peonies.

Bowing, he addressed Gabriella first. "Your Grace, I thank you for inviting me into your home. These are for you."

He held the flowers toward Gabriella, who stood so she could accept them properly. "What a beautiful bribe, Your Grace." She looked over at Juliette. "Come along. I believe the duke would like a word in private with your sister."

Amelia gave Gabriella a disapproving look, but it was to no avail. She and Juliette hastened from the room and even managed to close the door completely behind them. Well! Amelia glanced at Coventry and saw that he now appeared somewhat uncertain— almost shy—which she found not only peculiar but also a little unnerving. The man had always been the very picture of aristocratic confidence.

"I am pleased to see you looking so well," he said. A hesitant smile formed upon his lips.

Amelia studied it, unsure of what it might mean. "Yes," she said. "The wound is healing quite nicely. I am able to move about now without any pain or discomfort."

He nodded. "That is excellent news."

Glancing at the sofa where she sat, he seemed to consider the spot beside her, which prompted her to rise. Having him that near would not do at all, not when she felt her resolve wavering even as they spoke. She'd spent three long days and nights reminding herself why marrying him would not work. *But he will be yours and you will be his.* That little voice rose to the front of her mind again. There had to be more than that, though. She would suffer for it if there wasn't; she knew she would.

"And how have you been?" she asked, walking away from the seating arrangement, adding distance. Perhaps he could distract her with an outline of his daily routine.

"Not good," he said. "Terrible, actually."

Surprised, she stopped to look at him, not only at his physical presence, but at the details of his face. His eyes were muted, the usual spark there reduced to a simmer. His skin had turned the palest shade she'd ever seen on him. It made him look sickly, which prompted her to move toward him.

"Are you ill?" A thought struck her. "Is Jeremy all right? I hope nothing has—"

"He is fine."

"And your mother?"

"She is also well." He stepped closer to her, reminding her of his much larger size and of the pull that invariably brought them together. She'd made a tactical error when she'd approached him, for there was no longer time for her to flee. He caught her hand and brought it to his lips, kissing her knuckles before turning the palm against his cheek. "I am the only one afflicted."

Her heart shook with the tremor his words evoked. "Afflicted?" He nodded, his eyes meeting hers. "By what?"

"Love." Turning his head, he placed a kiss against her wrist. The effect was as dizzying as his words.

"Love?" She could not credit it, nor could she

avoid the buzz of joy that spiraled through her as his meaning took hold of her senses.

"I love you, Amelia." Tentatively, he glanced at her. "I cannot imagine my life without you in it."

She could feel tears pressing against her eyes. Her throat tightened around the words she wished to speak. All she could do was nod while her lips trembled against the sob she was trying to swallow.

His thumb brushed her cheek. "I hope these are tears of joy and not sorrow."

She nodded again. "Joy," she managed to say. One word that brought her into his arms.

Winding one arm around her waist, he held her to him. His fingers nudged at her chin, tilting it upward until their eyes met. His were warm shades of chocolate swirling with tender amazement. It was a look she would not soon forget—a look that expanded her chest and made her feel cherished.

"I love you too. Did I tell you that?"

He shook his head. "Not until now. In fact, considering your resistance to marriage, I feared you might not feel the same way at all."

A tremulous laugh pushed its way past her lips. "How very wrong you are, Thomas, for I have loved you since the very first time we danced. And as much as I wanted to stop loving you at times, my heart refused to allow it."

Smiling, he dipped his head toward hers. "I am glad, so very glad indeed." His mouth met hers, tentatively at first and then with greater assurance. She felt his hand move to the back of her head, holding her steady. A hot burst of tremors swept through her body, beckoning her to surrender, and surrender she did. Her arms went around his neck as she arched against his solid form, pressing to him for greater purchase. He responded with a hungry groan that had her lips parting and granting him entry.

What followed was hot and decadent; a meeting of unrestrained feverish passion. It set Amelia's world on fire, burning along every limb and turning her body to liquid. She wanted his hands to move and to touch, yet they remained infuriatingly still.

"Thomas," she murmured when she managed a breath.

He responded by capturing her lip between his teeth and giving that plump piece of flesh a careful nibble. "I want more, as well," he told her, reading her mind. He placed a kiss upon her cheek, then kissed his way along her jaw until he could whisper in her ear, "But we are in your brother's house with the door to this room wide open." His hand stroked upward in a teasing caress. "I will not go any further than this at the moment," he added, "but once we are married and alone in our bedchamber, you may be certain that I will have you in every wicked way I can possibly imagine."

The effect of his comment was nothing short of scandalous. It evoked a sigh of longing she could not hold back, tightening the air around them to a heady crackle.

"Amelia, the things you do to me . . ." He shook his head as if confounded. "Let us plan this wedding with haste, my love. The sooner we get it done, the sooner I can see to your pleasure."

"Not only mine," she said, daring herself to be bold, "but yours, as well, *Your Grace*."

The heat that ignited his eyes was intense. "I can scarcely wait."

Neither could she, and yet they had no choice but to do precisely that. It would be at least three weeks until their vows would be spoken because of the banns that would have to be cried in church. As she kissed him once more before pulling away, she wondered how she would ever survive the wait.

Unfortunately, three weeks turned into four because of a delay ordering the fabric for Amelia's wedding gown. She'd gotten so exasperated over the matter that she'd suggested wearing another one of her dresses, but Thomas had wanted the day to be perfect for her, so he had suggested postponing the service until everything was completely ready—a suggestion he'd made between gritted teeth right before excusing himself and leaving her company. It had been one of many signs of his growing agitation.

She herself wasn't faring much better. Her days were filled with errands pertaining to the wedding and her nights with thoughts of what would transpire between herself and Thomas when they were finally alone as husband and wife.

Finally, when she'd begun to wonder if her wedding day would ever arrive, it did. Gabriella and Juliette attended to her along with her maid before departing for the church. When Amelia descended the stairs to where Raphe stood waiting for her, the depth of emotion that shone in his eyes tightened her heart. In that moment, she was glad she and Thomas had forgone a hasty marriage by special license. Her brother had earned the honor of giving her away properly, of seeing her settled, and she would have regretted not giving him that.

Raphe bent to place a kiss upon her cheek. "You look stunning," he told her sincerely. "I still can't believe this is actually happening."

"Neither can I," she assured him. "It is a miracle, is it not?"

Meeting her gaze with a stiff nod, he made no effort to hide the moisture that gathered at the corners of his eyes. "Shall we?" He offered her his arm.

She happily accepted it and allowed him to lead her out of Huntley House and toward the future that awaited her at the church.

The ceremony had been briefer than she'd expected, not that she'd minded. When it had been completed, they'd enjoyed a lovely breakfast with friends and family in a private dining room at Rules. Everything had happened in a daze. Amelia could scarcely recall what she'd eaten besides the cake, which had been delicious. And then her husband had whisked her off with some half-hearted comment about being exhausted that no one had seemed to believe. The two of them were now heading toward Mivart's Hotel on Brook Street, where Thomas had reserved a suite for their wedding night.

"Are you ready?" Thomas asked. He sat beside her in the ducal carriage—*their* ducal carriage.

"Very much so," she assured him, catching his meaning.

"Has Gabriella spoken to you about . . . what you are to expect?"

She smiled in response to his obvious discomfort with the subject. "She did."

He expelled a breath. "Good. I was concerned since you do not have a mother with whom to discuss such things. The last thing I want is to frighten you."

Sensing he was as nervous as she was about what would soon transpire and touched by that thought, she shifted enough to allow for some eye contact. "You needn't worry about that. If you recall, I did grow up surrounded by whores and their patrons, so I did have some idea of what goes on between men and women, even before Gabriella gave me the details and showed me a rather surprising book."

His eyes widened a notch. "A book?"

"It contained some very colorful depictions of various positions along with descriptions." She couldn't help but grin in response to his shocked expression. "So perhaps it is *I* who will teach *you* a thing or two?"

Nostrils flaring, he attacked her with his mouth. It was really the only way to describe the plundering roughness of the kiss that followed. His hands moved over her, touching, feeling, caressing, until she squirmed with wanton discomfort.

"Four weeks," he murmured against her ear. "Do you have any idea how hellish that time has been for me?"

She nodded while pleasure rolled through her, igniting a thirst that would not be denied. "Yes," she confessed. "For it has been the same for me."

He froze, his eyes locked with hers as the words sank in. The carriage rocked, and then his hand moved, lowering to the place where she needed him most, the firm touch replacing the ache with a rush of pure pleasure.

Leaning back against the squabs, she sighed with relief. "Yes."

His eyes stayed on hers as he increased the pressure. "Tell me how you feel," he said, taking her higher.

"Incredible," she confessed on a rush of air.

His lips met hers for the briefest of seconds, then his breath blew softly against her cheek. "I have thought of you each night for as long as I can remember, Amelia, of how you will sound as you come apart in my arms." Another kiss and another touch had her begging for him to continue. "I think it is time for me to find out."

He pushed against her skirts while she arched into his hand, the pressure creating a frisson of heat that expanded and burst on a wave of spiraling bliss. She clutched him while tremors rolled through her, relishing every exquisite part of the moment.

He held her until they had ceased, replaced by

a soothing calm. "You're splendid," he said as the carriage swayed to a halt. He was out the door and helping her down before she could blink, his haste to have her alone evident in his brisk stride. Five minutes later, they were shown into the suite he'd reserved.

The porter who'd helped with their bags departed, and the door clicked into place behind him. Amelia felt the first hint of nervous trepidation. "This is lovely," she said, going to look out the window. She shouldn't have mentioned that book or the fact that she knew a thing or two about lovemaking. Now he would likely expect some experience when she in fact had none.

"Perfect," he murmured, coming up behind her.

She felt his hand on her hip right before his lips touched the side of her neck. Her exhalation of breath ruffled the gauzy curtains. "Thomas," she chastised. "Someone might see."

"If that is your concern, you had best come away from the window, wife, for I have no intention of waiting another second to make you mine." A playful nibble on her earlobe made Amelia's insides fizz with anticipation.

The nerves that had formed were chased away when he turned her in his arms and covered her mouth with his in a languid kiss that vanquished all thought. His hands slid along her sides while he deepened the kiss with increased urgency, then toward her back until she suddenly felt her gown slide off her shoulders. She'd no idea how he'd managed to unfasten all the buttons without her taking notice, and she really didn't care, her body now clamoring for increased contact—for skin against skin—for the intimate touches they would soon share.

Tugging urgently at his jacket, she wrestled it off his shoulders. A sleeve caught on his arm and he laughed against her mouth—a momentary easing of tension while he helped her deposit the garment on the floor.

"Willful hoyden," he murmured. He nipped at her shoulder while she tugged his shirt free, slipping her hands underneath.

Ahhh.

He felt divine, his back an unforgiving plane of solidity against the pressure of her fingers. Spreading them wide, she ran them toward his sides and felt his muscles ripple in response. Then up across his chest, pressing between them in a slow slide of exploration that forced a gruff sound from his throat.

A series of blistering embers erupted against the touch of his lips as he claimed her mouth once more. They rained through her with fiery anticipation, prompting a sigh of pure and uninhibited pleasure. And then she felt her stays loosen around her and the cool air brushing her skin when he drew her chemise up over her head and sent the silk piece of clothing flying.

Breaking their kiss, Thomas drew away a little, eyes dark beneath lowered lashes. His lips drew up with wolfish hunger. "God, you're beautiful," he murmured. Stepping back, he allowed his gaze to trail the length of her body.

An unfamiliar vulnerability shook her—this sense of being completely exposed and watched as strange and uncomfortable as it was provocative. But then she saw him raise his hands to his cravat, unknotting and unwinding the fabric with a slow deliberation that made her ridiculously impatient. His shirt followed, revealing the chest she'd felt with her hands. He was just as stunning as she'd expected, with toned muscles defining his abdomen, and arms strong enough to hold her forever.

"So are you," she whispered, her eyes riveted on the movement of his fingers as he undid the fall of his trousers and pulled them down over his legs. When he paused to meet her gaze with gleaming eyes that seemed to devour, she sucked in a breath and then daringly asked, "What about the rest?"

A wicked smile slanted his mouth. "As my lady commands."

He stripped off his smalls, discarded his stockings and stood before her, magnificently nude. "Perfect." No other word could describe him.

All humor slipped from his face. He went to her like a pirate determined to claim his treasure. That thought alone sent a thrill shooting through her, more so when he scooped her up, his mouth seeking hers. With a sure stride, he carried her straight to the bed.

"Amelia." His voice caressed her brow as he laid her upon the silk-covered mattress and climbed in beside her.

Reaching for him, she pressed herself to his

warmth, removing the distance and adding close-ness. "Yes?"

"I am the most fortunate man in the world." His hand found her hip and stroked over her thigh, ex-ploring her body while she explored his. A sense of calm had settled over them, bringing with it the delicate touches of being adored and savored. "I will do my best to be gentle with you—to make this new experience as good for you as possible."

He kissed her then, touching her for long languid moments until she got drunk on his essence. When she explored him, he seemed to grow increasingly restless, his strokes demanding an arousal that made her desperate for what came next.

Shifting, he settled between her thighs, and as she ran her hands down his back, clutching him to her, he eased his way forward, forging a path that would join her body with his. A smile broke on her lips, not of humor, but of deep and profound satisfaction, because the man she loved was finally hers, and nothing in the world had ever felt more glorious than that.

"Amelia." Her name was a pure benediction.

"Yes," she said on a sigh. If there had been pain, she'd been oblivious to it. All she could do now was beg for more.

Moving gently at first, he gradually increased the pace, bringing her to that wonderful place where clouds parted and sunshine spilled through. And then he sent her soaring, taking flight with her while clutching her tight.

When his body sank over hers, hugging her to

him as he rolled over onto his side, she set her palm against his chest and felt the rapid beat of his heart.

"I love you," Amelia whispered. The dim afternoon light faded and darkness descended upon the room.

"As I love you," he said for what had to be the hundredth time. "I always will."

Chapter 24

❧

"This is wonderful," Gabriella said as she came to stand beside Amelia. "Is it everything you imagined it would be?"

"It is even better," Amelia said. Glancing around, she admired the transformation the house she had bought had undergone. Six months had made a tremendous difference. It looked just as presentable as any town house she had ever visited, with polished wood moldings and floors that gleamed from waxing. "I could not have done it without Thomas, though."

Gabriella responded with a knowing smile. The glow of pregnancy suited her tremendously. Raphe was naturally ecstatic with the thought of becoming a father soon. Another couple of months and the child was due to arrive. Gabriella had apparently kept that secret safe until she and Raphe had been alone together in Paris. "It would appear that he cared for you greatly long before he knew it himself," she said.

Studying her husband who stood in conversation with Raphe and his friends, the Earl of Wilmington and Baron Hawthorne, Amelia felt her heart swell with joy.

Sensing her perusal, he turned his gaze toward her, excused himself to the others and came to join her. "Your school will be a success when it opens," he told her. "Everyone I have spoken to agrees."

They had invited all the investors to come to visit the building before the opening, which would take place that coming Monday. Lowell and Burton were naturally in attendance, as was half of Mayfair, it would seem. Apparently the two gentlemen had acted as ambassadors, encouraging everyone they'd come into contact with to donate to Amelia's cause. She'd scarcely known how to thank them when she'd discovered their efforts.

"It does appear to have made the world forget about my heritage," she said. It still surprised her how little gossip there had been about her and Thomas. Apparently, a duke could withstand almost anything without scandal, even marrying a woman who came from the slums of St. Giles.

"It just goes to show that you had nothing to worry about," Gabriella said.

"Worry about?" Thomas asked.

"She did not think herself deserving enough to be your wife." With that remark, Gabriella removed herself to go to speak with her husband.

Thomas's arm came around Amelia without

hesitation. He did not seem to care how inappropriate such a public display of affection might be. "You are more deserving than any other—a perfect wife and mother."

Before she could respond, Doctor Florian approached. "My apologies for intruding, but there is something I must tell you."

His grave expression threatened the happiness still bubbling up inside Amelia. She glanced at Thomas who looked just as apprehensive as she felt. "What is it?" he asked.

Florian eyed them both, then lowered his voice. "Can we speak privately?"

Nodding, Thomas led the way toward the headmaster's office. Once there, he closed the door and waited for Florian to speak. Amelia felt her stomach tighten with nervous anticipation. She couldn't imagine what this might be about, but the tension in the room was definitely unwelcome.

"It is about Bartholomew," Florian began.

Amelia shared a look with Thomas before he said, "Last I heard, he was charged with tax evasion, smuggling and counterfeiting." Once the accountants had begun their investigation into Bartholomew's financial affairs, they'd opened up a path that had led to other criminal activities. "The magistrate told me personally that he is to be hanged."

Florian nodded. "Someone accused of those crimes certainly will be."

Amelia frowned with incomprehension. "What are you saying?"

"Simply that the man being held at Newgate—the man everyone believes to be Bartholomew—is not."

"What?" Thomas glanced at Amelia with concern before facing the doctor once more.

"I attended the trial," Florian said. "The man accused of Bartholomew's crimes bears some resemblance to him, but I can assure you that the wrong man has been apprehended."

"Did this individual claim to be someone else?" Amelia asked.

"No. When I brought the matter to the magistrate's attention, I was told that this man insists he is Bartholomew. He is going along with the ploy, and I was told that I had to be mistaken."

"Could you be?" Thomas asked.

"No. Bartholomew will go free, and another man will hang in his place."

"That makes no sense," Thomas muttered. "Why would someone give up his life like that?"

Florian shrugged. "Perhaps the real Bartholomew offered him something—an assurance that the man's family might be well cared for in return. It is possible that this impostor is already suffering some ailment and has nothing to lose. I can only theorize."

Thomas stared at Florian. "You're doing more than that." He took a step forward. "How is it that you know so much about Bartholomew that you are aware of his finances and his exact appearance? What interest did you have in attending that trial?"

Florian didn't flinch, nor did his expression change. "All I will say is that I have my own reasons for wanting to see him swing. I hoped I would finally do so, but the bastard outsmarted everyone once again by getting some poor sod to take his place." He glanced toward Amelia and apologized for his language.

"No need," she said, waving away his words.

Thomas sighed. "I don't suppose there's a chance of us catching him then."

"He has left London," Florian confirmed. "I have already checked."

"So he's in the wind and still as guilty as ever. That's just bloody perfect."

Amelia had to agree. Having Bartholomew on the loose was not the ideal conclusion she'd hoped for. "Do you think he might return and threaten us again?"

"I doubt it," Florian said. "As far as the authorities are concerned, he is going to die soon. It would be foolish of him to let anyone know the wrong man was apprehended, so if you ask me, he'll be starting a new business elsewhere, far away from here."

"I suppose there is a little bit of comfort in that," Thomas said, "though it is hardly enough."

"I couldn't agree more," Florian said. He turned toward Amelia. "I am sorry to bring you such depressing news, but I thought you ought to know."

"Your forthrightness is greatly appreciated," she told him.

Returning to the party, Thomas drew Amelia

aside. "I do not like this development one bit," he told her.

"Neither do I, but I also refuse to let it ruin our lives when we have so much to be grateful for." She made an effort to smile. "Speaking of which, we should probably leave soon. Given the beautiful weather, I thought it might be nice to take Jeremy out to the park."

"He would enjoy that, Amelia, but there is no need for us to rush if you would like to remain here a while longer and see to your guests. Your sister and Lady Everly are with Jeremy as we speak. They have proven to be extremely attentive where he is concerned."

She gave him a look. "They spoil him rotten when we are not there."

He grinned. "They do so even when we are. Did you not see Lady Everly pass him a piece of chocolate under the table yesterday?"

"After I told him he could not have any more?" She would clearly have to set down some rules. Again. "That only proves my point."

"I suppose it does." He looked around. "I cannot wait to see this place filled with children next week. There is nothing quite like their joy and laughter."

She smiled in response. "How would you feel about having one of your own?"

A frown appeared on his brow. "I already do."

"Well yes, Jeremy is your son." And would always be considered as such since no one besides Amelia, Thomas and the dowager duchess would ever know the real truth. "But . . ." She placed her hand upon her belly.

Thomas followed the movement with his eyes, then looked up at her face. "Are you telling me that . . . you are . . . I mean . . ."

Taking pity on him, she decided to clarify. "We are expecting a child, Thomas."

She was in the air half a second later while he whooped and spun her around. Returning her to the floor, he lowered his lips to hers and kissed her soundly, right there in the foyer of Coventry School and without a care for what anyone else might think. It wasn't until they returned home that reality seemed to kick in.

That night, he held her quietly in his arms, his mood completely transformed as he gently asked, "What if I lose you?"

She understood his fear. His sister had died in childbirth. "I suppose the possibility exists, though I expect it to be decreased with Doctor Florian's help. That man is a miracle worker if you ask me."

"Yes. We will stay close to him during your confinement."

"And all will pass as it should."

Which it did, allowing them both to hold their daughter in their arms nine months later after a surprisingly quick delivery.

"I have never been happier," Amelia told Thomas as she watched him place a tender kiss upon Baby Melanie's head. Beside him stood Jeremy, who'd painted a series of colorful pictures to hang by his sister's crib.

Setting Melanie down, Thomas came over and touched his lips to Amelia's. Affection flowed between them, filling her with all the warmth he carried for her in his heart. "Neither have I, my love. Neither have I."

Chapter 25

St. Agatha's Hospital, one year later

Seated in the crowded office to which she'd been granted entry, Juliette wondered if she'd made a mistake by coming here. Following protocol, she had taken the precaution of bringing a maid with her. She had, however, neglected to relay the real reason for her outing to her brother. He was under the impression that she had gone to the British Museum, which she would do right after this meeting so there would be some truth to what she had told him.

Biting her lip, she glanced around at all the books and various objects strewn about.

"Is that a real skull?" her maid asked from the spot where she sat some short distance away.

Juliette looked at the item to which Sarah pointed and found a pair of empty eye sockets staring back at her. "Yes, I believe it is."

"Good grief!"

The door burst open and the man Juliette had

come to see walked in. "My lady." Doctor Florian acknowledged her presence with a polite nod, then smiled at Sarah before making his way around his desk and sitting down. "To what do I owe this pleasure?"

"First of all, I should like to thank you for seeing me," Juliette said. "I hope you will forgive me for coming like this without warning."

He met her gaze and held it until a distinct edge of discomfort forced her to look away. "My profession does provide me with a busy schedule. I would appreciate it if you would tell me how I might be of service."

In other words, he wanted her gone as quickly as possible so he could continue with his day. She decided not to keep him too long. "It is my understanding that there has been a recent outbreak of typhus in St. Giles. I have been following the news of it in the paper."

Florian frowned. "That is correct. Yes."

When he said nothing further, Juliette leaned forward slightly in her seat. She did not miss the way his eyes sharpened with interest or how his posture appeared to stiffen. Curious man, he'd intrigued her since the moment she'd first met him, his view of medicine so apart from the norm that she found herself drawn to a subject she'd never before considered remotely interesting.

"I would like to know what is being done about it."

He did not flinch, but she could tell that he was thinking—dissecting her words and turning them over in his head. "You have an interest on account of your history with the place."

"I know what it is like to be sick and unable to afford proper treatment. Fortunately, my ailments were never too serious. Others, like my sister, Bethany, were not as lucky."

She might as well have told him it often rained when she was a child. His expression remained unchanged, though he did say what was required. "I am sorry."

"Thank you." She would not blame him for his indifference. Death had no doubt become such an ordinary part of his life that he failed to be affected by it.

"As to what is being done," he said, moving on with the conversation, "the affected streets have been closed off in the hope of halting further contagion. Regarding treatment, however, resources are limited, the people suffering, too poor to cover the necessary costs. I believe there are even those who think it would benefit the City if we let nature take its course and allow the slum to perish."

"Then it is as I feared," she said, "which is why I would like to make a proposal."

He gave her a steady look—one that blatantly assessed her. "Does your brother know you have come here?"

"No. I thought to acquire your help before going to him."

He winced. "Even if you manage to do so, considering I have yet to discover your intent, I would prefer to avoid a duke's wrath. Now that there are two dukes in your family, I wish you would have sought some approval."

Nodding, she blurted, "I want to fund a health plan for the poor."

He stared at her. "What?"

"A means by which to cover the cost of their treatment—any treatment—for the duration of their lives." When he said nothing, she continued. "Fortune has smiled on me, Doctor, and I now have the means required to help. Please tell me you will allow it." If he denied her, she would fail. Countless lives would likely be lost, which was something she wasn't prepared to accept.

Author's Note

Dear Reader,

I hope you've enjoyed the second book in my *Diamonds in the Rough* series. Writing Amelia's story turned out to be a lot more challenging than I'd expected. In fact, it required a complete rewrite from start to finish, but in the end I have to say that I'm extremely pleased with how it turned out.

As you may have suspected, Jeremy is autistic, but since the term *autism* wasn't used prior to 1911 and the condition had not been described or researched at the time in which this story takes place, my characters could only conclude that Jeremy was "different" and in need of special attention.

Since Amelia did spend the majority of her life in St. Giles, I really loved the idea of her giving back to that community. Buying a rundown house with the intention of turning it into a school gave her purpose. It was also inspired by hours of binge-watching HGTV episodes in the evenings, and in case you're curious, my favorite show there is *Fixer Upper,* featuring Chip and Joanna Gaines.

In general, my intention and hope for this series is to explore class differences during the Regency period by getting the very rich and the very poor to mix and mingle. Right now, I'm about to start writing Juliette's story. As the youngest Matthews sibling, she has always felt overprotected and like Amelia, she desperately needs to find a place for herself in this new life she's been given. Prone to sickness during her time in St. Giles, she's been used to feeling weak and helpless, but she's about to turn that into an asset now. And with Doctor Florian by her side, who knows where her plan to do so might lead?

I'm having fun with it, and look forward to sharing this new romance with you soon.

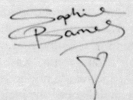

Acknowledgments

It takes more than an author to grasp an idea and transform it into a book. My name might be on the cover, but there's a whole team of spectacular people behind me, each with their own incredible skills and experience. Their faith in me and in my stories is invaluable, and since they do deserve to be recognized for their work, I'd like to take this opportunity to thank them all for their constant help and support.

To my editor extraordinaire, Erika Tsang, and her wonderful assistant, Nicole Fischer: your edits and advice have helped this story shine. Thank you so much for your insight and for believing in my ability to pull this off.

To my copy editor, Cathy Joyce; publicists Katie Steinberg, Emily Homonoff, Caroline Perny, Pam Spengler-Jaffee and Jessie Edwards; and senior director of marketing, Shawn Nicholls, thank you so much for all that you do and for offering guidance and support whenever it was needed.

I would also like to thank the amazing artist who

created this book's stunning cover. Chris Cocozza has truly succeeded in capturing the mood of *The Duke of Her Desire* and the way in which I envisioned both Thomas and Amelia looking—such a beautiful job!

To my fabulous beta readers, Rhonda Jones, Marla Golladay, Judy Barrera and Dee Foster, whose insight has been tremendously helpful in strengthening the story, thank you so much!

Another big thank-you goes to Nancy Mayer for her assistance. Whenever I'm faced with a question regarding the Regency era that I can't answer on my own, I turn to Nancy for advice. Her help is invaluable.

My family and friends deserve my thanks as well, especially for reminding me to take a break occasionally, to step away from the computer and just unwind—I would be lost without you.

And to you, dear reader—thank you so much for taking the time to read this story. Your support is, as always, hugely appreciated!